FALLING FOR A CHRISTMAS COWBOY

Cover Design and Interior Format

Falling for a
CHRISTMAS
COWBOY

A TENDER HEART TEXAS NOVEL

KATIE LANE

"Dax Davenport didn't like hanging around towns. He much preferred a campfire beneath the starry Texas sky with only wild coyotes for company. But it had been impossible to ignore the letter he'd received. So he'd come to Tender Heart . . . and waited."
—Tender Heart, Book Eleven

CHAPTER ONE

❧

THE COLD FRONT THAT SWEPT in from the plains three weeks before Christmas didn't bring snow. It brought something worse.

In his travels, Raff Arrington had driven in Minnesota blizzards, Washington rainstorms, Arizona heat, and even a Louisiana hurricane. But damned if this Texas ice storm didn't beat them all. The highway outside of Bliss was slicker than an Olympic bobsledding run and sleet flew from the night skies like incoming artillery fire. Raff was creeping along at thirty miles per hour, and the back end of his '67 Chevy pickup still fishtailed around every curve.

He hadn't planned on stopping in Bliss. He liked to be as far away from his hometown as he could get during the holidays. But the weather had caught him by surprise on his way from Houston. Now it looked like he'd have to postpone the delivery he planned to make in Austin.

He glanced over at the 1873 Winchester rifle

lying next to him on the bench seat. It was referred to as "the gun that won the west." But in this case, it was more like the "the gun that tamed Texas." He'd been looking for this particular gun for the last two years. And there had been a moment when he'd held the smooth wooden stock and cold steel barrel in his hands that he'd thought about keeping the gun for himself. But then he remembered his golden rule.

Never get attached to anything.

He planned to sell the gun and use the proceeds to build a house. A house that would hopefully ease the guilt that ate away at him. But it looked like he'd have to deal with the guilt another day. Ice had started to accumulate on the windshield so quickly it looked like the inside of a snow-cone machine. Luckily, he was only a quarter of a mile away from the turnoff to his ranch. Not that his acreage was still a ranch.

At one time, the Arrington Ranch had been the biggest ranch in Texas, but then his father and two uncles ended up in a dispute over how the ranch should be run—or Cole and Zane's fathers ended up in a dispute. Raff's father, Vern Arrington, was the easygoing middle son who didn't fight for any-thing. Even things he should fight for. When the other two brothers had decided to split the ranch three ways, Vern had been stuck with the land least suitable for ranching and his great-great-great-grandfather's old rundown cabin. Raff's father had named the ranch after the famous Tender Heart book series written by his Aunt Lucy.

Lucy Arrington wrote the series in the 1960s and based it on the mail-order brides brought to Texas to marry the cowboys who worked the Arrington Ranch. As a kid, Raff had loved the series. He stopped loving it when he grew up and realized that happily-ever-afters were purely fictional.

Once he turned off the highway and onto the road that led to the Tender Heart Ranch, Raff switched the radio from the weather station to country oldies. Loretta Lynn was singing *Country Christmas*. Raff remembered the song from one of the many Christmas albums his grandmother had played during family holidays. He'd never been much of a singer, but that didn't stop him from belting out the song. He cut off in mid-verse when a flash of red caught his attention.

At first he thought it was one of his cousin Becky's Hereford cows running across the road. Too late, he realized it wasn't a cow but a woman in a red dress. And she wasn't running. She was standing right smack dab in the middle of the road.

"Shit!" He slammed on his brakes. The mud wasn't as slick as icy asphalt, but it was slick enough to cause the tires to skid straight toward the wide-eyed woman who stood frozen in place. Raff cranked the steering wheel to the right, and the truck slid up a bank and straight into a wooden fence post.

If he had been in a new truck with airbags and a locking shoulder strap, he would've come through the accident without a scratch. But his vintage truck didn't have those amenities. It had a lap belt that kept him in the seat, but didn't keep his head from flying forward and smacking the steering wheel.

For a moment, he saw stars.

Then he saw nothing.

When he came to, it took him a moment to get oriented. His head hurt. His body was being jostled around. And he could smell chocolate . . . and wet animal?

He slowly opened his eyes. Two fuzzy red mountains greeted him. He blinked. No, not mountains. Boobs. A set of big boobs covered in red knit that showed off every luscious curve. Some guys like legs. Some guys like asses. But Raff had always been a boob man. He was thinking about burying his entire face between those lush melons of delight when his fantasy was interrupted by the woman's hysterical voice. A voice that was sweet as southern tupelo honey and extremely familiar.

"Sweet Baby Jesus! Everything has just gone to heck in a handcart. First, Miles runs out on my beautiful August wedding, ruining my plans to become a perfect southern wife and mother. Then my interior design business almost goes bankrupt, ruining my plan to be a successful, independent woman. And when I finally come up with a plan to fix at least one of those problems, I end up stranded on a muddy country road in a freezing snowstorm that completely ruins my cashmere sweater dress and Valentino leather shoes. And if that isn't enough to make a grown woman cry buckets, I'm now responsible for keeping a jerk of a cowboy alive." Her breasts rose and fell in an exasperated huff. "If I didn't know better, Lord, I'd think you were out to get me." She tried to shift gears, and the loud grinding noise finally had Raff sitting up.

Pain ricocheted through his head like a pinball, but it was the needling pain knifing through his balls that got his attention. He glanced down to see a soaking wet cat using his lap as a scratching post.

"What the hell!" He shoved the fur ball to the floor. It yowled as the truck swerved to the side of the road and barely missed hitting another fence post before it slammed to a stop. Raff grabbed on to the dash and put an arm out to keep the woman from suffering the same fate that he had. Soft breasts pressed against his forearm as he turned to her.

In the dashboard lights, she looked like the victim of a drowning. Her wet hair was darker than the usual vibrant red and plastered to her head like a skullcap. Mascara ringed her big blue eyes. And freckles that he hadn't known she had peppered her pert little nose and high cheekbones. The only makeup that had survived the storm was her lipstick. Her lips looked like they always did. Like an early summer strawberry that had been smashed just enough to spread out the corners but leave the center all plump and juicy.

"Savannah." The word came out sounding like a death knell. Which was appropriate. Of all the women he'd met in his life, there was only one that annoyed him to distraction. This one. And it appeared that the feeling was mutual.

She pushed his arm away and looked at him like he was a bug stuck on the sole of the sky-high heels she always wore. "Well, at least we know that the accident didn't knock you senseless—or not any more senseless than usual." She reached down and lifted her Persian cat from the floor and hugged it to her generous breasts. "Miss Pitty Pat? Are you okay, honey? Did big bad Raff hurt you?"

"Hurt her? That beast sank her claws into my

balls."

Savannah glared at him. "Gentlemen don't talk about their private parts in front of a lady. And the only reason Miss Pitty sank in her claws was because you frightened her when you sat up like Dracula from his coffin." A splatter of sleet had her looking at the windshield. "Good gravy, it's a nasty storm. I thought Bliss didn't get snow."

"This isn't snow. It's ice. Now would you like to explain why you were standing in the middle of the road in an ice storm?"

She flapped a hand as if she were sitting on the front porch of an antebellum mansion swatting flies. "Carly invited me to spend the holidays with her and Zane. I told her no at first, because the holidays are an extremely busy time at my interior design shop in Atlanta—what with all the people wanting to decorate for Christmas, Hanukah, New Year's, and such. But then . . ." She paused and bit on the lower half of that plump strawberry mouth. "I had a change of heart. I mean the holidays should be spent with friends and family, don't you think?"

"And since I was coming out," she rattled on. "I thought why not come out early and help Gracie decorate her new house and Emery decorate the baby's room." Raff's eyes felt like they wanted to roll back in his head. And not from his injury. Listening to Savannah always made him feel like he wanted to lose consciousness. "I was thinking of a pony theme because of Cole's horse ranch. But not the dirty, shaggy kind of ponies with wild eyes. I was thinking more of glittery pink ponies with fluffy manes all dancing in a meadow of flowers. Wouldn't that just be the cutest?"

He stared at her. "So that's your plan to save your business? You're going to charge Emery a fortune for decorating her kid's room with stupid ponies?"

Her eyes widened. She had weird eyes. One second, they could look a startling bluebonnet blue, and the next second, a deep lavender. They were bluebonnet at the moment. "Who told you my business was going bankrupt?"

"You did when you were blabbering about all your woes."

She blinked. "I do not blabber. Nor would I ever take money from a friend. I have other plans to save my business."

"Let me guess. You're searching for another sugar daddy after your first one left you at the altar."

"Miles did not leave me at the altar." She tipped up her chin. "He left me three days before. And he wasn't my sugar daddy."

He arched an eyebrow. "Really? It seems like more than a coincidence that your business is going bankrupt right after your fiancé leaves you at the altar." The flush on her cheeks confirmed his suspicions.

She cleared her throat. "It's bad manners to talk about money with a stranger. Now if you're done with your interrogation, we need to get you to the closest hospital." She settled the cat on her lap, and then ground the gears as she tried to shift into first.

Raff wasn't attached to possessions, but he couldn't sit there and let the vintage truck he'd spent months restoring be abused. He covered her ice-cold hand with his and stopped her from changing gears. "I don't need to go to the hospital."

She cocked an eyebrow. "Have you gotten a good

look at that goose egg on your head? You look like one of those Klingon guys in that Star Trek movie. You could be hemorrhaging internally. Or have a cracked skull."

"Stop with the dramatics. I'm fine. Now move so I can drive."

"Sorry, no can do." She forced the stick into first gear and took off down the road. "While I don't particularly care if you brain hemorrhage to death, the rest of your family will. And I wouldn't want to offend the Arringtons. I like them. You I merely tolerate."

He couldn't tolerate her for a second longer. He reached for the key and turned off the engine. Before his truck rolled to a stop, he had Savannah on his lap—cat and all.

She was wet. Not just a little wet, but soaked. The front of his jeans immediately grew damp . . . and snug. Because while Savannah was the most annoying female on the face of the earth, she was also built like a brick shithouse. Being a man, it was hard to ignore the full curves of her wiggling ass against his crotch or the weight of her generous boobs brushing his arm.

"What the heck do you think you're doing?" She struggled to get out of his hold, and the cat jumped over to the driver's side. "If you think that just because I've been without a man for one hundred and seventeen days that I'm interested in a little slap and tickle, you can think again. I have standards and you do not come close to meeting—"

His arm tightened around her waist, and when she stilled, he held one finger to his lips. Her mouth spread into a thin line of angry strawberry jam as he spoke. "I'm not interested in a little slap and tickle." It wasn't a lie. His brain wasn't interested. His cock was a different story. But Raff never let his rooster make his decisions. "Nor do I care about how many days you've been without a sugar daddy to buy you diamonds and furs. All I care about is getting you to Zane and Carly's and me home to my nice quiet—" He froze. "Dammit!"

"Don't cuss." She swatted at his shoulders. "And would you release me?"

"Believe me, I'd like nothing more. Unfortunately, it looks like we're stuck with each other for a while longer." He plopped her none too gently on the passenger's side, picked up the cat and set it on her lap, and then slid behind the wheel.

"What do you mean we're stuck?" she asked.

He started the truck. "I forgot that Carly and Zane aren't home. Zane texted me to tell me that one of the ranch hands hurt his shoulder this afternoon, and he and Carly were taking him into Austin for x-rays. With this storm, I figure they're not coming home tonight. Didn't Carly call you?"

"I ran my phone battery out using GPS. Which is why I couldn't call 911. I guess you'll just have to take me to Cole and Emery's."

He put the truck in reverse so he could turn around. "They're Christmas shopping in San Antonio."

"Dirk and Gracie's?" Her voice had a frantic pitch to it, and he knew how she felt. He was getting pretty frantic himself. But there was no help for it.

"Same shopping trip." He headed down the road toward his cabin.

When it finally registered where they were going, she slowly shook her head. "Oh, no. Miss Pitty and I are not staying in that shack of a cabin with you. I'd rather stay at that hideously decorated motor lodge in town."

"Sorry, but I'm not getting back on the highway. The trip from Houston was hell." A thought struck him, and he glanced around. "Where did you put my Winchester?"

"Your what?"

"My gun?" He pointed at the bench seat between them. "The gun that was sitting right here."

She petted the wet cat more rapidly. "Oh, that gun. Well, I couldn't stretch you out on the seat with a big ol' gun in the way. So I had to move it."

A bad feeling crept up his spine. "Move it? Where? Behind the seat?"

"Oh, I could never actually pick up a gun. My Aunt Lily told me she blew her left pinkie toe right off when she picked up her husband's gun to put it away in the gun safe. And even a good pedicure couldn't hide her disfigurement. No, I just sorta pushed it."

He stopped the truck and turned to her. "Where. Did. You. Put. My. Gun?"

That pretty strawberry mouth tipped up in a smile. "About a mile up the road."

"Melanie Davenport didn't know what to expect when she stepped off the stagecoach, but it wasn't a dusty little town with only a few dilapidated buildings. It was a far cry from her comfortable southern home in Atlanta. But she wasn't here for comfort. She was here to prod a tiger."

CHAPTER TWO

❦

SAVANNAH DEVLIN REYNOLDS HATED MEN with bad tempers. Probably because her daddy and brothers had the worst tempers on both sides of the Mississippi. As a child, she'd hidden in the coat closet whenever her daddy and brothers had lost it. As a teenager, she'd run away and never looked back.

There was no place to hide in Raff's truck—unless she crawled under the seat. And she didn't think she'd fit under there. Especially with Miss Pitty. Nor could she run away. The truck was moving too fast, and even if she did survive the jump, she wouldn't get far in this weather. She was already soaked to the bone, her dress and shoes completely ruined. Which left only one option: Sit there and act like Raff's loud bellows weren't making her stomach cramp like she'd eaten too many of her Aunt Bessy's fried green tomatoes.

"What kind of a lamebrain leaves a gun worth one hundred and fifty thousand dollars out in an ice storm?"

She tried to keep her voice firm and steady. "Like I told you before, I had no idea it was worth so much money. It just looked like an old gun to me."

Raff glanced over at her. "That's what makes it worth so much money!"

His angry features made her heart skip. While her daddy and brothers were average height and build, Raff was big. He was well over six foot with bulging muscles that were outlined by his gray thermal shirt. If he lost control and started swinging, Savannah was going to be in a world of hurt.

She scooted closer to the passenger door. "I really appreciate your offer to let me stay at your cabin for the night, but I must insist that you turn around and take me to the motor lodge in Bliss."

"You are not going anywhere until we find my rifle."

"I told you that I pushed it out of the truck right where you had the accident." She nervously stroked Miss Pitty's fur. "It's not my fault that it wasn't there. Obviously, someone stole it."

"No one stole it. No one in their right mind would be out in this kind of weather."

She shrugged. "Maybe a pig carried it off. I saw this show once about pigs. A middle-aged pig can be as smart as a three-year-old human. And three-year-olds are pretty smart." She glanced over just in time to see him clamp his lips together.

He had nice lips for a man. They were full and soft looking—even when they were frowning. Which was most of the time. Although he couldn't really help frowning on one side.

A scar ran along the left side of his face from the bottom of his cheekbone to the side of his mouth.

It wasn't the kind of puckered, deep scar that drew your attention right away. With the dark scruff that covered his jaw, it was hard to notice until he smiled and one side of his mouth didn't lift. Since he didn't smile often, it wasn't all that disfiguring. Not like the knot on his forehead that looked like it was growing bigger.

"I think you should go to the hospital. Or at least see a doctor," she said.

"It's just a little bump." He touched his head and winced.

She might not like him, but she hated for anything to suffer. She grabbed her travel purse and searched through it until she found the bottle of ibuprofen. She shook out three in her hand, and then searched for the bottle of water she'd bought at the airport. When she found it, she held out both. "Here."

He glanced at the pills. "What are those?"

"Strychnine. I gave you three to make sure your death is quick and painless."

A wink of a smile lifted the right side of his lips before it was gone. He took the tablets and popped them in his mouth, then reached for the bottle of water. Keeping an eye on the road, he tipped it back and drank every last drop before handing the empty bottle back to her.

"Thanks."

She stared at the empty bottle, suddenly extremely thirsty. What if the truck broke down like her car had? Or what if his bump really was serious and he died and they crashed? Then she'd be stuck out in the middle of nowhere with no food or water. She could live without water. She couldn't live without food. And all she had was the candy bar she'd bought at the airport. The thought of the candy bar was too tempting, and she reached in her purse, sneakily snapped off a piece, then popped it into her mouth. She'd share her painkillers and water, but never her chocolate.

"Look, I'm sorry for yelling," Raff said abruptly, and she almost choked on her candy. "But damn, woman, that rifle means a lot to me."

The apology was unexpected, but greatly appreciated. She'd always believed that one good turn deserved another. She quickly chewed and swallowed before replying. "And I'm sorry for leaving it behind, but at the time, I wasn't concerned about the gun as much as you dying."

He gave a brief nod. "Fair enough." He reached out and turned on the radio that she'd turned off earlier. Gene Autry singing "Rudolph the Red-Nosed Reindeer" came through the speakers. She was surprised when Raff started singing along. He hadn't seemed like the kind of guy who sang, especially about cute little red-nosed reindeers. There was something soothing about his deep, off-key baritone voice. And before she knew it, she was singing along with him.

When it was over, he glanced over and laughed. "That had to be the worst rendition of that song in its history. You sing as badly as I do."

She straightened her posture. "I'll have you know that my singing voice was what helped me win the title of Miss Georgia."

"Then the judges must've been tone deaf." His eyes reflected the lights from the instrument panel. While all the other Arringtons had deep blue eyes,

Raff's were a mixture of wild grass green and Kentucky whiskey gold. "Let me guess. The judges were all men."

"As a matter of fact, they were, but what does that have to do with anything?"

"A lot. How much of your boobs were showing?"

Her eyes widened as she stared at him. "Are you saying that I won Miss Georgia because of my breasts?"

"I'm saying that men can overlook a lot of flaws when presented with a nice set of . . . breasts. And you have chocolate on your teeth."

She turned away and ran her tongue over her teeth before looking back at him. "You are ill-mannered and disgusting."

He laughed. "I'm just being truthful."

She huffed and crossed her arms over her breasts. "I think it's best if we don't talk."

"I agree." He turned up the radio. Dolly Parton and Kenny Rogers were singing *Christmas Without You*. Savannah loved Dolly and Kenny, and it was a struggle not to sing along. Especially when Raff sang the rest of the way to his cabin.

Raff's cabin hadn't changed much since the last time she'd seen it. It was still as old and dilapidated as it had been a few months earlier when she and Gracie Arrington had come looking for lost chapters of the final Tender Heart book.

There was supposed to be eleven novels in the series, but Lucy had died before the eleventh book was published. Her family had looked high and low for the last book after Lucy died, but not one chapter had been found . . . until fifty years later.

Now chapters were popping up all over Bliss, Texas. And being a big Tender Heart fan, Savannah had high hopes of finding one herself. She would've already found one if Raff hadn't gotten to it before she and Gracie could. Just one more thing to hold against him. Thinking about the Tender Heart books made her break her vow not to talk to him.

"Have any more Tender Heart chapters been found?"

He pulled the truck up to the sagging porch. "Not that I know of. But you probably know more than I do about the final book, being that your friends are the most enthusiastic Tender Heart fans in town."

It was true. Emery, Carly, and Gracie loved Tender Heart as much as Savannah did and were dedicated to finding all the chapters of the final book. At least, they used to be dedicated. Now that they were all happily married, they weren't as enthusiastic as they'd once been about searching for the chapters. Emery was busy with her freelance editing business and planning for the arrival of her first child. Carly was busy with the diner she'd opened in town and helping Zane on the ranch. And Gracie was busy writing her own novel and preparing for her first child.

If Savannah's life hadn't gone to heck in a handcart, she would be as busy as they were. She'd be back in Atlanta happily married, going to Christmas parties with her wealthy husband's family, and decorating her interior design shop windows with twinkle lights and shiny ornaments. Instead, she was here. She stared out the ice-coated window at the dilapidated cabin with its scarred front door and cracked windows. It reminded her of the run-down shack she'd grown up in. The day she left her childhood home, she'd sworn that she'd never live in such poverty again. And yet, here she was.

"I guess you don't decorate for Christmas," she said.

"Why decorate when I'm not going to be around for the holidays. I'm only staying one night." He grabbed the black felt cowboy hat off the dash and hopped out of the truck, leaving the engine running.

A second later, her door opened. He plopped the hat on her head, and then took Miss Pitty Pat and tucked her under his thermal shirt. Savannah was about to complain about the manhandling of her cat, but then she stepped out in the driving sleet. It felt like icy needles hitting her, and she suddenly wished that she was protected beneath Raff's shirt.

He did protect her with his body, hovering much too close as they climbed the steps to the porch. He radiated heat like a space heater and smelled like rain and something more potent that she couldn't put her finger on. Probably Alpha Male.

Inside, the cabin wasn't much warmer than outside. Raff flipped a switch on the wall, and then muttered a curse. "The storm must have the power out." She stood shivering by the door as he handed her Miss Pitty then headed to the dark kitchen. He returned with two flashlights. He clicked on one and handed it to her. Her hand shook as she took it. For a second, he smothered it with his large hand, rubbing heat into it. The man certainly had enough heat to spare.

"I'll start a fire when I get back. In the meantime, take a hot shower to warm up."

"When you get back? Where are you going? You can't leave me here alone. What if the storm gets worse and I get snowed—iced in for days with no food?"

"You won't get iced in, and I'll be back." He grabbed a sheepskin jacket from a hook by the door and pulled it on. The wooly coat made him look even bigger and more imposing. "I'm just going to find my rifle. It has to be there somewhere." A smile tipped one corner of his mouth, and in the light of her flashlight, it made him look sinister and evil. "Unless a middle-aged pig carried it off." He took his hat from her head, then opened the door and was gone.

Savannah stood there in the dark hovel of the cabin shivering in misery and clutching Miss Pitty. "Oh, how we have fallen, Miss Pitty." The cat meowed as if in complete agreement.

By the grace of God, the water in the shower was deliciously hot and the pressure strong. She tried to talk Miss Pitty into the shower with her, but the cat refused and instead sat on the counter next to the flashlight grooming her wet fur. Savannah stayed in the shower until the water started to turn cold, then got out and dried off. After hanging her wet clothes on the shower rod, she took the flashlight into the bedroom. Raff had been so angry about the gun, she hadn't wanted to anger him further by asking him to stop by her car and get her luggage. So she was stuck borrowing one of his flannel shirts and a pair of wool socks.

Once dressed, she could've climbed into bed and

gone to sleep. It had been a long day and she was tired. But she was also hungry. So she headed to the kitchen. While the small bedroom and bathroom had seemed cozy, the living room and kitchen seemed creepy. The sleet splatted against the windows and the wind whistling down the chimney like the desperate moan of a ghost. Miss Pitty took one step into the room before she turned tail and raced back to the bedroom.

"Chicken liver," she called after the cat. But Pitty didn't return, and Savannah had to search for food in the spooky cabin on her own.

The refrigerator held only three bottles of beer and a pickle jar with no pickles. But the freezer had frozen dinners and bags of vegetables. She had a chicken dinner out of the box and in the microwave before she realized that she couldn't microwave without electricity. She put it back in the freezer and looked in the pantry. She found canned goods, stale crackers, and a jar of peanut butter. Since she was allergic to peanuts, she had to settle for the stale crackers and a can of peaches. She was searching for a can opener when a noise outside caused her to jump.

"Get a grip, Savannah Reynolds," she muttered to herself. "It's probably just a broken shutter." Or a serial killer who was looking for a redhead to add to his collection. Her knees shook as she walked to one of the front windows and peeked out. Through the icy rain she saw a beam of light coming from the barn a second before the big door slammed shut.

Bad Boy Raff was home.

"Before she reached the boardinghouse, Melanie spotted him. He sat in front of the general store with his boots propped on the hitching post and his black hat tugged low. He looked like he was sleeping, but her tingling skin told her different. Dax was watching her."

CHAPTER THREE

𝕮

SAVANNAH CONTINUED TO WATCH OUT the window. Raff was no doubt parking his vintage truck. She couldn't blame him for wanting to protect it from the weather. It was a cool old truck—one she'd love to dismantle just to get her hands on the parts. The chrome grill would look awesome above the bar of Mr. Carlisle's man cave.

The Carlisles were the main reason Savannah had come to Bliss three weeks before Christmas. They were one of the oldest and wealthiest families in Atlanta and were looking for an interior designer to decorate the thirty-room southern mansion they were building. A job like that would pay extremely well, and numerous Atlanta designers were vying for the job—including Savannah. But Savannah had an edge those other designers didn't have.

She knew that Mrs. Carlisle was a diehard Tender Heart fan.

When Savannah had purposely mentioned in her interview that she was friends with the

Arrington family, Mrs. Carlisle had almost had a coronary. She'd started asking Savannah a barrage of questions. Was there really a little white chapel? Did Savannah think Lucy wrote the final book of the series? Had she seen the desk where Lucy had written her books?

Savannah answered all the questions in the affirmative, and she'd wanted the job so badly that she'd added a little white lie.

"Of course, I've seen Lucy's desk," she'd said. "And if you hire me, I'm sure I can get it for your new study." The words had just popped out, and Mrs. Carlisle had jumped on them like a ravenous dog on a soup bone.

It would've been a great plan if Savannah could've gotten the desk. But there was no way that Emery and Cole would part with Lucy's desk. And even if they did, Savannah couldn't stand the thought of the infamous desk being anywhere but in Bliss, Texas. So she'd come up with another plan. She couldn't get Lucy's desk, but she might be able to find other furniture in Bliss that had once belonged to Lucy. A chair. A lamp. Anything that would make Mrs. Carlisle happy. If she couldn't find something, Mrs. Carlisle would think Savannah was a liar. Not only wouldn't she hire her, but she'd also blackball Savannah to all her wealthy friends. Then there would be no way to save her business from bankruptcy.

Darn her pride. If she hadn't been in such a hurry to pay Miles back the money he'd loaned her to start her business, she wouldn't be in this predicament. But she couldn't stand the thought of owing a man who had left her three days before their wedding. Especially when his reason for breaking their engagement was because his mother thought she was a gold digger. Savannah was no gold digger. She had worked hard for everything she'd gotten in this life. And she would continue to work hard. She wasn't about to let a little bump in the road keep her from getting the life she wanted.

She released the curtain and walked back to the kitchen to look for the can opener. Once she had the peaches opened, she decided to share some with Raff. He was annoying, but he had offered her refuge from the storm. She searched through the cupboards and drawers for pretty dishes to set the table with. Her Aunt Sally had always taught her that a beautiful table setting made everything taste better.

Aunt Sally had been one of Atlanta's premier interior designers in her day. The old photographs she'd shown Savannah of the beautiful homes she'd decorated were the reason Savannah decided to become an interior designer. She wanted to make beautiful places for people to live. She didn't just want to dress up houses with pretty things. She wanted to make homes. Homes where families could laugh and love without fighting and abuse.

Which was why she needed to save her business.

Once she had the peaches in two stoneware bowls, the crackers on a plate, and the candles she'd found in a drawer lit, she smiled with contentment and took a seat at the table.

Etiquette dictated that she wait until Raff got there. She glanced at the door. But what was taking him so long? Last she'd heard he didn't have any animals to tend to. And what else would he be doing in the barn? Unless he wasn't doing anything. Unless he was lying on the ground dead from his head injury.

"Sweet Baby Jesus," she breathed before she jumped up. She slipped into the muddy cowboy boots by the door and put on the jean jacket hanging on the hook before grabbing the flashlight.

Once outside, she bent her head against the icy rain and ran across the yard to the barn. She had to set her flashlight on the ground and work to get the door to slide open. The barn was huge and smelled like moldy hay. She expected to find Raff's truck parked right in front. But there was no truck. She flashed the light over an old tractor, a couple bales of hay, a lawn mower, a worn saddle, and a workbench with tools. She moved further toward the stalls, but even she knew that a truck couldn't fit through a horse stall door. Still, she leaned over the Dutch door and flashed the light inside.

Her breath caught.

"Holy crap on a cracker," she breathed as she stared at all the furniture jammed in the stall. And not junky furniture, but solid four-poster bed frames and dressers made of rich mahogany and delicate china cabinets and buffets made of luscious cherry wood. In the next stall, there was a sturdy oak harvest table loaded with antique lamps, quilts, and vases. The next stall had needlepoint rockers and gold-gilded mirrors.

Savannah moved from stall to stall like a six-year-old in the Disney Store. Every stall she peeked in was packed with antique furniture she'd give her right arm to have in her shop. Or in the Carlisle mansion. Even if nothing in the barn had belonged to Lucy, there was a good chance that a few pieces had been owned by the townsfolk of Bliss whose ancestors were the cowboys and mail-order brides who Lucy had based her fictional books on. And owning furniture that had once been a mail-order bride's should be enough to impress Mrs. Carlisle.

She moved to the next stall and peeked in. She was disappointed when all she found was a pile of hay and a rumpled quilt. Had Raff bedded down in the barn? If so, where was he? And where was his truck? She started to call his name when she realized that the hay had the distinct shape of a body. She pointed her flashlight at it, then froze when the light caught a glimmer of eyes through the yellow straw.

She wanted to turn and run, but she couldn't seem to move her feet. All she could do was stand there and stare at the eyes that were staring at her. The hay shifted as the monster beneath sat up. Savannah screamed and ran like the hounds of hell were after her. She ran until she hit a solid wall. A solid wall that issued an order in a commanding, familiar voice.

"Be quiet!"

Savannah had never been so happy to hear Raff's voice in all her life. She flung her arms around his waist and clung like a koala bear to its mama.

"Thank God you're here," she spoke into his wet sheepskin coat. "There's a hideous hay monster chasing me."

His chest lifted as he heaved a sigh. "Something is really wrong with you. Like seriously wrong. Did you get dropped on your head when you were a kid? I leave you for two seconds and you go wandering around in my barn looking for . . . hay monsters. That's strange. Just plain strange."

She stepped back. "I'm not kidding. There's something in that stall." She pointed the flashlight. "It was looking at me."

"I really don't have time for this. I'm cold. I'm wet. And I'm exhausted. Not to mention, pissed that I couldn't find my Winchester rifle that you tossed out of my truck. So if you're done with the theatrics, I'd like to take a hot shower and go to bed."

He turned to leave, but she grabbed his coat and held tight. "You are not going anywhere until you look in that stall, Mister."

He slowly turned, the beam from his flashlight momentarily blinding her. "Fine. But if it's a mouse, you're going to feel pretty stupid." He moved her out of the way and strode toward the stall. She heard the door creak open and then nothing. She'd started to worry that it was just a mouse and her imagination had gotten the best of her when she heard a muffled grunt, followed by Raff's cussing.

"Why you little shit!"

Savannah didn't know whether to run to the stall or run for the door. Before she could decide, a flashlight beam appeared. She turned her light on Raff as he stepped out of the stall with the hay monster. On closer inspection, not a monster so much as a teenage boy with hay sticking out of his hair and clothes.

"You better have a good excuse for breaking into my barn," Raff said as he dragged the young man closer. "And for hitting me in the shin with the handle of that pitchfork."

"I should've used the other end," the teenager grumbled.

Raff walked past Savannah on his way to the door. "Good idea. Then you'd be thrown in jail for murder rather than assault."

"I'm not going to jail." The teenager struggled, but Raff seemed to have a good hold on him. He pushed him through the open barn door and out into the icy rain. Savannah had to hurry to catch up. She wasn't even sure Raff knew she was behind them until they reached the porch and he gave her an order.

"Open the door, Savannah."

She clomped up the porch steps in her clunky boots and held the door as he guided the teenage boy inside. She followed to find Raff trying the light switch. When he discovered that the power was still out, he pushed the boy toward the couch in the living room. "Sit your butt down and don't move." Then he pulled off his hat and coat and hung them on a hook. "There's a kerosene lamp in the pantry on the top shelf, Savannah. Could you please get it?"

The "please" made her a little happier about being ordered around. She got a chair so she could reach the top shelf and took down the kerosene lamp. Her father had kept one handy for when he'd failed to pay the electric bill so she knew how to light it. Once lit, the lamp illuminated the cabin in its warm, flickering glow. Raff seemed to be standing guard by the door. When she returned with the lamp, he gave her a thorough once over.

"Nice outfit."

"Thanks. I call it Cabin Man Chic."

The side of his mouth lifted for a second before he took the lamp and carried it into the living room where the young man was belligerently slumped on the sofa picking at a hole in the knee of his jeans. Raff set the lamp on the coffee table, then stood in front of the fireplace with his feet spread and his arms crossed. Savannah had to admit that the pose was intimidating.

"I'm waiting," he said.

"Go to hell," the teenager said.

Raff pulled his cellphone out of his back pocket and started to dial. "I guess we'll just wait for the sheriff."

"Fine!" The teenager sat up. "I wasn't doing anything in your junky old barn but sleeping."

"And why were you sleeping in my barn?"

The young man sent him a belligerent look. "Duh." He motioned at the window where the sleet was still coming down.

Savannah couldn't stop the giggle. It was kind of fun to see someone go up against arrogant Raff Arrington. The teenage boy glanced over and blushed bright red as if she was making fun of him. His bashfulness made him a little more endearing. As did the scared look in his big brown eyes.

"He has a point, Raff," she said. "He couldn't sleep outside in this weather." She moved into the living room and sat down on the couch next to the teenager. "What happened, honey? Did you have car trouble like I did?"

He hesitated for a brief second before he nodded. "Yeah, that's exactly what happened. I had car trouble. I was headed into Austin when my car broke down."

Raff finished the story for him. "And you just happened to walk ten miles off the main highway and stumble upon my barn."

The young man's gaze flashed over to Raff and his expression turned angry. "Are you calling me a liar?"

"If the shoe fits."

Savannah cut in. "Raff, don't you think this poor child has been put through enough tonight without you adding to it?"

"I'm not a child. I'm eighteen."

Raff snorted. Savannah didn't believe the young man was eighteen either. He was sixteen tops. But she did believe that he needed a warm, safe place to sleep for the night. And she knew all about needing a warm, safe place to lay your head.

"Don't mind Raff, honey. He always has a burr up his butt. Now, are you hungry?"

The young man slowly nodded. "Yes, ma'am."

She got to her feet. "Well, then come on into the kitchen. I have some peaches and you can make yourself some peanut butter and crackers. I'd make them for you, but if I touch anything with peanuts in it, I swell up like a blowfish."

Raff grabbed his coat and hat and headed out the door. "I'm going to go get some firewood."

When the door slammed behind him, the teenager grumbled. "Asshole."

"Watch your mouth," Savannah scolded as she got the jar of peanut butter out of the pantry. "There will be no potty mouths around me." She handed him the jar before she took the chair across from him. "What's your name, honey? Mine is Savannah."

He hesitated. "Dominic Toretto."

"Nice to meet you, Dominic." She handed him a knife. The teenager only waited a second before he opened the jar and scooped some peanut butter out on a cracker. Her stomach grumbled. What she wouldn't give for a big bite of peanut butter . . . or better yet, a Reese's Peanut Butter cup. She picked up her fork and speared a peach.

Dominic ate like he was starving. He finished off the entire jar of peanut butter, box of crackers, and his bowl of peaches before he finally sat back. "Thank you," he said.

"You need to thank Raff. It's his food and his house."

He glanced around. "More like a dump. How come the barn has better furniture than in here?"

Dominic had a good point. The furniture in the barn was twice as nice as the furniture in the cabin. Raff's big body would fit much better on the four-poster bed in the barn than on the small double bed in his bedroom. But maybe the furniture wasn't his. Maybe he was just storing it for someone else. But who? And would they be willing to let Savannah purchase some of it?

The door opened, and Raff walked in. And she had to admit that there was something extremely virile and sexy about a man carrying an armful of wood. It didn't take him long to start a fire. Once he had it going, he just stood there and stared into the flames. She didn't know why the image struck a chord with her. Maybe because, with his hat and sheepskin coat, he looked like a Tender Heart hero standing by a campfire. Or maybe because there seemed to be a tinge of sadness in his features illuminated by the fire. But it must've been her imagination, because when he turned, he was the same Grumpy Gus he'd always been.

He sent her a sour look as he took off his hat and coat and hung them on the hook. "I'm going to take a shower and go to bed." He picked up the kerosene lamp from the coffee table before he pointed a finger at Dominic. "When I wake up, if anything is missing from my house or my barn, I swear to God, I'll hunt you down. You got it, kid?"

"Wait," Savannah stopped him. "Where am I sleeping?"

"I don't care, but not in my bed." He turned and walked into the bedroom.

After the door slammed, Dominic muttered. "Your boyfriend is a real—butthole. And a lousy writer."

"Raff is *not* my boyfriend," she said. "I only date southern gentlemen, not uncouth cowboys. And why would you think Raff is a writer?"

He spoke around a mouthful of peaches—peaches he'd obviously swiped from her bowl when she'd been ogling Raff. "Because of the chapter of the book I found in the barn. The part about the gun-slinger was cool, but the part about the mail-order brides was just plain stupid."

"Melanie was as beautiful as she'd always been, which explained why all the cowboys clustered around her like ants on honey. When one horny cowboy took her hand to help her up the boardinghouse steps, Dax had to keep his hand away from his gun and his mind focused on four words—she's not yours anymore."

Chapter Four

❧

AFTER HIS SHOWER, RAFF HOPED to find both his unwanted guests gone. But considering that the sky was still spitting ice, he knew it was just wishful thinking. When he walked out of the bathroom with the kerosene lamp, he saw the white ball of fur sleeping on his pillow. And Savannah wouldn't go anywhere without her precious cat. Miss Pitty opened one green eye and watched him as he dropped the towel and pulled on a pair of clean boxers, then she closed her eye and went back to sleep.

He should've kicked the cat out of his bed and done the same. Instead, he opened the door and walked out into the living room. The candles on the kitchen table had burned down. The fire needed another piece of wood. And a steady snoring came from the living room.

He walked over to the couch and found the teenager lying on his back with one of Grandma

Arrington's quilts neatly tucked around him. Obviously, Savannah was one of those women who liked to mother any kid that came down the pike. Even delinquent runaways. And there was little doubt in Raff's mind that the kid was a runaway.

He should call the sheriff. And he would. But on a night like this, he figured Waylon Kendall had enough to deal with. Morning was soon enough to call his childhood friend. His brow knitted as he glanced around the cabin. Unless he had to call him to look for a crazy woman who wasn't smart enough to stay in out of the cold.

He shook his head as he walked back to his room to get dressed. Was this night ever going to end?

He had just opened the dresser drawer to get a pair of jeans when he heard the front door open. He closed the drawer and walked out to find Savannah stepping inside. She was wearing his cowboy hat, sheepskin coat, and old boots. Ice crystals glimmered in her messy red hair and the tail of his flannel shirt flapped against her bare thighs as she pulled the door closed.

"Where the hell have you been?" He didn't speak loudly, but she jumped as if he'd shot off a canon.

"Sweet Baby Jesus!" She whirled and clutched her arms around her stomach. Her gaze traveled over his body, and her eyes widened. "Don't you have any manners at all? You don't run around in your underwear when you have guests."

"I do if it's my house and the guests are unwanted. Now where were you?"

"I just went out to . . . get some more firewood."

"And where is the firewood? In the pocket of my jacket?"

She giggled nervously. "Of course not, silly. I couldn't find where you keep the wood."

He tipped his head and studied her. She was lying through her pearly white teeth. Women like her didn't bring in firewood. Nor did they go out in an ice storm to look for it. Especially when there was still some of the firewood sitting in the wood box. "Okay, what were you really doing?"

She glanced over at the kid on the couch and lowered her voice. "If you must know, I was talking on the phone and I didn't want to wake Dominic."

"Dominic?" He looked at the sleeping boy. "That's his name?"

She nodded. "Dominic Toretto. He must be Italian."

Raff laughed. "Or a big fan of the movie *The Fast and the Furious*. Dominic Toretto was the character Vin Diesel played."

She blinked before she sent an annoyed look at the couch. "Why that little liar. And after I let him get away with stealing my peaches."

"That wasn't the only thing he lied about. He didn't have car trouble. I'm guessing he doesn't even own a car. And speaking of liars, I thought your phone was dead."

"Well, I must've been mistaken because it seems to be working now." She slipped out of his boots, then took off his hat and placed it on a hook. She kept his jacket on and hugged herself like she was freezing. He walked over and added more wood to the fire. When he turned, she had her eyes glued to the front fly of his boxers.

"You realize that boxers are out of fashion, right?" she said.

"And do you realize that I don't give a rat's ass about fashion? Unlike you, who travels with your entire wardrobe. You really needed to bring four large suitcases?"

"How do you know—" Her eyes widened. "Did you get my bags from the rental car?"

"I got your bags, and the keys you left in the ignition." The fool woman didn't have any sense at all.

"So where are they?"

"The keys are on my dresser and your suitcases are out in the truck."

"Why didn't you bring them in?"

"Because before I could, someone started screaming like a banshee." He wouldn't admit that her screams had scared the crap out of him. She had sounded like someone was killing her. "Then I had my hands full with a delinquent runaway."

"He's not a delinquent. Kids don't run away unless they have a good reason. Especially in God-awful weather like this. Instead of bullying him, you should show him a little kindness."

"I did show him kindness by not kicking his ass when he almost broke my leg with the pitchfork."

She glanced at his leg. "Ooh, that bump looks about as nasty as the one on your head. You should probably put some ice on that. In fact, why don't you go lie down and I'll get you some." She inched toward the dark kitchen.

"I don't need ice."

"Nonsense. Now go on." She flapped a hand.

He thought about arguing, but then decided it was a losing battle. Besides, the knot on his leg throbbed like a sonofabitch, and he probably did need to ice it. When he got to the bathroom, the cat was still sleeping on his pillow. Figuring the pillow was already covered in the feline's hair, he moved around to the other side of the bed.

A few moments later, Savannah sailed in carrying a bag of frozen corn and one of peas. She had taken off his coat and the jean jacket she'd been wearing earlier. He hated to admit it, but she looked hot. The soft flannel of his shirt clung to her breasts, outlining each sweet curve while the unbuttoned collar revealed a tempting shadow of deep cleavage. Her long legs were bare from the short hem of the shirt to the slouched top of the wool socks. She wasn't skinny. But she wasn't fat either. She just looked soft and tempting.

His cock stretched awake.

His physical reaction didn't surprise him. He was a man, after all, and Savannah was sexy as hell. But in the last year, he'd learned to control his baser instincts. Or at least hide them. He reached for the edge of the quilt and flipped it over his lower half.

"It's a little late to be bashful, isn't it?" She walked around to his side and removed the quilt so she could place the bag of corn on his shin. It was the wrong shin, but he didn't say a word. He wanted her gone. Like now. Unfortunately, she didn't seem to be in a hurry.

"For your head." She handed him the peas and sat down on the edge of the bed. The opening at the bottom of her shirt split wider, revealing soft upper thigh. Before he'd taken a shower, he'd had to remove her wet clothes from the shower rod—including a lacy red bra and a tiny scrap of matching underwear. His cock stretched a little more, and he reached for the quilt. Unfortunately, the cat decided to relocate. The animal stepped right up on his stomach and plopped down in a ball of damp fur.

"What the hell?" he said. He started to move the cat, but the animal growled low in its throat.

Savannah laughed. "I'd leave her where she is if I were you. Pitty doesn't like being disturbed once she gets settled." She leaned over and scratched the cat's ears. "So what's up with all that furniture in your barn?"

He wasn't surprised that she had seen the furniture. It was everywhere. He really needed to do something with it. And he was going to—as soon as he had enough money to rebuild the house. He thought about the missing gun and wanted to cuss a blue streak. Instead, he answered Savannah's question. "It's just a few antiques that I've picked up here and there."

The flame of the kerosene lamp reflected in her eyes like twin suns shining on fields of bluebonnets. "That's not a few. It's a warehouse full. What are you going to do with it all?"

"That's none of your business." He looked away from her hypnotic eyes. "Look, I'm pretty tired so—"

She cut him off. "How would you like to sell it? Or at least, a few pieces." When he looked back, she was smiling sweetly. A little too sweetly. "Like maybe the white provincial desk."

He knew exactly what desk she was talking about. He'd just bought it not more than a month earlier. "Sorry. It's not for sale. And neither are any of the other things in the barn."

"I'll give you a thousand dollars for it."

"No."

She leaned closer, giving him a much better view of her cleavage. "Two thousand?"

His gaze lifted from the sweet swells of her breasts, and his eyes narrowed. Of all the furniture, why had she picked that desk? The only answer he could come up with was that she knew who it had once belonged to. But that didn't seem likely. "Why do you want the desk so badly?"

She shrugged. "I'm designing a house for a woman in Atlanta, and the desk would look amazing in her study."

He was surprised. "So you really do work for a living? I thought you just mooched off your rich boyfriends."

He knew he'd hit a sore spot when she stiffened like he'd just slapped her fanny. "Of course I work for a living. I have supported myself since I was seventeen."

He should've left it alone, but he hadn't invited her into his room. And he was a little annoyed at the woman for giving him a semi-erection when he didn't even like her. He didn't like her designer clothes. Or her prissy manners. Or her sweet as sugar speech. He liked his women real. And Savannah was about as real as a plug nickel.

"When you say supported are you talking about living by yourself? Or are you talking about living with some sap who was willing to pay the rent and your gigantic credit card bills for a chance to touch your boobs?"

Her eyes widened. She opened her mouth, but then quickly snapped it shut.

"That's what I thought," he said. "Now if you'll excuse me, I need to get some sleep."

She got up in a huff. "You just can't be nice, can you? I came in here offering friendship and ice for your injuries, and in return I got nothing but spiteful words and insults. Come on, Miss Pitty." She leaned over to scoop up the cat. He didn't know if it was the feel of her soft hand sliding along his lower stomach muscles or the flash of swelling cleavage that finally brought his cock to full attention. But once she had the growling cat in her arms, Raff looked down to discover his boxer shorts tented like Barnum and Bailey's big top.

"You are nothing like your cousins," she continued. "You are mean and hateful and . . ." She glanced down, and the sentence drifted off as her eyes widened. "Sweet Baby—"

With a muffled curse, Raff grabbed the quilt and got up. "Take the damned bed. I'll sleep out in the chair." For once, she had nothing to say. She just stood there staring down at the quilt he held in front of him as he skirted past her and strode out of the room.

In the living room, the fire had died down again. He dropped the quilt in the chair and added another log. He stood there staring at the leaping flames, silently chastising his second brain for being a horny bastard with no self-control. Of course, there wasn't a man alive who wouldn't desire a body like Savannah's. And it didn't help that Raff had gone without sex for so long. It had been close to a year since he'd been with a woman.

He should've had sex with the pretty bartender in Santa Fe. Or the aggressive cowgirl in Amarillo.

Or the free-spirited skier in Vail. Or the dozens of other women who had offered him a warm bed and no strings. There would be strings with Savannah. Her high-maintenance type always came with strings. And Raff wasn't about to get tangled up in a relationship. He had enough to worry about without adding a woman to the mix.

He turned and discovered that the kid was sitting up on the couch and watching him with fearful eyes. When he spoke, his voice quivered. "If you're some kind of a psycho and thinking about picking up that poker and cracking me over the head, you should think again. My dad's a cop, and I just called him and told him where I am."

Raff lifted an eyebrow. "Really? And just where are we?"

The kid swallowed, his Adam's apple bobbing in his skinny neck. He was scrawny. His chest was almost concave, and his arms looked like he hadn't done a lick of physical work in his life. But he had some guts. Raff had to give him that. He hiked his chin. "I'm just south of Austin."

"Yeah, I bet that will help the FBI a lot when they come looking for your body." The flash of stark terror in the kid's eyes had Raff backing off. "Relax. I'm not going to murder you in your sleep. I'm too damned tired." He walked over to the chair and flopped down, leaning his head on the back. "Bad choice in names, by the way, Dominic Toretto. Vin's character is a little too memorable."

The kid sent him a sullen look. "She fell for it."

"She's gullible."

"She's also smokin' hot."

Since it was the truth, Raff didn't try to deny it.

"You can say that again."

"She's also smokin' hot."

Raff lifted an eyebrow, and the kid shrugged his shoulders as if accepting it was a bad joke. "So why are you out here?" the kid asked, "instead of in there with your hot girlfriend? Did you get in a fight and she kicked your butt out of bed?"

"She's not my girlfriend."

The kid looked confused. "That's what she said, but I thought with the way you two glared at each other that she was lying."

"The only one lying here seems to be you. But I figure we'll find out the truth soon enough . . . Dominic. I'm calling the sheriff first thing in the morning."

The kid stared at the fire. "It's not like I broke into your barn. The door was open. And I didn't steal anything either. I just slept on your smelly old hay."

"And hit me in the shin with a pitchfork."

He glanced over. "I was scared, okay? Haven't you ever been scared and done something stupid?"

Raff had. More times than he could count. "If you're trying to keep me from calling the sheriff, it's not going to work."

The kid sent him a belligerent glare before he flopped back on the couch and pulled the quilt up. "Whatever."

Raff should've left it at that and gone to sleep. He didn't need to get involved in the kid's problems. But he couldn't seem to keep his big mouth shut. "So why did you run away?"

He didn't think the kid was going to answer. A long time passed with nothing but the crackle of the burning wood in the fireplace and the splat of sleet on the windows. When Raff was about to nod off, the kid finally spoke.

"Why does anyone run away? Because they don't like where they are."

"When Melanie got to the boardinghouse, she discovered only one other mail-order bride living there. 'The rest are hitched already,' the proprietor said, before he spat a stream of tobacco at the spittoon in the corner. 'And with the cold snap, I figure you two won't last long.'"

CHAPTER FIVE

❧

IT SEEMED LIKE IT TOOK forever for the pink tinge of dawn to lighten the skies outside the bedroom window. Savannah had not slept a wink all night. Not only because she didn't trust Raff and the lying teenager as far as she could throw them, but also because she was too excited to sleep.

She'd found another chapter of the final Tender Heart book!

She'd found the precious pages right where Dominic—or whatever his name was—had told her they were. The envelope had been tucked in the drawer of the small white provincial desk in the stall next to the one the teenager had been sleeping in.

The desk was another reason to be excited. Whoever was hiding the chapters only hid them in places that had to do with Lucy and her writing. So it made sense that the desk had been Lucy's at one time. Not when she was writing the Tender Heart series—Cole owned that desk and a chapter had already been found there. But maybe this desk was the one Lucy had used when she still lived with her family. And Savannah was hoping that would be enough to impress Mrs. Carlisle and her Tender-Heart-loving friends.

If—and that was a big *if*—she could get Raff to sell it to her.

An image popped into her head—or, if she were honest, had never popped out of her head—of his impressively tented blue cotton boxers. Raff might act like he didn't like her, but he did. Or at least his body did. And she could understand that. She didn't like him either, but as soon as she'd turned and seen him standing there in his underwear, her secret parts had hot flashed like a menopausal woman in ninety-eight percent humidity and almost melted her panties.

While Miles's body had been fit from hours spent with his personal trainer, Raff's body looked like it belonged to a personal trainer. His chest, arms, and legs bulged in all the right places and his stomach had hard ridges like Savannah's favorite potato chips. She'd always thought she hated tattoos. They seemed so tacky. But when covering a canvas of hard, bulging muscles, they weren't tacky so much as . . . art. Art she wanted in her home so she could stare at it whenever she wanted. And touch it. Yes, she wanted to touch Raff's tattoo. To slide her fingers over the spiked edges of the barbed wire heart and caress the licking flames of the orange fire that surrounded it.

Of course she would never indulge that fantasy. Raff was the last man she wanted to have sex with. She didn't go for aggressive men who had no obvious means of supporting themselves and lived in rundown cabins. She went for coolheaded, mannerly men who were business savvy and enjoyed the finer things in life, like she did.

Miles was one of those men. They had been perfectly matched. They agreed on everything and never argued about anything. Which was why it had been such a shock when he broke off their engagement three days before their wedding. He'd told her that he just wasn't ready to tie the knot. And he did have commitment issues. He couldn't even decide on an entrée for dinner without second-guessing his decision. But that wasn't the real reason he broke their engagement. After getting back to Atlanta, she'd learned that Miles's mother was not happy that her son had given Savannah a loan for her design business.

To prove her wrong, Savannah had paid Miles back every cent. Which had left her close to bankruptcy. But she wouldn't be close for long. Once she got Mrs. Carlisle as a client, her business would be out of the red and she could start working on the rest of her life plan. Marriage. Children. All she had to do was get Raff to sell the desk. It wouldn't be easy. But her aunts had always said she could charm a wolf out of its coat. And Raff was definitely a wolf.

She got out of bed and headed to the bathroom to shower. The light worked so the power was back on. Since she didn't have her luggage, after she showered, she had to wear the same clothes she'd worn the day before. Unfortunately, her dry-clean-only sweater dress hadn't weathered the storm well. The hem was a good three inches shorter and the tight knit clung to her hips and breasts like red holiday plastic wrap. With no make-up or blow dryer and styling tools to fix her hair, she did not look her best.

Since it was so early, she expected to find both Raff and the teenager sleeping. Instead, the teenager was nowhere in sight and Raff was standing at the stove cooking. She hadn't taken him for the type of man who cooked. And yet he looked extremely comfortable. He skillfully added seasoning to whatever he was making and used a spatula like a pro. Today he wore a black thermal shirt that hugged his biceps and soft jeans that hugged his butt.

She pinned on a smile. "Good morning."

He glanced over his shoulder, and his gaze slid down to her heels and back up. She tugged on the hem of her dress. "I know. It shrunk. Just an example of why you should always read the care instructions."

He shook his head before returning to cooking. "I brought your luggage in. It's sitting by the door. Hopefully, there's a coat and a sensible pair of shoes in one of your multiple suitcases."

"Define sensible."

"Low heels that aren't going to break your neck when you step out on the ice."

"Nope, I don't even own a pair." She watched his neck muscles tighten. The man definitely had some pent-up tension. "But no worries, I'm more balanced in high heels than I am in low. As for a coat, I didn't think it got so cold in Bliss." She glanced around. "So where is . . . Dominic?"

"Gone. And I say good riddance."

She wasn't particularly fond of the teenager, especially after he had lied to her, but she wasn't so coldhearted as to want him to freeze to death. "You kicked him out without a coat?"

"He has a coat. He stole mine. He also stole my favorite hat, a pair of gloves, a backpack, and a flashlight." He turned and slid two over-easy eggs onto a plate on the table. They looked perfectly cooked and extremely yummy. After eating only peaches last night, she was starving.

"Where did you get the eggs?" she asked.

"I drove over to Cole's and got them from Gracie's chickens. I also used the spare key and helped myself to some bread, sausages, and coffee."

She didn't know what sounded better. Sausage or coffee. Probably coffee. Hopefully, Raff was willing to share a cup. And maybe a few bites of food. She looked at the eggs and couldn't help thinking about the runaway teenager out in the cold and hungry. "We have to find Dominic, Raff. Something awful could happen to a young boy all alone."

Raff sighed as he put the pan back on the stove. "Twenty-four hours ago all I had to worry about was what truck stop to eat breakfast at. Now I have to worry about my lost gun, a runaway thief, a cat shedding all over my pillow, and an annoying redhead who doesn't know when to leave well enough alone."

She had set her mind to charming him, but it was hard to be charming to a man who was so irritating. "Fine. If you won't look for Dominic, I will. I just need to call the rental car company and have them bring me another car."

"That could take days. I'm sure you're not the

only one to have car trouble in the storm." He cracked some more eggs in the pan. "But don't worry about the kid. I called the sheriff this morning and gave a complete description of him and my clothes. Waylon and his deputies will have a better chance of finding him than we do."

Savannah's shoulders relaxed. "Thank you."

"Don't thank me. I'm hoping Way picks him up and tosses the little thief's butt in jail."

"He only stole because he's desperate. Maybe he didn't go far. Maybe he's in the barn." She moved to the window, then released an awed breath.

Everything was covered in ice. The tree branches looked as if they'd been dipped in glitter glue. Each waxy leaf and red berry of the holly bush by the porch steps looked like it was encased in glass, and the icicles hanging from the eaves sparkled like prisms in the early morning sun.

"It's prettier than snow," she whispered. "It's like an ice wonderland." Raff snorted, and she turned around. "You don't think it's beautiful?"

He glanced over his shoulder and gave her the once over. "It's not smart to think dangerous things are beautiful. That can get you in trouble in a hurry."

A giddy feeling jumped to life in her tummy. Did he think she was beautiful? Her dislike of him lessened just a smidge. It lessened even more when he slipped two more eggs onto another plate and set them on the table.

"Come and get it before it gets cold."

She placed a hand on her chest. "You cooked for me?" No man had ever cooked for her before. They'd bought her dinner. Given her chocolates.

But they'd never cooked for her. Especially not her daddy or brothers. They believed that cooking was women's work and wouldn't have been caught dead in the kitchen holding a spatula.

Raff stared at her as if she was losing it. "You want them or not? If not, I'll eat them."

"As long as you didn't cook them in peanut oil."

"Just butter."

"I love butter." She hurried over so quickly that she tripped on a wrinkle in the throw rug by the front door. She caught herself before she took a nosedive. When she glanced over, Raff was smiling.

"Yep, great balance in heels."

Breakfast was wonderful. The eggs were delicious and so was the sausage Raff pulled out of the oven where he'd been keeping it warm. But what tasted even more divine was the cup of coffee he poured her before he sat down. She preferred cappuccino, but caffeine was caffeine. And after her sleepless night, she needed a pick-me-up.

While she ate, she tried to pull Raff into a conversation, but the man seemed to be the type that preferred to eat in silence. He answered her questions with brief nods or head shakes, and when he was finished eating he got up and carried his dish to the sink. She quickly followed.

"Since you cooked, let me do the dishes."

He glanced at her. "I don't have a dishwasher."

"I don't need a dishwasher." She nudged him out of the way with her hip and reached for the bottle of dish soap on the edge of the sink. "Growing up, I had to do dishes by hand all the time. Talk about dishpan hands. I couldn't keep my nail polish from chipping to save my soul."

He leaned against the counter and studied her. "I got the feeling that you came from a wealthy family. I would've thought you had servants to do the dishes—and to paint your nails."

Obviously, the caffeine hadn't helped her sleep deprivation. She rarely slipped and talked about her childhood, even with her closest friends. The past was best left there.

"No servants. Just me."

"So you were an only child too?"

She started washing the plates. "I wish. I had two older brothers who were as mean as sin."

"Had? Did they die?"

"Did I say had? Roy and Jonas are alive and well." Still mean as sin, and still living in Louisiana right next to her deadbeat daddy and her poor browbeaten mama. "And what about you? How did you like being an only child? I bet you were spoiled rotten."

"Yeah, I was pretty rotten." He walked to the table and picked up the coffee cups. "With the sun shining, it will only take a few hours for the ice to melt, then I'll take you into town. I called Emmett at the gas station, and he said he'll tow your car and store it in his garage until the rental company can deal with it." He leaned over her to put the cups in the sudsy water. "I'm going to go out to the barn and do a little work."

She turned. "And what am I supposed to do?"

He shrugged. "Whatever you want to do. There are some books on the shelf over there. Or you could call your friends. I'm sure Emery and Carly would love to hear all about your night in the den of big, bad Raff."

"You aren't that big and bad." The image of his erection popped into her head. Okay, so maybe he was big, but he wasn't so bad. At least not as bad as she'd once thought. Cooking breakfast for her had covered a multitude of sins. "Besides, Carly and Emery like you."

"Meaning you don't."

"Meaning you're kinda growing on me."

He smiled slightly as he reached out to the hooks by the door. They were all empty, except for the jean jacket she'd worn the night before. He grabbed the jacket. "Damn kid."

Once he was gone, Savannah finished washing, drying, and putting away the dishes. Then she did her makeup, fixed her hair, and changed out of her dress and heels and into a sweater, skinny jeans, and impractical boots. She plugged in her cellphone to charge, then unpacked Miss Pitty's food, litter box, and fluffy bed. But once the cat had eaten and taken a potty break, she ignored her bed and jumped right back on Raff's pillow and went to sleep.

Savannah made the bed around her, smoothing out every wrinkle and perfectly folding the top sheet over the quilt before stacking all the pillows except Miss Pitty's against the wood headboard. Once she was through with that, she organized the clutter on Raff's dresser into some empty shoe-boxes she found in the closet and organized his shirts by color and print. She would've organized his underwear drawer, but that just brought up images she didn't need to think about.

When she was finished, she moved into the living room. There wasn't much to work with, but she folded the quilts and draped them strategically over the couch and chair, put the candles she'd used the night before on the mantel, and grouped framed pictures into more aesthetically pleasing arrangements on the shelves. For a man who acted like the black sheep of the family, he certainly had a lot of family photos, including sepia-toned ancestors with somber faces.

Once she'd done everything she could to the living room, she went to the bookshelf to look for something to read. Raff had a lot of books, but they were all antique and history books of the old west. There was not a romance in the bunch. She froze as a thought struck her. Why was she looking for something to read when she had a chapter from one of the best fictional series of all times?

She glanced out the window to make sure Raff wasn't headed back to the cabin before she went to the kitchen. She'd hidden the Tender Heart chapter in an empty cookie jar in the very back of a bottom cupboard. Once she had the jar in her hands, guilt set in. Carly and Gracie would yell at her for even thinking about reading the chapter. While Emery had to read the chapters to authenticate them, Carly and Gracie believed everyone else should wait to read them until the entire manuscript was found.

Savannah agreed with that in principle. It would be a little like opening a Christmas present early. But now that she actually had a chapter and time to read it without being interrupted, her principles went right out the window.

She wanted to know what was going to happen to her favorite character, Dax Davenport. Was he really the villain everyone made him out to be? Was he in Tender Heart to cause trouble? Or was he there for another reason? And why did the last mail-order bride to come to town have his same last name? Was she his sister? Or was it just a coincidence?

All these questions raced around in Savannah's head. And unable to resist a second longer, she snatched off the lid and reached in for the envelope. Her brows furrowed when her fingers touched nothing but the cold, smooth ceramic sides. Confused, she took her hand out and peeked in.

It was gone.

The chapter was gone.

"It was well after midnight before Dax climbed the trellis that led to the upper rooms where the mail-order brides lived. He'd thought he gotten the wrong room until he heard the click of a gun being cocked. He turned to see a derringer pointed at his heart. The very same derringer he'd bought his beloved wife."

CHAPTER SIX

THE WHISPERED SCRAPE OF SANDPAPER against wood soothed Raff, as did the smells of the barn. As a kid, he'd spent a lot of time in the barn—tending animals, playing in the hayloft, and watching his father make furniture. The pieces were never anything too complicated. A plain harvest table and benches. A bookcase for Raff's mom. A headboard and footboard for Raff. A cradle for his brother and three sisters, who had all died before they got a chance to use them.

Raff usually didn't let his mind wander down that path, but this morning he couldn't seem to stop it. Unlike Savannah, he'd been a lonely only child. The first time he remembered his mother being pregnant he was only four and so excited to have a sibling to play with. He also remembered being confused when his parents came home from the hospital with haunted looks and no baby. The second time, he was seven. Again he was excited.

And again, confused. The third time, he was ten. He hadn't been excited or confused. Because he'd understood what was going to happen. He understood that he wasn't getting a sibling. He was getting a father and mother who would be heart-broken for months. The final time, he was thirteen. Old enough to lose his temper and blow up at his mother and father's stupidity. He remembered the words he'd thrown at them.

"Just stop it already! Just stop the craziness!"

They had stopped—at least they had stopped trying. He didn't know if it had been because of his outburst or because they just couldn't deal with another loss. But occasionally, Raff had caught his father staring off into space or his mother crying, and he knew they were thinking about the children they had lost. It made Raff sad, but it also made him angry. They had a son. Wasn't he enough?

He stopped sanding and studied the chest that was lying on its side in the hay. It had been his great-aunt Lucy's hope chest. It was the only thing that had survived the fire that burned down his family home two years earlier. Everything else in the house had gone up in flames.

Becky and Gracie were convinced that Lucy's ghost had saved the hope chest. He'd thought that was just fanciful thinking until he'd found Lucy's illegitimate child's birth certificate in a hidden compartment at the bottom. The birth certificate was the only way his family would've found out about Lucy's daughter, Bonnie Blue. And Raff had to wonder if Lucy hadn't saved the chest so the truth would eventually come out.

The squeak of the barn door opening drew his

attention. A second later, Savannah peeked over the stall door. She was back to being the perfectly coiffed beauty pageant winner he'd first met. Her makeup was artfully applied and her hair styled to hang around the shoulders of her green sweater in fiery red waves. With her large diamond stud earrings, she looked like a sparkly Christmas package. One he would never open.

She opened the lower half of the Dutch door and walked in. He was relieved that she'd changed from the distracting dress, but his relief was short lived when she turned to close the door and he got a good look at her curvy butt in the skintight jeans. He'd been annoyed when she said she didn't own a pair of sensible boots. But sensible seemed overrated when she strode toward him in those brown knee-high boots with stiletto heels.

"You were absolutely right," she said. "Dominic is nothing but a little thief."

He pulled his gaze from her boots, made a brief—or maybe not all that brief—pit stop at the lush green hills that rose from her chest before finally meeting her eyes. They looked violet. Violent violet.

"And when I get my hands on him, I'm gonna whup his butt within an inch of his life."

Raff had wanted to kick the kid's butt earlier, but he'd gotten over his anger. He went back to sanding. "Calm down. Waylon will find him. The kid probably didn't even make it off Arrington land. What did he take of yours?" He glanced at her boots. "Sensible shoes?"

"He took . . . a journal."

He stopped sanding and lifted an eyebrow. "As

in a diary journal? Please tell me it wasn't like the diary of Lucy's that Gracie and Becky found—filled with your sexual exploits."

"You are just a barrel of laughs today. Obviously, you're a morning person. You certainly weren't this much fun last night." She looked down at the hope chest. "So this is how you make money? You refinish antique furniture?"

"I don't refinish as much as buy and resell."

"And yet you won't sell the desk to me."

"I sell other antiques. The furniture in this barn belongs to my family."

Her eyes widened. "All of it? This is an entire house full."

"Which is exactly what I intend to do with it. Fill a house." He glanced at the hope chest. "Except for this piece. This piece is Gracie's. I thought she might want to use it as toy box for their new kid." Although he had no intentions of giving it to her until the baby was a few months old and healthy.

Again Savannah looked surprised. "And here I thought you were nothing but a selfish Grinch." She took a closer look at the chest. "Isn't this the same hope chest that used to be in your bedroom? I remember it from the night Gracie and I were here."

"You mean the night you and Gracie broke in. And yes, it's where I found the Tender Heart chapter."

"You found the chapter in this chest? I just thought you'd put it in there for safekeeping." She walked around, examining it from all sides before leaning close to look at the bottom.

"You won't find a maker's mark or label. This

piece was built by Lucy's father for her thirteenth birthday."

Savannah gasped in awe.

Raff wasn't surprised by her reaction. Like her friends, she was a rabid Tender Heart fan. And true fans loved all things that had once belonged to Lucy. That was why Raff was working on the chest for Gracie. She would love having something from their aunt. He had earmarked three other pieces of furniture to work on for Becky, Emery, and Carly when he was finished with the chest.

Savannah moved closer. "This was Lucy's."

"When she died, she willed it to my father." He started to go back to sanding, but she jerked the sander out of his hand and stepped between him and the chest.

"What are you doing? You can't refinish this wood. Don't you know anything about antiques? Especially antiques that have been owned by famous people. This finish is the finish that Lucy Arrington once touched. To remove it would be like removing part of its value and charm."

He wanted to reply, but he couldn't. His brain had short-circuited as soon as she'd stepped between his spread knees and placed those tempting breasts within range of his mouth. The green sweater had a V-neck. Not a low V-neck, but low enough to show a hint of soft swells and the shadowy valley between.

All the blood in Raff's body relocated to his crotch and throbbed beneath his fly like a second heart. A needy heart. And what it needed was to feel those sweet melons cradled in his hands. To taste their tips against his tongue. To see them swaying in front of his face when his needy heart was thrusting deep inside her.

"It would be like stripping the cover off a first edition novel," she continued.

Stripping. Yes, that's what he wanted to do. He wanted to strip that sweater right off her body, followed by her bra, and drown between those heavenly clouds of plump flesh. And she didn't seem to have a clue what her close proximity was doing to him. She just kept on jabbering while he drew closer and closer to doing something insane.

"Or like washing the last article of clothing worn by a historical figure. Or painting over the brick of a historical—" She cut off. "Raff? Are you okay? You don't look well. You look all flushed and . . . hot."

Hot didn't quite cover it. He was on fire.

She placed her hand on his forehead. But it wasn't her cool fingers that made him lose his grip on reality. It was her breasts shifting closer. So close he could smell the scent of her flowery perfume. So close that he could count each one of her breaths. So close that all he had to do was lean his head two inches closer to touch the soft swell above her neckline with his lips.

She sucked in a startled breath. The sound snapped him out of his sexual haze, and he started to pull back. Before he could, her fingers tangled in his hair and held him in place. That was all the permission he needed to open his mouth and take a taste of her warm skin with his tongue.

She tasted tart and heady, like homemade apple wine. He kissed his way to the vee of her sweater, then he raised his hands and cradled each heavy piece of fruit, lifting and squeezing until sweet flesh embraced his face. The abundance made him a little crazy. He kissed and licked his way over every exposed inch, mumbling incoherent words of praise for such beauty. He didn't know if he would've ever stopped if his phone hadn't started chiming. They drew apart.

He opened his eyes to find Savannah staring at him as if he'd grown horns. He had grown one horn. It was prodding him to pull her back into his arms. He resisted and grabbed his cellphone out of the toolbox.

"What?" he snapped.

"What bug crawled up your butt?" Sheriff Waylon Kendall said.

Raff tried not to look at Savannah. "Sorry. I was busy."

"I know what you mean. I've been working all night and this morning dealing with broken tree limbs in the middle of the highway, stranded travelers, and a sullen teenager wearing your coat who claims he's your houseguest's nephew. You didn't mention that you had a woman staying with you."

"I'll be right there," Raff said.

He would've liked to drive to Waylon's office by himself, but Savannah insisted on coming along. Fortunately, it seemed she was too stunned to talk. He was a little stunned himself. Usually it was his temper he lost control of. It had never been his lust. Even when he'd been a green kid and Debbie Crawley had offered him a chance to play with her big boobies, he hadn't just dived in. He'd paid for her dinner at the diner and spent a good hour kissing her at Whispering Falls before he slipped his hand under her shirt. With Savannah, he'd gone straight for the prize without any romancing whatsoever. And he was more than a little embarrassed about that. His face felt beet red all the way to the jail.

The kid looked relieved when he saw Raff. Or maybe it was Savannah he was happy to see. As soon as Waylon opened the door of the cell, the kid jumped up and hugged her.

"I'm so glad you came, Auntie Savannah. I tried to tell the sheriff that I was visiting you and Uncle Raff, but he didn't believe me."

Waylon exchanged looks with Raff. "Maybe because a guest wouldn't sneak off in the early morning after he robbed his auntie and uncle blind."

The kid drew away from Savannah. "I didn't sneak. I just wanted to go for a walk and I borrowed a few things."

"Cut the crap, kid," Raff said. "No one is falling for it. The only reason I came down here was for my favorite hat."

"And my journal," Savannah spoke up. Raff had gotten everything the kid had taken from his cabin, but Waylon hadn't found any journal in the backpack.

Savannah took the kid's arms like a teacher trying to get her student's attention and leaned down close to his face. "I'm not going to get mad at you for taking it, honey. All I want is for you to tell me where you put it."

The kid smiled. "Sure. As soon as you and Uncle Raff get me out of here."

"That will happen when hell freezes over," Raff

said.

Savannah turned to Waylon and flashed a bright smile. "Do you think I could have a few minutes with Dominic?"

"Dominic?" Waylon shook his head and laughed. "He told me his name was Dax Davenport. As if I wouldn't know the name of the infamous Tender Heart villain."

Savannah's smile dimmed. "Dominic is quite the prankster. Just a few minutes," she wheedled. "I promise not to break him out of jail." She glanced at Raff. "That will give you and Raff a little time to catch up."

She was being so pushy and secretive, Raff had to wonder if it really was her journal the kid had stolen. Of course, women would be weird about their diaries.

"Let's give her a few minutes, Way," he said. "You got any coffee?"

"Always," Waylon said as he followed Raff out of the cell. But when they got to his office, Raff wasn't interested in coffee as much as what was going on in the jail cell.

"I'm assuming you have surveillance." He sat down in the chair in front of the desk.

Way took a seat behind it and tapped his computer keyboard a few times until Savannah's voice came through the speakers. "You'd better hand it over, you little thief, or I'll let the sheriff keep you here like Raff said—until hell freezes over."

The kid's punky reply came only a second later. "No you won't. You want it too badly." He paused. "And just so you know, everything we do and say is being filmed and recorded."

Way laughed. "Smart kid." He turned the monitor so Raff could see Savannah staring at the camera with those big bluebonnet eyes. "Damn, she is one good-lookin' woman. Where did you find her?"

"She's a friend of my cousins."

"Well, I'd like to make her my friend. Is she single?" Waylon pulled his gaze from the monitor and glanced at Raff. "Or have you already called dibs?"

"Believe me, you don't want dibs on Savannah. She's more trouble than she's worth. You couldn't ask for a higher maintenance woman."

"I wouldn't mind high maintenance if it came in a package like that."

Raff's neck muscles tightened, and he got up from the chair and walked to the window. "Suit yourself."

"Hey," Waylon said. When Raff glanced at him he was leaning back in his chair, grinning. "All you had to do was say you were interested."

"I'm not interested!" Raff changed the subject. "So what are you going to do with the kid?"

"What we do with all runaways. Send them to the state facility in Austin until their parents can be located." Waylon shook his head "Of course, in this case, he might not be going back to his parents. When I was patting him down before I put him in the cell, I noticed some bruises on his lower back. He claimed they were from football, but they don't look like any bruise I ever got from football. They look like belt marks."

Raff felt guilty for being so hard on the kid. "That explains why he ran away." He rubbed a hand over the back of his neck and massaged the tight muscles. Muscles that had been tight ever since a sassy redhead and a runaway had entered his life. "I hope you're not going to send him back to abusive parents."

"I'll file a report of my suspicions, and child protective services will investigate. But if the kid denies it and they can't prove they're belt marks, there's not much we can do."

"And if the parents never show up?"

"He'll go to the state facility in Austin."

Raff hated the thought of the kid going back to abusive parents, but he also hated the thought of him spending the holidays with complete strangers. The last few years, Raff hadn't spent Christmas in Bliss or with his parents in Oklahoma. It brought up too many sad memories. So he usually spent the holiday in some roadside motel with a six-pack of beer. But that was his choice. The kid didn't have a choice.

"It looks like they've figured out a way to communicate without us listening in," Waylon said.

Raff glanced at the computer monitor. Savannah and the kid were sitting on the bed sharing a pen as they wrote back and forth on a notepad.

Waylon shook his head. "That's what I get for being distracted by a pretty woman. I didn't even notice she had a purse. Good thing she wasn't packing or I'd be looking for another job." He got up. "I think it's time to crash their party."

When they got to the jail cell, Savannah had put the notepad and pen back in her purse and was standing by the door looking annoyed. The kid was stretched out on the bed looking smug. Obviously, she hadn't discovered where he had hidden her journal.

As soon as Waylon opened the cell, she stepped out and spoke to Raff. "We need to talk."

Waylon offered to let them use his office, but Savannah politely declined. No doubt because she thought it was wired. Once Raff had collected everything the kid had stolen, she practically dragged him out the front door.

"The brat refuses to tell me where he hid my journal until I get him out of jail," she said once they were outside.

"Not happening. Even if you wanted to, you couldn't. Waylon can only release him to family or a state social worker."

"Then you better find a social worker who owes you a favor." She took a piece of folded notepad paper out of her purse and handed it to him. "He wanted me to give you this."

Raff took the paper and opened it.

Get me out and you'll get your gun.

"In the last year, Melanie had spent hours daydreaming about having Dax on the other end of her derringer. Now that she did, she couldn't help but savor the moment. 'You don't look like such a big, bad gunslinger to me, sweetheart.'"

CHAPTER SEVEN

&

"**A**RE YOU LEAVING ME HERE?" Savannah hurried after Raff as he headed back to his truck. "I wasn't the one who stole your gun. Luke did."

Raff stopped so suddenly she ran into him. Her heels hit a slick patch on the sidewalk, and she would've slid right between his legs and landed on her bottom if he hadn't turned and caught her. He set her on her feet. "Get some sensible shoes before you kill yourself. And who is Luke?"

She tried to ignore the sexy feel of Raff's muscled body pressed against her, but it was difficult. He had really nice pectoral muscles. Like really hard and nice. She tried to focus. "Dominic. I told him if he didn't give me his real name, I wasn't going to help him get out of jail."

"Let me guess. His last name is Skywalker."

She laughed. "Maybe. But for some reason, I think he's telling the truth this time. He looks more like a Luke than a Dominic or Dax." She shrugged.

"Anyway, that's what I'm going to call him."

"I'm calling him Little Shi—"

She placed a finger against his lips to cut off the cuss word. It was a mistake. As soon as she touched those soft lips, she remembered the feel of them against her breasts—the moist warmth of his first kiss and the heated slide of all the ones after. She wasn't surprised that he'd gone straight for her boobs. Every man she'd ever dated had done the same thing. But those men had made her feel cheap with their rough fondling and gasping. Raff had made her feel worshipped. Like her breasts weren't sexual objects, but things of breathtaking beauty. Just the thought of the way he'd touched her made her nipples harden.

She removed her finger and pulled out of his embrace. "Calling Luke names isn't going to get your gun back—or my journal." She mentally kicked herself once again for believing that the kid was asleep when she'd hidden the chapter in the cookie jar. He'd been wide awake, and her actions had clued him in to the fact that the chapter held value. Sheriff Kendall had verified it with his statement about the infamous Tender Heart series.

A gust of wind swept over her, and she shivered. Raff sighed in exasperation and slipped the sheepskin jacket he carried over her shoulders and buttoned the top button. The brush of his hot fingers against the skin of her throat made her shiver again. Or maybe it was the gentlemanly gesture.

"Thank you," she said.

"You're welcome. And we'll find your journal." She should probably tell him the truth about the Tender Heart chapter. It wasn't like Raff didn't know about the chapters—he'd even found one. But for some reason, she kept her lips zipped as he continued. "He had to have hidden it and my gun back at the ranch. I can't see the kid lugging a long rifle down the road in broad daylight. They're probably in the same stall he slept in." He turned and headed for his truck, leaving Savannah to hurry after him.

"But what if they aren't there?"

"They better be or the kid is going to be in jail for more than being a runaway. I didn't press charges about my clothes and a flashlight, but I damn well will over my gun." He opened the passenger's side door of his truck with so much force that she thought he was going to pull it right off the hinges.

"You really need to do something about that temper of yours," she said as she climbed in. "Maybe you should try some deep breathing or hatha yoga. There has to be something that calms you down."

"There is. Leaving this town." He slammed the door.

She waited for him to slide into the driver's seat before she continued the conversation. "You can't mean that it's Bliss that stresses you out."

She glanced out the window. When she'd first laid eyes on Bliss she'd been thoroughly disappointed. It had been nothing like the quaint town of Tender Heart that Lucy Arrington had written about. Most of the businesses had been closed and waist-high weeds had filled every vacant lot.

But in the last nine months, Bliss had undergone revitalization. It had started with Gracie finding the first chapter of the final book and had grown with each chapter that had been discovered. Emery believed that finding the chapters had made the townspeople remember their heritage—Gus Arrington, who had started the town in the late 1800s, and the cowboys and mail-order brides who had helped tame the Wild West. And town pride grew when Emery sold a non-fiction book about those mail-order brides to a big publishing house. Businesses had started sprucing up their storefronts and quaint old-fashioned streetlights had been put up along Main Street. The street would look even quainter with a few Christmas decorations— some twinkle lights in the trees and some greenery around the lampposts.

"How can a cute little town stress you out?" she asked.

"It's not the town as much as the responsibility that comes with it."

She glanced over at him. "What do you mean?"

He started the truck. "I'm an Arrington. The townsfolk expect Arringtons to be bigger than life. I've fallen far short of their expectations."

"From what I can tell, you haven't fallen short of your family's expectations," she said. "They all love you. And maybe if you spent more time here, the people of the town would be a little less judgmental. Maybe all they want is for you to accept your heritage."

He pulled out onto Main Street. "I am who I am. Take me or leave me. I don't really care." The words were spoken with such vehemence that Savannah had to wonder whom Raff was trying to convince: Her or himself.

"But if you don't care about the people who live

here, then why come back at all?"

"I didn't say I didn't care about the people. I just don't care to spend my life trying to please them."

"Then you're nothing like me," she said. "I'm the biggest people pleaser on both sides of the Mississippi." She noticed a little old woman walking along the street in a down coat and a wide-brimmed hat. "Oh, look, it's Ms. Marble. Stop so I can say 'hi.'"

"I'm not stopping. I don't have time for a women's chat-fest. I want to find my gun."

But Ms. Marble wasn't a person you drove past. When she spotted them, she held up her white-gloved hand like a traffic cop.

"Great," Raff grumbled as he pulled to the curb.

"Don't be such a Debbie Downer," Savannah said before she climbed out of the truck to give Ms. Marble a hug. "It's so good to see you, Ms. Marble. How have you been?"

"Busier than a bee in a field of sunflowers, what with the diner and the orders for holiday baked goods." She squeezed Savannah's hand. "And what are you doing here in Bliss? I thought you weren't due in for another week." She glanced at Raff who was walking around the front of the truck, and a smile creased her wrinkled face. "And with the town bad boy, no less."

Surprisingly, Raff gave Ms. Marble a big hug. "Don't be calling me bad. My daddy told me about some of your exploits when you were younger. The rest of the town might think you were a sweet little schoolmarm, but I know better."

She pointed a finger at him. "You watch your p's and q's, young man, and show respect for your elders." Her words were stern, but her eyes twinkled. "Or I'll have to put you in time out like I did when you were in my first grade class. And get your hat off when you're in the company of ladies."

Raff rolled his eyes, but took off his hat. "Yes, ma'am." He glanced at the plastic-wrapped plate in her hands. "Are those your famous cinnamon-swirl muffins I'm smelling?"

"They certainly are." He reached for the plate, but she smacked his hand. "They're for Joanna Daily. She just suffered a gallbladder attack and had to have surgery."

Raff looked genuinely concerned, which verified his love for the people of the town. "Is she okay?"

"She just needs a little bed rest, and she'll be right as rain. But unless we can find someone to take over the Christmas pageant, we might have to cancel. You wouldn't know anyone who has pageant experience, would you?"

Raff's gaze shifted to Savannah, and before she could shake her head, he spoke. "As a matter of fact, Savannah was just telling me about her pageant experience."

"That was just a little ol' beauty pageant," she said. "It wasn't a big deal."

"Now don't be modest," Raff said with an evil lopsided grin that made her want to kick him hard in the shin. "You told me you won the title of Miss Georgia with your amazing singing voice. I'd say that's a big deal."

Ms. Marble's direct blue eyes pinned Savannah like a butterfly to an insect board. "Miss Georgia? That sounds like you're more than qualified to me. The children already have their parts in the nativity story, all you have to do is go to a few practices and organize them."

The last thing Savannah needed to worry about was a Christmas pageant. Not only because she needed to concentrate on getting Raff to sell her Lucy's desk, but because she wasn't all that comfortable around children.

"I'd love to," she said, "but I'm afraid I'll be too busy helping Emery decorate the baby's room and Gracie decorate her new house."

"But I was just at Cole and Emery's the other day," Ms. Marble's said. "And the baby's room looks like it's almost done. Emery said you'd helped her pick out all the paint and furnishings online. And Gracie and Dirk are in San Antonio as we speak picking out the furniture for their new house."

Savannah scrambled for another excuse. "I'm an atheist."

"Now, don't lie, Savannah," Raff said. "You can't be an atheist when all you talk about is Sweet Baby Jesus."

She wasn't going to kick the man. She was going to strangle him.

"It's fine, dear," Ms. Marble said. "If you really don't want to do it, we can cancel. I'm sure people won't be that disappointed." She paused. "Although it will be the first time it's been canceled in close to a hundred years."

The people-pleaser part of her folded like a cheap lawn chair. "I'll do it."

"That's wonderful!" Ms. Marble patted her shoulder. "The first auditions are tonight at seven." She directed her unyielding gaze at Raff. "You can come too, Raff. We need someone to help build the manger and stables."

Raff held up his hands. "I'll have to pass. Dirk is the handyman, not me."

"Dirk won't be able to make it. The highways are a mess with all the downed trees and ice, and he and Cole don't want to chance being stranded with two pregnant wives. Dirk called me this morning and told me they decided to stay another night. Besides, you're much better at carpentry than he is." She straightened her hat. "Now if you'll excuse me, I need to get these muffins to Jo." Without another word, she headed down the street.

"I told you we should've driven past the woman," Raff grumbled as he walked back to the truck.

"Don't you dare blame me. You were the one who had to go open your big mouth and get us stuck with the Christmas pageant."

He grinned as he held her door open. The impish smile made him look almost boyish with his tousled brown hair and twinkling hazel eyes. "It *was* fun seeing you squirm."

"You just wait, Raff Arrington. Paybacks are hell."

His smile deepened, bringing out a dimple in his cheek. "Did southern belle Savannah just cuss?"

She lifted her chin. "Hell is not a cuss word. It's a place. Now if you don't mind, I'd like to stop at the diner. I'm starving."

Lucy's Place Diner was decorated fifties style with a black and white checkered tile floor, shiny chrome and red upholstered barstools and booths, and plenty of pictures of Lucy Arrington and the Tender Heart novels. Savannah wanted to sit in the booth that Lucy had sat in to plot all her books, but Raff was in too much of a hurry to get back to the ranch and search for his precious gun. She was in a hurry to look for the Tender Heart chapter too, but not so much that she couldn't enjoy the ambience of the diner—and possibly a slice of Ms. Marble's double fudge cake for dessert.

Raff stood at the cash register and placed their order to go. He ordered a cheeseburger, but Savannah ordered the daily special of chicken and waffles the Sanders sisters had put on the wipe-off board. Carly had hired the sisters to help her out at the diner. When Carly was supervising, they stuck to her chic California recipes. But when their boss was gone, they went full-out country comfort food with plenty of butter.

While Raff was paying for their order, Savannah noticed Old Man Sims sitting at the counter eating his lunch. Mr. Sims claimed to have been Lucy's lover when he was younger, which made him the number one suspect for hiding the chapters. Savannah hoped it wasn't true. The man had been married numerous times and was rumored to be a horrible womanizer. Which was confirmed when he glanced over, and his gaze zeroed in on her breasts.

"You're that big-busted gal that's friends with Emery and Carly, ain't ya?"

She ignored his rudeness because of his age—and because she wanted to find out more about his affair with Lucy—and moved closer so he could hear her. The man was hard of hearing. "Yes, sir."

He nodded. "I dated a few big-busted women in my day, including my first wife. Worst mistake I ever made."

She sat down on the barstool next to him. "I heard you dated Lucy Arrington too."

His bushy eyebrows waggled like furry caterpillars. "I don't know if you'd call it dating. And Lucy wasn't one of the big-busted gals. Her boobs were no bigger than tangerines."

She wanted to ask if he was basing his observation on appearance or feel, but she figured that would be getting a little too personal. "How long did you and Lucy . . . see each other?"

"Long enough." He leaned closer. "You single?"

Before she could answer, Raff walked up with a large carryout bag. "Hello, Mr. Sims. I can see you haven't changed much since I've been gone."

Mr. Sims glanced at Raff, then back at Savannah. "You with him?" He didn't wait for her to answer before he leaned closer to whisper. Except it wasn't much of a whisper. His voice carried through the entire diner and had the Sanders sisters peeking out from the kitchen. "You better be careful with that one. He's a pyro. Burned his family's house right down to the ground."

"It had been difficult not to touch Melanie when she'd been fifty feet away. When she was within two feet, it was impossible. Dax gave in to the ache that had been eating him alive for the last year. Ignoring the gun aimed at his heart, he pulled her into his arms and kissed her."

CHAPTER EIGHT

&

RAFF DIDN'T FIND HIS WINCHESTER. He looked in every possible place in the barn the kid could've hidden it and came up empty. Savannah didn't find her diary either, and she looked as hard as he did. Maybe even harder. As he searched, he could hear her opening and closing drawers and moving around furniture. But while he was ticked off when he didn't find what he was looking for, she wasn't. In fact, she seemed quite happy. That happiness didn't even dim when Carly called and said that their ranch hand needed to see a specialist and they wouldn't be returning from Austin until the following morning.

Raff's displeasure over the news must've registered on his face because Savannah laughed. "You look like you just ate a lemon. Don't worry. I'm not staying with you. I'm getting a room at the motor lodge."

"Good," he grumbled as he stared down at the white ball of fur rubbing against his pant leg. "I can't take any more feline affection." Or any more of Savannah's sexy-as-hell body being in such close proximity. It was damned distracting. And it became even more so when they headed back to the house and she changed into another dress and heels. The off-white dress was long-sleeved with a hem that hit her mid-knee. It covered her entire body so it shouldn't have been seductive. But he was learning that everything Savannah wore was seductive.

In the red dress, she'd looked like a shiny Christmas ornament he wanted to hold in his hands. In the green sweater, a brightly wrapped package he anticipated ripping open. Now, she looked like a fluffy snowflake he wanted to catch on his tongue . . . and make melt. He blinked away the memory of his tongue on her soft, pale skin and grabbed two of her suitcases. The sooner he got her out of his cabin the better.

"Let's get a move on. We need to get you settled at the motor lodge before we have to be at the church."

As it turned out, they couldn't get her settled at the motor lodge. Mrs. Crawley made it perfectly clear that she didn't accept pets. Not even for Savannah's "pretty pleases with sugar on top" or the extra fifty Raff tried to slip her.

"I won't have cat hair all over my sheets," the annoying woman said. "Do you know how hard it is to get off?"

Raff knew. The cat had only been in his house for a day and his thermal shirts looked like they were made out of angora.

"Maybe we could use Emery and Cole's spare

key and I'll sleep there," Savannah said as they walked back to his truck.

Raff wanted to, but even he knew that would be rude. "One more night of your company isn't going to kill me."

She sent him an annoyed look. "Gee, thanks." She glanced across the street at the diner. "Do you think we could grab something to go?"

She was always hungry. It should annoy him, but there was something nice about a woman who enjoyed food as much as Savannah. Most the women he'd dated had eaten like birds and were constantly talking about diets and losing a few pounds. Savannah had a healthy appetite and didn't seem to be ashamed of it. At the diner, she ordered the fish and chips and a thick slice of chocolate fudge cake for dessert.

"Hmm," she hummed and closed her eyes from the first bite of cake to the last. He almost reached orgasm just watching her. It was a relief when she pushed her plate away and they could head to the church.

The First Baptist was located at the end of town. It wasn't a pretty church. Nothing like the little white chapel that sat on a piece of land that was owned by all the Arringtons. The chapel had been built by Gus Arrington to give the mail-order brides a place to be properly wed. It was tiny but beautiful with its stained-glass windows and tall spire. The First Baptist was a one-story stucco building with an Austin stone front and a pitched roof that looked like it needed major repairs.

Raff wasn't exactly happy about being forced into helping with the pageant, but he wasn't as upset as Savannah looked when she got out of his truck. She clung to her cat like she was standing on the deck of the *Titanic* and the feline was a life-jacket. He couldn't help but take pity on her.

"It's not a big deal," he said as he hooked his coat over her shoulders and buttoned the top button. The woman really needed to buy a coat. "You'll just listen as the kids run through their lines a couple times, offer a few suggestions, and that will be that."

He was wrong. There was a little more to being a pageant director than he thought. Like crowd control. When they entered the chapel, there was complete chaos. Kids were chasing each other down the aisles, teenagers were taking turns belting out rap songs on the pulpit microphone, and the parents were gossiping in the front rows, seemingly oblivious to what their rug rats were doing.

Savannah took one look at the mayhem and turned for the door. Raff stopped her with an arm around her waist as he whistled through his teeth.

Everyone froze and looked at him.

He turned Savannah around. "This is Savannah Reynolds. She's taking over as pageant director for Joanna Daily while Mrs. Daily is recuperating. I know y'all will welcome her and show her all the respect due a guest in our town."

One of the little kids toddled up to him and pulled his thumb out of his mouth with a succulent pop. "Who you?"

The mother hurried over and picked up the child. Raff had gone to high school with her. "That's Raff Arrington, sweetheart." Melba smiled at him. "Sorry, Raff, but you haven't spent enough time in town for him to know who you are."

She was right. Which meant he had no business making a speech like he was a resident of the town. He cleared his throat. "I'll just see about the nativity." He glanced at Savannah. "You okay?"

She nodded, but she didn't look okay. He noticed Pitty squirming in her tight hold, and he took the cat. "I'll keep a close eye on her." With Miss Pitty in tow, he went in search of supplies to build a stable. While he was searching, Emmett showed up with a load of lumber in the bed of his truck. When he noticed the cat's head peeking out of Raff's shirt as they unloaded the wood, he grinned.

"Joanna has a cat. Hated that damn thing at first, but they grow on you."

Waylon wasn't as nice when he arrived a few moments later. "Aww," he said as got out of his sheriff's SUV. "Does Raff have a sweet little puddy tat?"

"Did you come to help with the nativity or just to chap my ass?"

Waylon glanced back at his car, and Raff finally noticed the sullen kid sitting in the passenger's side. "He still won't give me his full name. All I got was Luke. Since the name and his description don't match up with any of the reported runaways in the area, I called child protective services. Unfortunately, they can't send someone out until tomorrow or the next day." He heaved a sigh. "Chances are it will be even longer." He paused, and his eyes narrowed on Raff. "Didn't I hear that Lucy's daughter, Bonnie Blue, works for the state in some kind of transitional home for kids? Maybe I'll call her and see if she'll take Luke."

Raff could've offered to call Granny Bon. He and Dirk's grandmother had gotten close when she had come to Bliss to visit Dirk. But he didn't want to get involved any more then he already was.

"Anyway," Waylon continued. "I felt bad leaving the kid sitting in the jail cell with nothing to do. So I thought maybe a little Christian socializing might do him good. Do you mind keeping an eye on him while I fill out some reports?"

"I mind," Raff said. "I don't want the responsibility of babysitting some punky kid."

"It's only for a few hours, Raff. And he asked to be with you. I think he feels a connection with you and Savannah." Yeah, a blackmail connection. Waylon glanced around. "Where is Savannah, anyway?"

For some reason, Waylon's interest in Savannah annoyed him. "She's busy directing the pageant. And the kid doesn't have any connection to me. He just likes to piss me off."

Waylon released his breath. "Fine. I'll take him back to jail. But I really think Luke just needs a little attention to open up. And unfortunately, I'm too damned busy with the after effects of the storm to give him that. But don't worry yourself about it." He turned and lifted a hand. "I'll manage."

The opening-up part registered with Raff. Maybe if he gave the kid a little time, he'd tell him where the gun was. "Fine," he said. "Leave him. But if he runs off again, that's your problem, not mine."

Waylon turned back around and grinned. "Thanks, man." He motioned with his hand, and Luke got out of the patrol car and shuffled over. The kid really was scrawny. Waylon, who had been a star football lineman in high school, dwarfed him as he placed a hand on his thin shoulder. "I'm going to leave you here for a few hours. You listen to Raff and help him with whatever he needs help with." He pointed a finger. "No running. You got that? You run and I'll put an all-points bulletin out on you, and the next sheriff you meet up with might not be as nice as me."

"You're not that nice," Luke grumbled. "And your food sucks."

Waylon rolled his eyes at Raff before he walked back to his car. Once he was gone, Raff pinned Luke with the meanest look he could conjure. "Where's my gun?"

The kid grinned. "You get me out of jail—and don't make me go home—and I'll get your gun."

"Sorry, kid. I can't do that even if I wanted to."

"I'm not a kid. And you can do anything you want to. The sheriff told me the entire story of how your great-aunt wrote those famous books and how your ancestors started this town. I figure with that kind of history you've got to have some serious clout."

"Not a nickel's worth. I'm just an antique dealer who travels around the country searching for deals."

Luke looked thoroughly disappointed for a second, before he called Raff's bluff. "Okay, I guess you just missed out on the sale of a really cool gun."

Raff scratched Miss Pitty's head. "I guess I did."

Emmett called over. "If you two are finished jawing, we need to get this nativity built. I'll be the one to hear about it from Joanna if it isn't ready for the pageant."

Luke turned out to be more trouble than he was worth. Not only was he sullen and belligerent, he also didn't know one end of a hammer from the other. Emmett started to teach him, but then Joanna called and he had to go home. Which left Raff alone in the church gymnasium with the kid.

Irritated about the gun, he had little patience with Luke. He snapped at him for just about everything . . . until the kid stretched up to hold the front eave of the stable and his shirt lifted. Waylon was right. The bruises on his lower back didn't look like a football injury. They looked exactly like belt lashes.

Anger welled up inside of Raff—along with a whole lot of guilt for being so mean to the kid.

"Hurry up and hammer it in place," Luke grumbled. "This frame isn't exactly light, you know?"

Raff put down the hammer and nails. "Then you nail it and I'll hold it." He took hold of the frame.

Luke stepped back. "I thought you said I couldn't hammer worth shit."

Raff cringed. "Yeah, well, you won't learn unless you try. Just don't hit your thumb."

Luke ended up hitting his thumb. He also bent more nails than he hit in straight. By the time the pitched stable front was connected to the side frames, Luke had gone through an entire box of nails and Raff's triceps burned from holding the wood in place. But when he turned and saw the pride on the kid's face, his strained muscles didn't hurt all that much.

"I did it." Luke grinned.

Raff nodded. "You sure did. Now let's add some screws to secure it and see about making a manger.

You ever use a drill and a hand saw?"

It was surprising how well a little patience worked. Luke lost his sullenness and actually looked like he was having fun. He seemed to like using the power tools more than he'd like using the hammer. And Raff couldn't blame him. Power tools were "awesome." Raff had loved learning how to use them with his father. A father who had always been patient and full of praise.

"You're doing a good job," Raff said when they were halfway through completing the manger. "You'd make a good carpenter."

Luke glanced up, and his cheeks turned red. "Yeah, well, who wants to be a stupid carpenter?"

Raff shrugged. "Jesus did."

"Only because his dad did it. Or I guess his step-dad." The sullen look came back. "I'd never want to do anything my stepdad did. I hate him."

Raff turned over the manger and handed Luke another screw. "Hate is a pretty strong word."

"It's not strong enough for that asshole." He placed the screw in the hole Raff had drilled earlier. "And my mom just can't see it." He shoved the drill in and pressed the trigger until the screw embedded in the wood and the drill bit clattered against the metal.

Raff waited for him to pull the drill back before calmly handing him another screw. "Is this stepdad the one who hit you with the belt?"

Luke's head came up. His brown eyes locked with Raff's before he tossed down the drill and got to his feet. "Take me back to jail. I'm done with this shit."

Raff could've pushed for the truth, but he didn't

need to. Luke's reaction said it all. "I'll take you back when we're finished." He picked up the drill and held it out.

Luke hesitated for a second before he grabbed the drill and knelt back down to finish the manger. They didn't talk after that. There was nothing Raff could think of to say. No words that would change things or make a difference. When they finished, Raff gathered the tools and carried them back to the janitor's closet. He turned to find Luke staring down at the manger.

"I bet Joseph hated Jesus," the kid said. "First his wife comes to him already knocked up, and then he has to raise the kid as his own."

"As the story goes, an angel appeared to Joseph in a dream and explained things."

Luke turned to him. "And you'd completely believe some ghost showing up in a dream and telling you that your girlfriend was going to give birth to the Son of God?"

The kid did have a point. "If it were me, I'd probably continue to have a few doubts. But maybe God didn't judge Joseph on his doubts. Maybe God only judged him on his ability to love. There are a lot of dads and moms out there who love their stepchildren as if they were their own blood."

"I wish I knew one." Luke glanced over at him. "If you drive me to Austin, I'll tell you where I hid the gun."

Before Raff could answer, Waylon walked through the door. "Wow. This looks great." He walked around the false front of the stable. "Good job, you two."

The kid didn't say a word. He was back to being

sullen, no doubt angry that he hadn't had a chance to talk Raff into taking him to Austin. Not that Raff would've done it. Dropping the teenager off in a big city could be worse than sending him back to his stepdad. He could end up prey for all kinds of vultures. But would Luke fair better in the foster system? Luke wasn't exactly a warm and fuzzy kind of kid. Raff hadn't been either, but his parents had loved him regardless. And while his father had given him more than a few stern lectures, he'd never lifted his hand to Raff. Even when Raff had deserved a good spanking. What would it be like to live in terror of being physically abused?

The question rolled over and over in his head as he watched Waylon herd the kid out the door. And when Raff finally turned away, his gaze landed on the manger.

An empty manger waiting for a child.

"At the first touch of Dax's lips, it was like all the years melted away and Melanie was sixteen again kissing the cutest boy in Atlanta. But the dream quickly faded to be replaced with their last kiss. The kiss she'd given her new husband before he rode off to deal with an uprising of Sioux Indians. He'd never come back."

CHAPTER NINE

C

"YOU LOOK LIKE YOU SURVIVED," Raff said as they drove away from the church.

"Barely. It was like trying to corral a pack of wild wolverines." Savannah slipped off her high heels and snuggled back into Raff's sheepskin jacket. It smelled like him. Manly and . . . wooly. The scent was soothing. As was the country Christmas music that played on the radio. And she needed soothing as she recapped her night.

"Mary is a boy-crazy teenager who thinks the story would be more realistic if she and Joseph kissed every time they looked at baby Jesus. Joseph wants no part of the kissing or the pageant. He'd rather play violent videos games on his phone and throw me nasty looks. The wise men are three football jocks who forgot their lines every time they looked at my breasts. The shepherds decided to use their staffs for some kind of Kung Fu fighting. And the cute little angels were more like Satan's demons.

If they weren't pooping their pants and stinking up the place, they were letting out blood-curdling screams that sent shivers up my spine. One little terror bit my leg when I got after her for trying to eat her halo. But I was only worried she was going to choke to death on the glitter." She covered her face with her hands. "I swear I'm totally reconsidering having kids. And I'm not going back. I'd rather walk over hot coals and jump into a lake of fire then to have to deal with those hellions again."

She waited for Raff to have some snide comment. When he didn't, she glanced over. He was looking out the window as they passed the jail and absently stroking Miss Pitty, who was curled up on his lap. It seemed her precious cat had developed a fondness for Raff. Savannah could understand why. For all his grumpiness, there was something about him that made you feel secure and safe.

"Obviously, you couldn't care less about my horrible experience," she said.

When they had passed the jail, he turned to her. "I doubt it was that bad."

Now that she was all cozy in Raff's truck, she reevaluated her evening and realized that there had been a few precious moments. Mary might be boy-crazy, but she was a good actress. Tears had sprung to Savannah's eyes when the pretty young girl had cradled the plastic baby doll in her arms and looked at it with adoration and love. And the angels were adorable, even if they were loud and stinky . . . and quick to bite. Not to mention how appreciative the mothers had been about her taking over for Joanna Daily.

"Okay," she said. "I guess it wasn't that bad. But

I'm still not going back. There has to be someone else in town that has time to do it. What about your cousin Becky?"

Raff shook his head. "Becky would hogtie all the kids and call it a night. Besides, she has her hands full with the renovations she and Mason are doing on their ranch. You agreed to do it so I'd say you're stuck." He paused. "Just like I am."

"At least you don't have to deal with those wild rug rats." She sat up and grabbed her purse, searching for the candy bar. After her night, she needed a chocolate fix desperately.

She took a bite. "Sheriff Waylon stopped by to say 'hi' and told me that Luke was helping you. How did that go? Did he tell you where your gun and my journal were hidden?"

Savannah wanted the chapter Luke had taken more than ever. While looking in the barn, she had discovered four more chapters. All in different pieces of furniture—a baby cradle, beneath the cushion of a rocking chair, in a dollhouse, and behind the headboard of a white four-poster bed. Which proved that Raff owned more than a desk of Lucy's. Enough to make Savannah the talk of Atlanta if she could score the furniture for Mrs. Carlisle's house.

She should feel a little guilty about taking the chapters. But it wasn't like she was actually stealing them. Once all the chapters were found and Emery authenticated them, she planned to give the book to the Arrington family. Like her friends, she believed that the Arringtons deserved the royalties. Especially since Lucy had willed the royalties of her other books to the Texas state library system.

Savannah just didn't want Raff knowing where she'd found the chapters until after she struck a deal with him for the furniture. She knew it was devious, but she really needed those pieces and she wasn't sure he would sell them if he knew they were Lucy's. She would give him a good price. And selling them to someone who would appreciate them like Mrs. Carlisle was better than letting them sit and rot in a musty old barn.

"No," Raff said. "Luke didn't tell me where either were."

Savannah sighed. "He's one stubborn, angry teenager."

There was a pause before he spoke. "Maybe he has a reason to be."

Since it was the first time he had ever shown any sympathy towards Luke, Savannah glanced over at him with surprise. "Do I detect a hint of kindness inside Raff Arrington's hard tattooed shell?"

He didn't smile at her teasing. He just stared straight ahead with a somber look on his face. In fact, now that she thought about it, he'd been somber ever since leaving the church. He wasn't a smiley kind of guy, but he'd never looked so depressed before.

"What has you so grumpy?" She asked. "Building the nativity couldn't be as bad as being the pageant director."

His hands tightened on the steering wheel. "I think Luke's stepdad is physically abusing him."

"What makes you think that? Did he tell you?"

"No. But Waylon mentioned seeing bruises on the kid's back. Luke said they were from football. But when I saw them tonight, they didn't look like bruises you get from being tackled. They look like belt marks. And the way Luke hates his stepfather, I would say he's the one who dished them out." He slammed a fist on the steering wheel, causing Savannah to jump. "I'd love to get my hands on the asshole and show him how it feels to get beaten with a belt."

Savannah knew how it felt. She also knew how it felt to get beaten with a switch, a coat hanger, and anything else within her father's reach. No longer hungry, she rewrapped the candy bar and put it back in her purse. "We need to do something. We can't let him go back into an abusive situation."

"Waylon's already called children's protection. That's all we can do."

Savannah stared out the windshield and tried to convince herself that Raff was right. They weren't related to Luke. They had only known the teenager for less than a day. And yet, she couldn't help feeling responsible for him. Or maybe what she felt was empathy. She had been there. She knew what it was like to be left with no choice but to run. She'd been lucky. She'd found her aunts. But Luke had no one. His only choice was to go back to the hell he'd run from or to go into foster care.

"What about Granny Bon?" she asked. "Doesn't Dirk's grandmother work for an orphanage or something like that? Couldn't we have Dirk call her and see if she can take Luke? She's such a sweet, nurturing woman. I'd feel so much better about Luke being with her for the holidays than with strangers"

"I already called her after Luke left with Waylon."

"And?"

"And there's no room at the inn. The home where she works is completely full." He paused. "She did mention another option, but I don't see it as being viable in this instance."

"What is it?"

"If Luke is sixteen or over, he can file for emancipation from his parents. But in order for a judge to agree to that, Luke will need a job and a place to live. And the kid seems too irresponsible to hold down a job and too sullen to be a good houseguest."

Savannah turned to him. "Maybe he just needs a chance to prove himself. I was pretty irresponsible when I first moved to Atlanta. But then the aunts took me under their wings and I became a changed person."

Raff glanced over at her. "I thought you grew up in Atlanta."

She could've lied, but lying wouldn't help Luke. She needed to convince Raff that Luke was worth helping. "I was born in Louisiana. I didn't move to Atlanta until I was seventeen."

"With your parents' permission?"

"My mama knew where I was." She could feel Raff's gaze boring through her, but she didn't glance over. "What about Carly? I bet she'd hire him to bus tables at the diner. Or he could work for Zane at the Earhart Ranch. Or help Cole with his new horse ranch."

Raff shook his head. "I'm not saddling my family with a belligerent thief. They have enough to deal with."

"But maybe he wouldn't steal if he were around people who were patient and non-violent. Maybe he just needs a little attention and love."

"That's what Waylon thinks too. And I'm not going to argue the point, but who has time for that? All my cousins have their own lives and family to worry about. You are only staying for the holidays. And I don't plan to stay long, either. Once I find the gun, I'm gone."

She couldn't argue with him. After the holidays, she had to head back to Atlanta and convince Mrs. Carlisle to hire her. "Maybe Ms. Marble could be his mentor." When Raff cocked an eyebrow at her, she nodded. "You're right. We can't expect her to have to deal with a teenager."

She spent the rest of the trip back to Raff's cabin trying to figure out a solution to the problem. But there didn't seem to be one. When Raff pulled up to the barn, she was reminded that she had her own problems to worry about. She needed to get Raff to sell her the furniture. Her plan of becoming his friend wasn't moving along as quickly as she would've liked. While they were no longer enemies, she wouldn't exactly call them friends. She felt like Raff was just putting up with her until he could get rid of her.

Which meant she needed to up her game.

"You can take the bed tonight," she said when they got inside the cabin. "I'll be fine on the couch. Would you like me to make you some coffee? Or maybe some hot chocolate?"

He set two of her suitcases by the door before he helped her out of his coat. "Coffee keeps me up. And there's no chocolate or milk for hot chocolate." He hung the coat on the hook. "And I'll take the couch. I prefer sleeping without a cat on my head." He walked into the bedroom and closed the door. A second later, she heard the shower turn on.

While he was in the bathroom, she made up the couch, spreading one quilt over the cushions and another on top. She even gave him the pillow from the bedroom that was not covered in Pitty hair and plumped it up before leaning it perfectly against the arm of the couch.

After she folded down the top quilt, she got ready for bed. She chose the most modest nightgown she'd brought, a simple white floor-length made of silk charmeuse. She had just finished brushing her teeth at the kitchen sink when Raff came out of the bathroom in his boxers. They were light green this time, but just as sexy as the blue ones. With the power back on and the lights working, she could see him much clearer than the night before. There were no words to appropriately describe the perfection of his sculpted muscles. Some bulged while others rippled or stretched out in hard, lean plains.

"Do you work out at a gym?" The question popped out before she could stop it. He froze and finally noticed her standing by the kitchen sink. His gaze ran over her body before returning to her face.

"I run when weather permits and work out with the punching bag in the barn when I'm here."

"A punching bag?"

"My dad got it for me after I got in my first fight at school. He wanted me to take my aggression out on it rather than other people."

She tried to keep her gaze above his neck, but it was as hard as his pectoral muscles. "And did it work?"

"No. I still got in fights."

"Is that how you got the scar?"

He nodded. "I misjudged how many pissed off bikers I could handle at a bar in Houston. My mama completely lost it when she saw her son's disfigured face." He reached up and ran his thumb along the scar, stopping at the corner of his sensual mouth. A hot tingle settled in Savannah's panties, and she pressed her legs together.

"It's not that disfiguring," she said. "In fact, it's barely noticeable with your sexy growth of beard." Had she just said sexy? If his stunned look was any indication, she had.

His eyes narrowed as he studied her. "What are you doing?"

"What do you mean?"

"What's with the compliments and the sheer nightgown and the ogling?"

"Ogling? I was not ogling you. I was just . . . making conversation."

"When a man is in his underwear and a woman in some flimsy nightie that shows her nipples, that's not a conversation. That's foreplay."

She glanced down at her breasts, and sure enough, her nipples were poking out through the thin silk material like two soldiers standing at attention. She quickly crossed her arms. "Obviously, you don't know how to be polite company so I guess I'll just go to bed." She walked toward the bedroom with her head held high. But before she could get past him, he reached out and pulled her against his chest. Below his lowered lashes, his hazel eyes glittered with heat. When he spoke, his breath fell hot and moist against her lips.

"Do you want company, Savannah? Is that what the wide-eyed sweet southern belle look and sexy nightie are about? Because I'll be happy to join you in bed. But know this, it won't be polite. It will be raunchy." He nipped at her bottom lip. "Hot." He licked the spot. "And satisfying." He kissed her.

The kiss was raunchy and hot. But not quite satisfying. It was like the first bite of chocolate cake—rich and decadent and addictive. And Savannah wanted more. Much more. She slid her arms around his neck and pulled him closer. With a deep growl, his hands tightened on her waist and his tongue slid into her mouth in a sensual dance that left her lightheaded and weak-kneed.

He continued to kiss her as he scooped her up in his arms as if she weighted nothing and carried her into the bedroom. Once there, he set her on her feet by the bed and pulled away from the kiss. His eyes looked hot and greedy as his hands reached for the straps of her nightgown and slowly slid them off her shoulders. The silk slipped and then caught on the tips of her breasts. It hung there like the breath in her lungs as Raff reached . . .

Her phone rang. Or not rang as much as chimed out the song "Hey Good Lookin', Whatcha Got Cookin'?" It was the ringtone Savannah had attached to Carly's number. She hadn't realized how annoying and distracting the song was at the time. But she could ignore it for hot kisses. Unfortunately, Raff couldn't. He pulled back. Once there was space between her and his sizzling lips, she realized the mistake she'd been about to make.

She couldn't have sex with Raff. Not only because he wasn't even close to being her type, but also because he was the one thing standing between her and getting Mrs. Carlisle as a client. And if she'd learned anything from her relationship with Miles, it was never mix business with pleasure. While sex might work in her favor, she wasn't about to prostitute herself for a piece of furniture. Even for raunchy sex with a hot bad boy.

She clutched her nightgown to her breasts and pinned on her best beauty-pageant smile. "If you'll excuse me, honey, I better get that."

"Dax sat by the window of Miss Loretta's Saloon, nursing a glass of whiskey and staring across the street at the boardinghouse. There was no denying that he still loved Melanie. But he didn't deserve her. After his cavalry regiment's attack on the Indian village, he'd become a different man—a shell of a man who couldn't erase the memories of screaming women and children."

CHAPTER TEN

RAFF TURNED UP THE RADIO as he drove toward Bliss to meet with his cousins and sang along with Brenda Lee's "Rockin' Around the Christmas Tree." His voice sounded even flatter than usual. Or maybe it just sounded that way because he didn't have a worse singer joining in with him. He glanced over at the empty passenger's side.

Savannah was gone. Carly and Zane had gotten back from Austin and swung by to get her, her shedding cat, and her four suitcases. And just in the nick of time. If Carly hadn't called, Raff would've made a major mistake—sunk into that delectable body like there was no tomorrow. While there was little doubt he would've enjoyed it, Savannah wasn't the type of woman who did one-night stands.

She was the type who tried on wedding gowns just for the fun of it, had her colors and flowers picked out by third grade, and who heard wedding bells when she reached orgasm. And Raff wanted no part of marriage. Or maybe what he wanted no part of were children. It wasn't that he didn't like kids. He just wasn't strong enough to go through what his father had gone through. He couldn't stand by and watch a woman he loved have her heart broken again and again. He'd had a hard enough time watching his mother deal with her miscarriages.

He knew that the chances of a woman he married having the same problem as his mother were slim to none. And even if she did have the same problem, with medical advances, she might not have the same outcome. But he still wasn't willing to chance it. He was glad his cousins had all found happiness, but his happiness would be found repaying his parents for what he'd taken from them. Not with a woman . . . no matter how hot she looked in a thin nightgown.

He switched the radio station from Christmas music to a sports station and spent the rest of the trip to Bliss listening to the analysts talk about football. Once in town, he pulled into the parking lot of the Watering Hole Bar and parked between Dirk's and Zane's trucks. Inside the bar, it looked like Hank had done some decorating for the holidays. Cheap silver garland hung over the bar in uneven loops, a pathetic artificial tree with no more than ten ornaments stood next to the jukebox, and a laughing Santa wearing a tropical shirt and board shorts sat on the bar.

Being that it was early evening and wasn't Twofer Tuesday, when you got two beers and two wings for the price of one, the place was mostly empty. Only a couple guys sat at the bar talking with Hank, the owner and bartender.

When Hank saw Raff, he motioned with his head. "The boys are in the back."

Raff headed toward the poolroom. It looked like his cousins had started a game without him. And Zane and Cole had never been able to play a game without getting into an argument.

"You hit the eight ball in," Cole said. "Which means you just lost."

"Like hell," Zane said. "I hit it in on the break so that doesn't result in a loss." He glanced at Dirk who leaned against a barstool with a bemused smile on his face. "Tell him, Dirk."

Dirk blinked. "What? Sorry, I wasn't paying attention. I was thinking about what Gracie and I did last night—"

Cole cut him off. "Shut up! I don't want to hear what you and my sister do at night." He glanced over and saw Raff standing in the doorway. "Well, if it's not Better Late Than Never. I swear you'll be late for your own funeral."

"I hope so." Raff moved into the room. "So who's winning?"

"I just won. Zane hit the eight ball in."

Before Zane could start arguing, Raff refereed. "If he hit it in on the break, then he's right. He doesn't lose. It's treated like a scratch." He glanced around. "So where are the girls? I thought they would be here too."

Zane leaned on his pool cue while Cole took his shot. "They're decorating the chapel. They're all aflutter about getting it fixed up for Christmas Eve.

This is the first time we'll have a church service in it since before we were born. And speaking of church services, I heard you got wrangled in to helping with the Christmas pageant." He flashed a smile. "I hope you don't plan on sneaking out and smoking cigarettes behind the dumpster like you used to do when we were in junior high."

Cole laughed as he leaned down to take another shot. "I'd forgotten about you ditching Sunday school to smoke."

"I only did it a couple times," Raff said.

Dirk lifted an eyebrow. "And I guess you never inhaled?"

That got all the cousins to laughing. Raff waited until they were done. "If you're finished, I'll explain why I asked you to meet me here. I have a favor to ask."

A big favor.

After Savannah had left, he'd had trouble falling asleep. Some of it had to do with the desire pumping through his blood. But most of it had to do with Luke. He couldn't stop thinking about the bruises. About midnight, he'd realized that he couldn't let Luke go back to his stepdad. The only solution seemed to be emancipation. While he couldn't ask one of his cousins to take full responsibility for the kid, he could ask them to help Luke get a job and a place to stay. But before he could explain about Luke, Zane jumped in.

"I bet I know what favor he wants. He wants us to talk our wives into putting in a good word for him with Savannah?" When Raff sent him a surprised look, he laughed. "Don't try to act like you don't know what I'm talking about. I knew some hanky-panky was going on as soon as I walked in the door of your cabin. Both you and Savannah looked like kids caught with your hands in the cookie jar."

"Raff and Savannah?" Cole lifted his eyebrows at Raff. "Well, I'll be damned."

"Probably," Raff said dryly as he sat down on a barstool next to Dirk. "But there's nothing going on between me and Savannah."

"That's what I tried to tell him," Dirk said. "Savannah doesn't go for small town cowboys. From what I can tell, she likes big city men with money and power."

Raff should be glad he wasn't Savannah's type. And yet, he couldn't help feeling a little annoyed. "And look at how well that worked out last time. Miles sounded like a real catch."

"Carly can't stand the man," Zane said. "She wanted to seriously hurt him after he dumped Savannah." He paused. "Maybe you shouldn't set your sights on Savannah. Carly will rip your heart out if you hurt her friend."

"I'm not getting involved with Savannah," Raff said a little too loudly. He took a deep calming breath and lowered his voice. "I only gave her a place to stay while you guys were out of town."

"Then what favor do you want?" Cole asked.

"I was hoping you'd help out an abused kid."

Without another word, Cole and Zane placed their pool cues in the rack on the wall and joined him and Dirk at the table. Once they were seated, Raff told them the story of Luke, starting from the barn and ending with Granny Bon's proposal.

"I think filing with a judge for emancipation is a

bad idea," Zane said. "I can't see a sixteen-year-old kid being ready to live by himself."

"I was fifteen," Dirk said, "when I went to live with my father. And that was pretty much living by myself. I worked, paid bills, cooked, and cleaned the apartments we lived in. It was tough, but it has to be better than living with an abusive parent."

"What about a foster home," Cole said. "Couldn't Granny Bon make sure he got with some good people?"

Raff had thought the same thing. Unfortunately, he didn't know the system as well as Granny Bon. "She said the foster system is overwhelmed right now. There are a lot of children they need to find homes for. With Luke being so much older, he'll be the last one to get placed. And chances are, they won't get him in a home for months." He paused. "That's if Luke is willing to turn his stepdad in for abuse. Which I don't think he will. Especially if he thinks it's going to put him in foster care. And I can't blame the kid. I'd rather deal with the known than the unknown."

His three cousins nodded before Dirk spoke. "Then I guess emancipation is the only way to keep him safe. He can live with me and Gracie."

Cole shook his head. "No. You and my sister just got married. You need time alone. Besides, your house doesn't even have any furniture in it. He can live at the Arrington Ranch with me and Emery."

Zane spoke up. "I thought Emery's family was coming for the holidays. That's why you couldn't have Savannah stay with you. He can stay at the Earhart Ranch. My folks and Carly's are coming in this week, but I'm sure we can squeeze in one more." He shook his head. "Damn, I forgot that Becky and Mason are staying with us too. A water pipe in their house burst during the ice storm. But no worries, we can have Luke sleep in the bunkhouse."

Raff was grateful and proud that his cousins were so willing to help. But for some reason, he didn't like the thought of Luke sleeping in the big bunkhouse all alone. Before he could put much thought in it, he spoke.

"He can stay with me at the cabin through the holidays."

"You're staying here for Christmas?" Cole asked. "I thought you were headed out soon."

"I changed my mind." When Zane exchanged looks with Cole, Raff got a little annoyed. "What? Do you have a problem with that?"

"No," Zane said. "No problem. It's just that this will be the first Christmas you've spent in Bliss since . . ."

He left the sentence hanging, but the three cousins knew what word should be there. The only one who didn't know was Dirk. He hadn't been living in Bliss at the time of the fire. He hadn't seen the flames shooting into the sky that fateful Christmas Eve. He hadn't heard the sirens. He hadn't seen the total destruction. He hadn't witnessed Raff being handcuffed and carted off to jail.

Raff pushed down the emotions that always swelled whenever he allowed his mind to drift to the fire and got back to the subject at hand. "I'll only be here until New Year's. After that, I think Luke should stay with Zane and Carly. They don't have to worry about new babies, and I was hoping Carly could give him a job at the diner." He looked at Zane. "But I have to warn you that Luke is a sullen teenager with an attitude."

Zane grinned. "If I remember correctly, you were a sullen teenager with an attitude and we got along just fine. We'll work it out. We always do." He pulled a gold chain out of the collar of his shirt and held up the Native American arrowhead. An arrowhead similar to the one on Cole's keychain, the one attached to the braided band around Dirk's cowboy hat, and the one lashed with leather to Raff's wrist.

He, Zane, and Cole had found the arrowheads as kids and made them part of a secret pact to never become like their fathers. Their fathers had let a disagreement split up the Arrington Ranch and the family. Their sons made a vow not to make the same mistake. Dirk was now part of their family, and they had presented him with his own arrowhead on his wedding day. He took his hat and held it up. Cole held up his keychain. And Raff held up his fist.

"Arringtons . . . straight and true."

"Straight and true," his cousins echoed.

Normally, Raff would've stayed and played a few games of pool. But now that he had his family's support, he couldn't wait to talk with Luke and see what the kid thought of their plan. Since the jail was only a couple blocks from the Watering Hole, he walked. He was almost there when Ms. Marble called his name.

He turned to find her hustling across the street in her big down coat and bonnet. This one was decorated with a red ribbon and a cluster of holly berries that jiggled as she walked. Why the older woman was out after dark, he didn't know. But since she was coming from the direction of the diner, he figured it had to do with dropping off her baked goods for the following morning. Her tote bag was slung over her shoulder, and as soon as she stepped up on the curb, she opened it and pulled out a plastic-wrapped plate.

She held out the plate. "When I saw your truck parked at the Watering Hole, I thought I'd bring you a thank you for a job well done. I went by the church earlier today and saw the stables."

He took the plate and sniffed the plastic. "Cinnamon-swirl muffins?"

"Of course."

He smiled. "Thank you. But I still have a little sanding to do and the star to attach before the nativity is finished."

"I'm sure it will be perfect." She paused. "Waylon told me that you had a little help building the stables." The way she said it made Raff wonder if that's all Waylon had told her. She quickly confirmed his suspicions. "What a shame that a young man would feel like he had no choice but to run away. There has to be something we can do for that boy. And we certainly can't leave him in jail during the holidays."

"If all goes to plan, he won't be in jail. He'll be staying with me at the cabin."

A bright smile lit her wrinkled face, and she patted his arm. "You don't know how happy that makes me. You needed a reason to forget the past and stay where you belong."

He held up a hand. "Now don't be getting any

ideas. I'm only staying through New Year's. After that, Luke will live with Zane and Carly, where he'll be much better off."

Her steely blue eyes narrowed on him. "And why would your cousins be better mentors for that young man than you are?"

"I think you know the answer to that. I'm not exactly what you would call a good role model. I've always had a rebellious streak."

"Because you didn't fall into the townsfolk's crazy notions of how an Arrington should act? Some people might call that rebellion. I call that individuality. You chose to go your own way. Make your own choices." She paused. "And your own mistakes. While it's taken your cousins years to figure out how to separate themselves from the Arrington name and become their own men and women, you were always your own man. That takes strength and honesty. Two admirable qualities that every young man needs. So no, I don't think Luke would be better off with your cousins. I think he would better off with you."

She pointed a finger at him. "And in return, I think he would help you to realize that going your own way is fine . . . until it's time to come home. And this is your home, Raff Arrington."

"It's not my home. It's my parents' home. They are the ones who belong in Bliss." He didn't add that they would still be there if not for him. But for some reason, maybe because she had always been intuitive, Ms. Marble heard the words without him saying them.

"Maybe what happened on Christmas Eve was meant to be? Every time I talk with your mother, she seems happier than she's ever been. And so does your father. They needed to leave Bliss. There were too many sad memories here to deal with."

He knew Ms. Marble knew about his mother's miscarriages. She was the one person in town who everyone confided in. But like most people, she thought the only ones affected by those loses were his parents. She didn't realize that he'd been affected too. He'd had to watch the two people he loved most in the world suffer. She was right: There were too many sad memories here in Bliss. And that's why he couldn't live there. But his parents could. And he intended to make sure they did.

He tipped his cowboy hat. "Thank you for the muffins, Ms. Marble."

"There was no china. No finger sandwiches. And the teapot had a large crack that ran along the spout. But the tea party Melanie had been invited to by the wives of Tender Heart was the best party she'd ever been to. Probably because soon after she told the mail-order brides about her situation, the tea became more of a strategy meeting on how to catch a gunslinger."

CHAPTER ELEVEN

❦

SAVANNAH WAS IN HEAVEN. SHE was getting to do what she loved most—decorate—in a place that had filled her dreams since she had started reading the Tender Heart series as a young girl. The little white chapel in the books symbolized happily-ever-afters to Savannah. And the fact that it had actually existed and been the wedding site for eleven real-life mail-order brides made it all the more special.

Gus Arrington had built the white clapboard church in the late 1800s. And Savannah believed that the vows those mail-order brides and cowboys exchanged still hung in the air around the church like a magical love spell. Whoever made a wish for love at the chapel would receive it.

Savannah had made a wish the very first time she came to the chapel. It was just another reason that she believed that she would eventually find the man of her dreams. But for now, she wasn't worried about men. She just wanted to enjoy decorating the chapel with her friends for her favorite holiday.

Becky and Carly were hanging swags of evergreen branches over one of the stained-glass windows. Gracie and Emery were stringing lights on the Christmas tree in the corner.

"That brings the total number of chapters found to eleven," Emery said as she handed Gracie the string of lights to wrap around the other side of the tree. Savannah had given Emery the chapters she'd found in Raff's barn, and Emery had verified that they were indeed written by Lucy. So the decorating party was also a celebration. They were that much closer to finding the entire book.

"Twelve with the one that Luke stole." Savannah turned a potted poinsettia she was decorating the altar with to the fuller side, then stepped back to make sure she was satisfied with the arrangement. "But I can't really blame him for taking it. He was the one who found it first."

Carly finished hanging the evergreen garland and climbed down from the ladder. "I can't believe five chapters were in Raff's barn and he didn't even know they were there."

"He could've known they were there and just not cared." Becky picked up a box of red ornaments and started hanging them on the tree. Although she didn't seem to have a clue on placement. She was clustering the balls way too close together, which would put the entire tree off balance. "The men in our family have never cared anything about the Tender Heart series," she continued. "They think we're foolish to even waste our time looking for the book. But, of course, *they* aren't stupid when they look for Indian arrowheads."

"I know what you mean." Gracie finished hooking the lights on the bottom boughs of the tree. "Dirk thinks that silly arrowhead my cousins gave him is the best thing ever. He only rolls his eyes when I talk about the final Tender Heart book."

"Which is why Carly and I haven't told Zane and Cole about the other chapters we've found." Emery moved over to the table Carly had set up with snackies and picked up a carrot and dipped it in ranch dressing. "I can't wait to see their faces when we find the final chapters and present them with the entire book. Where exactly in the barn did you find them, Savannah?"

"In that pile of furniture Raff has collected." Savannah moved over to the tree and, as inconspicuously as possible, started rearranging Becky's balls. "It was just like an Easter egg hunt. One envelope was taped behind the headboard of an antique bed. Another under the seat of a needlepoint rocking chair. Another in an adorable dollhouse. And the last in a cradle. I'm assuming all the furniture once belonged to Lucy."

"But I thought the chapters were only hidden in places that had to do with Lucy's writing and the Tender Heart stories," Becky said.

"A writer's work is the culmination of all their life experiences." Emery munched on a ham and Swiss cheese wrap. She had gotten over her morning sickness and was back to eating. "Technically, Lucy's entire life has something to do with Tender Heart. Do you remember anyone in the family mentioning the items?"

Instead of answering, Becky stared at Savannah with her deep blue Arrington eyes. "Hey, are you touching my balls?"

Savannah didn't know Zane's sister as well as she knew the other women and was still a little scared of her tough cowgirl persona. "Umm . . . I was just doing a little rearranging to balance the tree."

Becky laughed and punched her playfully in the arm. It hurt. "Just kidding you, Red. You can touch my balls all you want. I hate to decorate as much as I hate to cook. Poor Mason got the boobie prize of wives when he married me."

"He did not." Carly joined the women at the tree. "You might not like to cook or keep house, but you know how to run a ranch. While Mason has been setting up his law practice in Bliss, you've single-handedly started your own cattle business."

Becky shrugged. "It's not that big a deal."

"Yes, it is," Gracie said. "The entire family is proud of you." She gave her a big hug before she answered Emery's question. "I remember the doll-house. I saw it in a picture of Lucy as a little girl. When I asked my stepfather if it was still around, he said that all of Lucy's childhood things had been sold or given away long before anyone knew how famous she would be."

Savannah was confused. "But how did they end up in Raff's barn? I thought he'd just inherited them."

"He must've discovered them while he was junk hunting. Anything of Lucy's that his family inherited was destroyed in the fire." Becky moved over to the food table and picked up a chocolate pep-

permint brownie. Savannah had already had two
so she tried to ignore the ooey-gooey bite Becky
took. "I don't know how he would've ended up
with Lucy's things. But I'm with Gracie, I remember the dollhouse from pictures."

Savannah should've taken the opportunity to ask
how Gracie and Becky felt about her buying the
dollhouse and the other pieces of furniture for Mrs.
Carlisle. But right now, she wanted to hear more
about the fire. She'd tried to talk to Raff about
it on the drive back to the ranch after Mr. Sims's
accusation, but he'd turned up the Christmas music
and pretended not to hear her. Obviously, it was a
tender subject.

"How did the fire start?" she asked.

Gracie and Becky exchanged looks as if they
were hesitant to discuss the fire at all. Which made
Savannah even more intrigued. Carly and Emery
looked as interested as she was. They moved closer,
their eyes intent as Becky spoke.

"It happened two years ago Christmas Eve.
Raff was visiting his parents for the holidays. After
college, he bought a Harley and started traveling
around the country. He was a bartender in Austin
for a while. Worked on an oil rig in the Gulf. Spent
some time in New Orleans working on a shrimp-
ing boat. He had almost as many jobs as Dirk."

The bad boy biker went with the first impres-
sion Savannah had of Raff. But it didn't go with
the man she'd come to know in the last few days.
Raff wasn't a bad boy. In fact, for all his tattoos and
gruff talk, he was a bigger pussycat than Miss Pitty.
He was gracious enough to offer Savannah a place
to stay, made her breakfast, and allowed her cat to

sleep on his pillow. He was chivalrous enough to open her doors, loan her his coat, and give up his bed. And he was kind enough to build the stables for the Christmas pageant and worry about a runaway. He might not be the type of guy she wanted to date, but he was a nice guy.

"It was an accident," Gracie said. "Raff started a fire in the fireplace after my aunt and uncle went to bed. I guess an ember flew out and caught the Christmas tree on fire."

Savannah's eyes widened. What a horrible accident. Poor Raff.

"Raff got his parents out and called 911," Becky took over the story. "But by the time the fire department got there, the house and everything, except for Lucy's hope chest, were gone. Which ticked off Raff. He got in a fight with one of the firemen and was tossed in jail. The charges were finally dropped, and Raff left soon after and didn't return until recently." Her eyes narrowed. "At least, that's what everyone thought. But if his barn is filled with antiques, he must've stopped by and just not let anyone know."

"Like he did when he came to see me after my horseback riding accident," Gracie said. "He slipped in and out of my hospital room without anyone else seeing him." She picked up the angel tree topper. "As much as he tries to act like he doesn't want to live in Bliss, I think he loves this town and is upset that his family no longer lives here."

"But why didn't his family rebuild their house with the insurance money?" Savannah asked.

"Because the insurance investigators claimed it

wasn't an accident. And speaking of accidents . . ." Becky walked over and took the angel from Gracie. "You're not getting on the ladder to put this on the tree. If you fell and something happened to those babies, I'd never forgive myself."

Carly stared at Gracie's rounding stomach. "Babies?"

The smile on Gracie's face was euphoric. "It seems I'm going to have triplets. I was going to tell y'all tonight." She shot an annoyed glance at Becky. "But Beck beat me to it."

Everyone took turns hugging and congratulating Gracie. The conversation turned to babies, and then husbands and married life. Savannah couldn't help feeling a little like an outsider. She, Carly, and Emery had known each other since college, where they'd bonded over their love of the Tender Heart novels. Even though they'd moved to different cities after they'd graduated, they made a point of facetiming or texting nearly every day and meeting up for girls' trips at least once every couple months.

Their last girls' trip had been to Bliss. Emery, who was an editor for a big publishing company at the time, had received a letter from Gracie saying she'd found the final Tender Heart book. It turned out that Lucy had written only one chapter of the book. But while figuring that out, Emery fell in love with Cole. Then Carly got fired from her job in San Francisco and decided to reopen the diner. She fell in love with Zane. Now they were part of the Arrington family and sister-in-laws with Becky and Gracie.

Savannah was the only one who no longer fit

into the group. Not only because she wasn't married to an Arrington, but also because she didn't live in Bliss. She couldn't just run over to one of the ranches and sit on the porch for sweet tea and a chat. Or stop by the diner for a girls' lunch. And when the conversation moved to all their families coming in for the holidays, she really started to feel like the odd woman out.

"I didn't think my parents would want to come," Carly said. "But my dad fell in love with the ranch when they came for the wedding and jumped at the chance to come back when Zane invited them for the holidays. They get here on Friday." She glanced at Becky. "Are you sure you and Mason don't mind sleeping on the sleeper sofa in the study while they're here?"

"It's better than sleeping in our flooded house."

Savannah hadn't even thought about the sleeping arrangements now that Becky and Mason had to move out of their house because of the busted water pipes. Carly's house would be filled to the brim with family . . . and one friend who no longer fit in.

"I don't mind sleeping on the sleeper sofa," she said. "You and Mason should have your old room, Becky. And Carly's parents should have the guestroom. In fact, why don't I just get a room at the motor lodge? That way I don't have to bug anyone to drive me into town for the Christmas pageant rehearsals—since the rental car company has yet to send me another car."

"You're not staying at the motor lodge for the holidays. There's plenty of room at my house," Carly said. "And I don't mind driving you into town for rehearsals. I need to close up the diner anyway."

"I still can't believe that you let Ms. Marble talk you into being the director," Becky said. "Although that woman could talk a sinner into church."

Carly laughed. "And Savannah is one big sinner." She glanced at her watch. "And speaking of the rehearsal, we'd better finish up here if you want to be on time."

Everyone pitched in to finish the tree, and Savannah continued to do a little rearranging to make everything perfect. When they were finished, they turned off the overhead lights and plugged in the tree. The clear glittering lights danced off the ornaments and the stained-glass windows, giving the chapel even more of a fairytale look.

"It's beautiful," Savannah breathed. "I wish Lucy had written a Christmas story. I know she would've written the chapel just like this—except with candles on the tree instead of lights."

Emery stepped up and took her hand. "Maybe the last book does end on Christmas. We won't know until we find all the chapters."

"Who do you think is hiding them?" Gracie asked. "Who would know that Lucy's furniture is in Raff's barn?"

"Maybe the same person who sold it to him," Becky said.

Carly moved next to Savannah. "My bet is still on Mr. Sims. He claims he dated Lucy. He worked a short time for the Arringtons. And he also lived at the Reed Place where Becky and Gracie found Lucy's diary."

"I'm sorry," Becky said, "but I can't stand the

thought of Old Man Sims being Lucy's Honey Bee. It sounds like he was trying to get into every woman's pants in town. I just can't see Lucy falling for a man like that."

"Maybe he had a really nice body," Savannah said. "Women can lose all rational thoughts over a really nice body." At least, she had lost all rational thoughts over Raff's body. If Carly hadn't called, there was little doubt that she would've had sex with Raff. A part of her was thankful, but the other part wished her cellphone had gone dead.

"He's still our only lead to who's hiding the chapters," Emery said. "And we can't just come out and ask him. If he's being so secretive about hiding the chapters, he'll just lie. We need to get inside his house."

Carly glanced over at Emery, her brown eyes reflecting the lights from the Christmas tree. "Are you talking about breaking and entering?"

"Of course not. I'm talking about taking him a Christmas gift basket." Emery smiled deviously. "And possibly slipping away to go to the bathroom and checking out the rooms in his house for envelopes or more chapters."

"I am not stealing from an old man like Savannah stole from Raff," Carly said.

"I did not steal, Carly Sue!" Savannah glared at Carly. "The chapters belong to the Arringtons. I just want to make sure they get published so I can find out what happened to Dax. And knowing Raff, he would leave the chapters in his barn to rot with the furniture."

"What chapters?"

Savannah froze at the deep voice, then slowly

turned to see Raff standing in the doorway of the chapel looking like a desperado with his black hat, form-fitting black t-shirt, and faded jeans. Miss Pitty, who had been fast asleep under one of the pews last time Savannah checked, was rubbing against his legs. Raff didn't seem to notice. His attention was directed on Savannah. And he looked mad. Real mad.

She pinned on a big smile and motioned at the tree. "What do you think, honey?"

He didn't even glance at the evergreen. "I think you and I need to have a little talk."

"Dax knew what Melanie was up to. She was trying to make him jealous by flirting with every cowboy in town. He was jealous, but he wouldn't let that jealousy keep him from the reason he'd come to Tender Heart. He intended to find Mellie a better husband than he was."

CHAPTER TWELVE

❦

"WHY, IT WAS JUST SO sweet of you and Luke to pick me up for church, Raff. Some people might think you're nothing but a big ol' meanie, but I know better." Savannah flashed a bright smile over at him.

She might be all bright smiles and southern charm, but it was obvious she was nervous by the way she was fidgeting with the straps of her purse. And she should be nervous. Raff was fit to be tied that she'd lied to him about finding chapters of the final Tender Heart book in his barn. But he was having a hard time concentrating on his anger with her sitting so close.

He hadn't really thought things through when, after he picked up Luke from the jail, he decided to swing by and get Savannah. His Chevy had one bench seat, and with Luke refusing to give up shotgun, that left Savannah in the middle. Every time he shifted gears, he had to make sure to keep his arm from brushing against her breasts. Then there was the way she smelled. He couldn't pinpoint a scent tonight. It was more a mixture of all things woman—flowery lotion, clean shampoo, and expensive perfume.

He tried to ignore the scent and her breasts that filled out her pink sweater to perfection and concentrate on her deception. "Cut the butt kissing, Savannah. It's not going to work."

She crossed her arms, poking him sharply in the ribs with her elbow and causing her cleavage to swell over her neckline. Didn't the woman have a clue what her body could do to a man? He clutched the steering wheel and tried to keep his gaze on the road.

"I do not bottom kiss," she said. Okay, that wasn't an image he needed at the moment. "I was just trying to lighten the mood. But if you want to continue to be grumpy about a little old fib, that's your prerogative."

"A little fib? I think you mean a huge lie."

"Fine. I lied. I should've told you about finding the chapters."

"You didn't find the first one. I did."

Raff glanced over at Luke, who was slumped down in the seat with a sullen look on his face. On the ride to the Earhart Ranch, he hadn't talked much. Raff and Waylon had told him about his option to file for emancipation. Luke had immediately jumped on the idea until he found out that the judge would probably want to talk to his mother. Once he'd learned that, he'd immediately shut down, and Raff could understand why. It had to be hard to have to tell your mom that you didn't want to live with her anymore. Which was why

Raff had invited Luke to rehearsal. He hoped that a little woodworking would distract the kid from his problems.

"Where did you find the chapter?" he asked.

Luke glanced over, and his eyes widened when he noticed Savannah's cleavage. Raff should've gotten after the kid for staring, but he really couldn't blame him. It was a distracting sight. Savannah finally noticed and quickly lowered her arms and tugged up the neckline of her sweater.

"It is impolite to stare, young man."

Luke blushed before answering Raff. "I found it in the top drawer of the old desk in the first stall."

Raff nodded. "I should've guessed that it would be in Lucy's childhood desk." He downshifted to make the turn onto the highway. He would've avoided Savannah's boobs if she hadn't lean up at the same time. The back of his arm brushed against soft resilient flesh. He pulled back as if burned, but she didn't seem to notice.

"So it *is* Lucy's desk?" she asked in an excited voice. "And the dollhouse, bed, rocker, and cradle where I found the other chapters, those were Lucy's too? Where did you find all her childhood furniture? Becky and Gracie said that most of it had been sold long before Lucy became famous. Did someone in town have it? Mr. Sims?"

He glanced at her. "Why would Mr. Sims have it?"

She shrugged and smiled innocently. "Just a guess. So where did you find it?"

"Different antique dealers around the state."

"You mean you just stumbled upon it?"

He hadn't stumbled upon it. He'd been pur-

posely searching for Arrington artifacts to replace
the ones that had been destroyed in the fire. He'd
taken old pictures of his ancestors and zoomed in
on saddles, furniture . . . or guns. Then he'd placed
the pictures in antique magazines and with online
dealers. He used an alias. He didn't want them
knowing the value of the antiques he was searching for. Especially the ones owned by Lucy. There
were too many rabid Tender Heart fans around
that would up the price until he couldn't afford to
buy them.

His search was what started his antique business.
He figured while he was looking for Arrington
artifacts, he might as well make some money. But
that wasn't something he wanted Savannah to
know. His father didn't even know why his only
son had become an antique dealer. He didn't know
that Raff was trying to assuage his guilt by giving
his father back some of his heritage.

Thankfully, before he had to lie to Savannah,
Luke jumped into the conversation. "So this Lucy
hid all the chapters of her book for people to find?
That's fuckin' weird."

"Watch your mouth, young man!" Savannah
snapped.

Luke shot her a mean glare. "So it's okay to steal
the chapters from Raff, but not to cuss?"

Her cheeks got brighter, and Raff couldn't help
but smile as she cleared her throat. "I was not stealing. I have no intentions of taking any money from
the sale of the final book. That money should go
to the Arrington family. I just wanted to make sure
that the chapters got to Emery so the book could
be published . . . instead of becoming a nest for a

bunch of barn mice." She glanced at him. "How can you let Lucy's desk sit out in an old barn with a leaky roof? It needs to be in a beautiful home where it can be appreciated."

"It will be in a home. Just not your client's." The faint sound of Elvis singing "Blue Christmas" came through his truck speakers. He reached out and turned up the volume, then started singing along. Savannah soon joined in, singing as badly as he did. He thought she would've been mad about not getting Lucy's desk, but in the last few days, he'd learned that she wasn't one to hold a grudge. In fact, nothing seemed to take the smile off her face for long. She viewed life through rose-colored, southern-belle glasses. No matter how bleak things were, she always looked for the silver lining. At first, her brightness had been a little annoying. But now, he found himself kind of liking it.

When they got to the church, Savannah headed to the auditorium while Luke and Raff headed to the gym to finish the stables. But they had barely started on the sanding when Savannah came hurrying through the door, her high-heeled boots hitting the tile floor in rapid staccato clicks.

"The entire pageant is going to be ruined! Completely ruined!" She stopped in front of the manger Raff was working on and wrung her hands. "It's Joseph. He says he came down with the flu, but he didn't sound sick at all on the phone. He sounded as happy as bug in a rug that he could now stay home and play his silly video games. And there's no way we can have a Christmas pageant without Jesus's dad—"

She cut off as her gaze zeroed in on Luke. The

kid was staring at her boobs again, but this time, Savannah didn't get after him. Instead, she strutted over and placed her hands on his shoulders, giving him a smile that would bring most men to their knees. "Luke, honey, how would you like to do me a big favor? I promise it will be a lot more fun than sanding a piece of splintery ol' wood"

Luke was completely boob-stunned and didn't have a clue what was happening. Poor kid. "Okay. Sure." He followed after her like a sheep to slaughter, and Raff couldn't help going along to watch.

This time, when he walked into the church, there was a lot less mayhem. It looked like Savannah had organized the children into groups according to their parts. They weren't wearing costumes, but each group had something that distinguished them. The angels had halos. The wise men had crowns—and one a weird purple feathered hat. The shepherds had their staffs. The manger animals were on all fours. And Mary was holding a plastic baby. Each group had older teenagers supervising. Although the angels were still running amok.

Raff decided it was best to watch from a distance and took a seat in a pew in the back. As a child, he'd always sat in the front pews with the rest of the Arringtons. He remembered feeling a huge burden sitting at the front of the church—as if everyone in town expected him to be more godly. He felt the same way about being an only child. He felt like he had the burden of all his father's and mother's hopes and dreams. And maybe that was why he'd been so rebellious. If he couldn't be perfect, he'd just be perfectly imperfect.

"Oh, no"—Luke shoved the stapled pages

Savannah had just handed him back at her—"I'm not being Joseph. You can just forget that shi—" He cut off abruptly when Savannah's eyes shot fire.

"Watch your mouth in the Lord's house," she growled.

"Fine." Luke shook his head. "But I'm not doing it. No how. No way." He turned and headed up the aisle, stopping at Raff's pew. "You can't make me do it either. I don't want to wear some stupid looking sheet and ask if there's any room at the inn. If he was God's son, you'd think God would've make reservations for his mom and dad ahead of time."

Raff smiled. "You would think that, but I guess that wasn't how the story went."

"Well, it's stupid." Luke flopped down next to him. "And I'm not doing it."

Raff shrugged. "Okay with me. But I think you're making a mistake."

Luke glanced over at him. "The only mistake would be doing a dumb kid's Christmas pageant."

"Maybe, but a judge would probably be much more willing to emancipate a sixteen-year-old kid who played Joseph in a Christmas play than he would a belligerent kid who refused to participate. Besides, you can't tell me that you don't think Mary is kind of cute."

Luke slumped down in the pew and glared at the scuffed toes of his Nikes. "She's not as hot as Savannah."

"Savannah is way out of your league." He watched Savannah walk across the stage like she was Miss Georgia in a beauty pageant and pick up an angel who was crying about something. "She's even way out of mine," he muttered. "She's after rich guys." Although, at the moment, he couldn't picture her with some wealthy dude in a designer suit. She looked right at home in the midst of all the pageant mayhem as she tried to sweet talk a wise man into being Joseph while the toddler wiped his snotty nose on her sweater.

Luke sat there for a few minutes before he spoke. "You really think it will make a difference with a judge?"

"I know it will."

Luke got up. "Fine. But I'm not kissing Mary. At least, not in front of an entire church."

Raff bit back a grin. "Fair enough."

Once Luke got over his pouting, he turned out to be a pretty good Joseph. His voice was strong and loud enough to be heard clear in the back and he had his lines down cold after only a few run-throughs. He even held the swaddled baby doll. Although he held it more like a football than a baby. Still, Savannah was smiling to beat the band by the time rehearsal was over.

"What did you say to him to change his mind?" she asked as she sat down in the pew next to Raff.

"I told him that I thought Mary was hot."

Her gaze swept over to him. "That is just sick, Raff Arrington. You don't talk about Jesus's mother like that."

"You don't think that Joseph thought Mary was hot?"

"No. He thought she was beautiful. You see hot with your libido. You see beauty with your heart." She smiled at a little angel who came tearing down the aisle with her daddy giving chase. "Now that's beautiful," she said when the daddy finally swung the angel up into his arms.

The swift punch of longing took Raff totally by surprise. After all his parents' painful losses, he had thought the desire for children wasn't in him. But as he watched the dad cover his daughter's chubby cheeks with kisses, a deep yearning flickered to life. It terrified him. He had seen the pain and devastation the yearning could cause. With a firm resolve, he doused the flame and looked away.

"Well, I'm just thankful Luke was willing to take over the part," Savannah said. "He's really a sweet kid deep down, and we can't let him go back to his abusive stepdad." She took a half-eaten candy bar out of her purse.

"I talked with my cousins, and Zane is willing to give him a job at the diner and a place to live if we can get a judge to agree with emancipation."

Her eyes lit up. "That's wonderful news! I knew the Arringtons would come through." She smiled. "And you." She started to eat the candy bar, but hesitated. She snapped it in two and offered him a piece.

Since he knew how much she loved chocolate, he was going to decline. But there was something about the way she passed the candy to him that was almost like a peace offering. He took it with a nod of thanks before popping it into his mouth. "I thought you were allergic to peanuts."

She closed her eyes as she ate the last of the candy bar and sighed. "I am."

"You must not be too allergic if you're eating a Butterfinger."

She opened her eyes. "They aren't made with peanuts, silly. They're made with butter. Butter-finger."

He lifted an eyebrow. "Are you sure you weren't dropped on your head as a kid?"

She sent him an annoyed look before she flipped the wrapper over. "It says right here that they're made with corn syrup, sugar, ground roasted pea—" She stared at the wrapper and clutched her throat. "Oh my God, I'm going to die."

He rolled his eyes. "You're not going to die. I'm assuming this is the candy bar you were munching on the other night. If you were allergic, you'd already be dead."

"But I don't understand. I could've sworn I was allergic to peanuts. My big brothers told me a story about how I swelled up and almost die when I ate a peanut at the age of three, and I did start to swell a little that time Carly used peanut oil. Of course, one Benadryl took care of it."

"I don't think Benadryl takes care of a nut allergy. And did you ever think that your big brothers might've been lying to get you to stay away from their candy?"

She sat there for a stunned moment before she giggled with glee. "Well, thank you, Sweet Baby Jesus. Now I can have Reese's Peanut Butter Cups."

Raff burst out laughing.

"The plan wasn't working. Dax wasn't acting the least bit jealous. In fact, he was pointing out men he thought would make her a good husband. And maybe that was the problem. Maybe she shouldn't go for a good husband as much as a bad one."

CHAPTER THIRTEEN

❧

MR. SIMS LIVED IN A huge Victorian-style house that looked much too big for one little old man.

"He lives here by himself?" Savannah asked Gracie as they walked up the pathway.

"Gossip has it that he inherited it from his third wife." Gracie glanced at the basket of holiday goodies Carly had packed for them to bring to Mr. Sims. "Are you sure you don't want me to take a turn carrying that? It looks heavy."

Savannah lugged the basket up the porch steps. "It is heavy, which is exactly why I'm not going to let you carry it. My Aunt Rue said that carrying heavy things when you're pregnant can give the baby a bad back—not to mention the mama a bad case of hemorrhoids. And you don't want hemorrhoids or three babies with bad backs." She stopped at the front door with the *No Solicitors* sign and whispered. "Maybe we should've called first."

Gracie shook her head. "We have a better chance

of finding proof that Mr. Sims is the one hiding the envelopes if we surprise him. And there's no need to whisper. Mr. Sims is hard of hearing. We'll be lucky if he hears the doorbell."

Gracie was right. It took Savannah pushing the doorbell numerous times before Mr. Sims jerked open the door. "Can't you read—" He cut off when he saw Savannah and Gracie. "You two beautiful ladies aren't selling anything, are you? Unless it's Girl Scout Cookies, I have enough junk as is."

Savannah held up the basket. "We brought you some holiday goodies."

His eyes narrowed on the wrapped baked goods in the basket. "I hope that old battle ax Ms. Marble didn't bake them. That woman has had it out for me since she thought I tattled to her mama about her having a crush on an Arrington ranch hand—as if anyone with eyes couldn't see how infatuated she was with that cowboy."

"No, sir," Gracie said. "Ms. Marble didn't do the baking. Carly and Savannah did." Savannah nodded, even though she wasn't sure if licking the frosting beaters and eating cookie dough qualified as helping. If it did, she'd more than done her fair share.

Mr. Sims held a hand to his ear. "What's that you say? You just came from Savannah?"

Gracie shook her head and yelled louder. "Ms. Marble didn't bake any of this."

He nodded. "Good." He glanced again at the basket. "You better bring it in. Last time I tried to lift anything that big I tipped over like a bowling pin and broke a hip." He turned and shuffled off, leaving Gracie and Savannah to follow.

The house was old, but filled with character. Intricate crown molding run along the coffered ceilings, beautiful antique light fixtures and sconces hung from the ceilings and decorated the walls, and the wood floors looked to be solid maple. Mr. Sims lead them into the front room that would've been referred to as the parlor in early times. The fireplace with the maple mantel and marble inset made Savannah want to weep with pleasure. But the rest of the room's décor was atrocious.

The furniture was an eclectic mix of decades, ranging from early twentieth-century end tables to a brand new Lazy Boy recliner. She thought Mr. Sims would sit down in the new recliner. Instead, he sat in an overstuffed chair with grease-stains on the arms. Gracie and Savannah sat down on the 60s-style orange sofa with the lumpy cushions.

"My grandson had that shipped to me for Christmas." He pointed at the new recliner. "It's got a remote that supposedly lifts your feet up." He shook his head. "I tried it once and almost got ejected like a pilot out of a plane." He turned to them. "Did I ever tell you about flying in the Korean War?"

The next hour and half was spent listening to Mr. Sims's war stories. Savannah had almost nodded off when Gracie elbowed her in the ribs. "Do you think I could use your bathroom, Mr. Sims?" she asked.

"Use my what?"

"Your bathroom!"

"Up the stairs and to your right," he said as he turned back to Savannah. "So where was I?"

Unable to listen to any more bragging about

his flying expertise, Savannah got up and headed to the shelves that were lined with pictures. "Are these all photographs of your family?" She spoke loud enough so he could hear her. "My, what a handsome lot."

Behind her, Mr. Sims snorted. "All except the oldest girl's family. She married that ugly boy from Big Springs and every one of her kids looks just like their daddy. Homely as mud fences."

Not knowing how to reply to that, she continued to peruse the photographs in silence. Surprisingly, she recognized numerous children that were in the Christmas pageant, including the young girl playing Mary. Obviously, Mr. Sims had done his fair share of populating Bliss. She was about to turn around and tell him about directing his grand-children—or great-grandchildren—in the pageant when she noticed a photograph in the back. She moved the framed pictures in front so she could get a better look.

It was of Mr. Sims when he was much younger. He was dancing with a pretty woman in a 50s-style dress. But it wasn't Mr. Sims or the woman who had caught her eye. It was Lucy Arrington. She danced in the background with a handsome cow-boy in a straw cowboy hat. The profile of the man looked familiar with his perfect features and cocky smile, but Savannah couldn't quite place him.

She carried the picture over to Mr. Sims. "Who is this?"

Mr. Sims glanced at the photo. "That's me and my first wife Roberta." He shook his head. "She was a lively one. Always wanted to go dancing. I swear it was the dancing that killed her . . . or it might've been the booze. She could drink any man right under the table."

Savannah held the picture closer to Mr. Sims. "And who's that with Lucy?"

"Lucy?" Mr. Sims squinted at the photograph. "Why, hell, I didn't even realize Lucy Arrington was in this picture. But sure as shootin', there she is." He looked up and winked at Savannah. "No doubt, she was hopin' for a turn with ol' Doug Sims."

It didn't look like Lucy was waiting for a turn to dance with him. She looked quite content with the man she was with. Savannah could understand why. The cowboy was as good-looking as sin. And familiar. She knew she'd seen that face before.

"The man," she said louder. "Who is the man Lucy's with?"

Mr. Sims squinted at the photograph again. "That's the cowboy I was telling you about. Maybelline Marble's first husband."

Savannah suddenly remembered where she'd seen the man before. She'd seen a picture of him on her last visit to Bliss when she'd been helping Gracie clean out the room above Ms. Marble's garage. "This is Ms. Marble's husband?"

"First husband. He died of a heart attack only a few years after they were married, then she married that schoolteacher. But she never was as crazy about him as she'd been about that Justin Bonner. Did I ever mention I was a cowboy? I worked on the Arrington Ranch right alongside Lucy Arrington's daddy and brothers."

Disappointed that she hadn't found Lucy's Honey Bee, she returned the photograph to the shelf and sat down as Mr. Sims went on and on about his cowboy days. She was relieved when Gracie appeared in the doorway.

"We probably better get going, Savannah," she said. "I promised Dirk we'd meet him over at the diner to go over some of your decorating ideas for the new house." She held up a hand when Mr. Sims started to get up. "No need to get up, Mr. Sims. We can show ourselves out."

"What's that?" he said.

"We'll show ourselves out! Enjoy the basket of goodies."

He nodded. "I hope you didn't put nuts in anything. I broke a crown on the last walnut I ate."

They said their goodbyes as they headed to the door. Once they were on the porch, Savannah quizzed Gracie. "Did you find anything?"

She shook her head as they walked down the steps. "I didn't get a chance to go through every room. The house is massive. But I did get to go through the downstairs study and Mr. Sims's bedroom. And I didn't find any chapters, envelopes, or anything that connected him with hiding the final Tender Heart novel." She waited until they were in the car before she asked. "Did Mr. Sims mention anything to you about Lucy?"

"Not anything of interest. He had one picture of her, but she was in the background. And he didn't even know she was in the photograph. After you left, he went off on a tangent about what a great cowboy he'd been. I think he was stretching the truth on some of those wild stories. Which makes me wonder if he was lying about having an affair with Lucy. I can't tell you how many boys lied about having sex with me in high school."

Gracie started the car and pulled away from the curb. "Maybe you're right. Maybe we need to start looking elsewhere for Honey Bee." For the next few minutes, Savannah took notes on her phone as Gracie went through the names of the elderly men living in the town. They crossed off the ones who hadn't been living in town when Lucy was alive, but still ended up with twenty names.

They were going over the possible Honey Bees when Savannah spotted Raff's vintage truck parked out in front of the sheriff's office. She didn't know what the happy, jumpy feeling was that settled in her stomach. Maybe she was happy to see his truck because she and Raff had become friends.

It was surprising. Raff was the type of man she normally steered clear of—the alpha type who reminded her too much of her father and brothers. But now that she thought about it, her daddy and brothers hadn't been alpha men as much as drunken hillbillies who thought that intimidating women made them manly. Raff looked intimidating, but he wasn't. He had only yelled at her once, and he'd had good reason to yell about losing an expensive antique gun.

Was that why he was working so hard to help Luke? He wanted his gun back? It made sense. And yet, he hadn't brought up the gun once in the last few days. Every night, he showed up at Zane and Carly's to drive Savannah to rehearsal. Last night, he'd taken her and Luke for chocolate shakes at the diner afterwards. As she'd chatted about the funny things the kids had done during rehearsal, she'd actually caught him smiling his cute lopsided smile more than once.

"I need to run into the post office and get some stamps for my Christmas cards," Gracie said as she parked across the street from the sheriff's office.

"I'll just wait here." Savannah kept her gaze on Raff's truck as Gracie got out. The draft of cold air caused Savannah to shiver. There hadn't been any more ice storms, but it was still freezing. She reached out to turn up the heater when she saw Raff coming out of the sheriff's office. The happy, jumpy feeling in her tummy intensified until it bordered on giddy delight.

The cold didn't seem to bother him. He didn't even have on his coat. His tattooed muscles flexed beneath the short-sleeved jade t-shirt as he held open the door for a woman. A pretty dark-haired woman with a slim body that looked like it didn't crave Butterfingers and chocolate cake. Although it was hard to see more than her legs with the coat she had on.

Raff's sheepskin coat.

Savannah's smile fizzled, along with the happy, jumpy feeling. It was replaced with a grumpy, annoyed feeling. A feeling that grew worse when Raff followed the woman to her car that was parked directly across from Gracie's. Savannah slid down in the seat and peeked out the driver's side window as he stepped into the street to open the woman's car door. They were talking, but Savannah couldn't hear a word. She leaned over and rolled Gracie's window down.

"I get it," Raff said. "I don't exactly look like the type of guy a mother would trust with her son, but I give you my word that I'll watch out for Luke.

And it's only for a couple weeks. Then my cousin Zane will take him."

Savannah's happy feeling came back. This wasn't a woman Raff was interested in. This was Luke's mom. Not that she cared if Raff was interested in another woman. Okay, maybe she cared a little. But she had no business caring, and she needed to remember that. Raff had no place in her plans. He was just a nice man she'd become friends with.

Luke's mom slipped off his coat and handed it to him. "For all I know, you're just some pervert who has a sick fetish for young boys. Gerry might not be the best of stepdads, but at least he's not a pervert."

Even from that distance, Savannah could tell Raff was about to lose it. His jaw tightened as he spoke between his teeth. "No, he just likes to beat the shit—"

Savannah jumped out of the car and waved her hand over her head. "Raff, honey!" She hurried across the street. "I've been looking all over for you. I wanted to thank you for the amazing job you did on Jesus's manger." She gave him a quick hug. "Why the Good Lord Himself would've felt blessed to have such a nice bed to lay His sweet head on." She turned to the woman and smiled. "Hi, I'm Savannah Reynolds, a friend of Raff's. And you are?"

Raff sent her a look that said he thought she'd been dropped on her head as a kid before he made the introductions. "This is Jennifer Slater. Luke's mother."

"Luke's mama!" Savannah gave her a tight hug, then pulled back. "Why it is a pleasure to meet the woman who raised that sweet boy. Did you know he helped Raff build the manger and stable for our town Christmas pageant? And not only that, Raff here talked him into being our Lord and Savior's father—not the Big Daddy, but Joseph."

Jennifer looked confused. "Luke is in the Christmas pageant?"

"He certainly is. He learned his lines faster than anyone else. That's one bright boy you've got there. I bet he gets all A's in school."

"Umm . . . actually, he's been having a little trouble in school."

Savannah tried to look shocked. "Really? Well, then it must be the teachers. Luke hasn't given us a speck of trouble." She glanced over at Raff. "Has he, honey?"

Raff studied her with narrowed eyes. "Maybe just a speck."

She swatted his chest. "Now stop with the grumpy bumpkin act. Everyone in town knows you're just a sweet little ol' teddy bear." She reached out and gave his cheek a good pinch. His hazel eyes darkened, but thankfully, he didn't say a word. "Now why don't you take me and Mrs. Slater to lunch at the diner. I am flat-out starving. But first let me run into the post office and tell Gracie Lynn what I'm doing."

Jennifer shook her head. "I'm sorry, but I can't go to lunch. Luke and I need to get back to San Antonio."

It was hard to keep the smile on her face, but Savannah did her best. "Does Luke want to go home?"

"He doesn't have a choice. He's my son, and I

love him."

Savannah knew that Jennifer wasn't lying. She knew it because she'd had a mama just like her. "Of course you do," she said. "But do you love him enough to let him go?"

Jennifer's face fell, and Savannah knew if she wanted to drive her point home, she'd have to talk about something she didn't want to talk about. "My daddy was a tough man. He was quick to anger and quicker to hit. My mama spent so many years justifying his behavior that she lost the truth. It took me running away before she found it again. While she wouldn't leave, she understood why I needed to go."

Tears welled in Jennifer's eyes. "Gerry isn't a bad man. He just doesn't know how to deal with Luke."

"Then don't make him," Raff said. "Luke has already told you that if you take him home, he's only going to run away again."

"He could run away from here too and end up on the streets somewhere."

"He could. But there's also a chance he could be happy here. All you need to do is give him that chance." He glanced back at the sheriff's office. "Why don't I go get Luke? I'm sure Sheriff Kendall has finished talking to him by now. Then you two can figure things out."

After Raff left, Savannah tried to lighten the mood by talking about the Christmas pageant, but Jennifer seemed too distracted to care about a kids' play. Savannah could understand. She had a lot to think about. So Savannah kept her mouth shut and left the woman to her thoughts.

She was studying the post office door across the

street and thinking it needed a Christmas wreath when Gracie came out. Savannah lifted her hand to get her friend's attention, but before she could, a handsome cowboy came striding down the street and scooped Gracie up in his arms.

Dirk swung his wife around before setting her on her feet and smiling down into her laughing face. The sight of Dirk with his straw cowboy hat pushed up on his forehead and his cocky smile stuck a chord with Savannah. In that instance, she realized why Ms. Marble's first husband had looked so familiar.

She knew him.

Or at least she knew his great-grandson.

"The unsavory drifter who rode into town was just the type of man Melanie was looking for. Unfortunately, he didn't give her a second glance when he swung down from his horse. His entire attention was focused on Dax."

CHAPTER FOURTEEN

C

HOLY CRAP ON A CRACKER! Ms. Marble's first husband was Lucy's lover. Savannah couldn't believe it. Or maybe she just didn't want to believe it. She idolized Lucy Arrington. And she couldn't idolize a woman who would cheat with her best friend's husband. Everyone in town knew that Maybelline Marble and Lucy had been friends. Ms. Marble's father had been the foreman of the Arrington Ranch for years. Lucy and Maybelline had grown up together. How could Lucy do that to her?

Maybe she hadn't. Maybe Savannah's mind was playing tricks on her. She'd just seen the picture of Lucy and Justin Bonner at Mr. Sims's. Maybe Dirk holding Gracie in the same pose had made her conjure up things that just weren't real. Like the same nose. And the same jawline. And the same cocky smile.

Dirk released Gracie, and when she glanced over and saw Savannah, she pulled Dirk across the street. "Are you ready to go to lunch?" She paused.

"Savannah? Are you okay? You look like you've seen a ghost."

Pretty much she had. Savannah pulled her gaze away from Dirk. "I'm fine," she said in a voice that didn't sound like her own. "I was just . . . thinking how cute you and Dirk look together." And how it would break Dirk's heart if he ever found out that his great-grandmother had cheated with Ms. Marble's husband. Dirk loved Ms. Marble like a grandma. Everyone did. She was the sweetest little old lady in town. And if Dirk was heartbroken by the news, just think how it would devastate Ms. Marble. Savannah had to be wrong. She just had to be.

But all the puzzle pieces fit. Lucy called her lover Honey Bee. Bonner started with a *B*. Lucy named her daughter Bonnie. Bonner. Bonnie. But maybe those were all just coincidences. Just great big coincidences.

"Is there a wart on my nose, Savannah?" Dirk asked.

She realized she'd been staring again and forced a laugh. "Sorry. I guess I'm not used to seeing such handsome cowboys."

Dirk arched an eyebrow. "Funny, but you've never been affected by my good looks before." He held out a hand to Jennifer. "Dirk Hadley."

Savannah suddenly remembered that Luke's mom was standing there. "Forgive my rudeness. This is Luke's mom, Jennifer Slater. Jennifer, this is Dirk and his wife, Gracie Lynn. Dirk and Gracie are Raff's cousins and can vouch for him." She looked at Gracie and Dirk. "I was just telling Jennifer about what a sweet, caring man Raff—"

Before she could finish, Raff came out of the sheriff's office with Luke. He didn't look sweet and caring. He looked annoyed and seemed to be getting after Luke. "You want the rights of a man, you better start acting like one. Men don't run from their problems. They face them. And they treat their mamas with respect."

Luke wasn't exactly respectful when he reached his mother, but Savannah couldn't blame him. She recognized the fear in his eyes. "I'm not going back to him."

Jennifer looked embarrassed before she pointed to the car. "We'll talk about this in private."

Luke held back, but when Raff sent him a stern look, he conceded and walked around to the passenger's side. Savannah watched them pull away and couldn't help being worried that they'd never return. She shivered at the thought of Luke being forced to go back to his stepfather.

Raff placed his coat over her shoulders. "Come on. Let's go get something to eat."

Dirk and Gracie followed them to the diner. Once they were seated in a booth, Raff filled them in on what had happened with Luke's mother.

"I just can't understand how a mother could let someone abuse her child and do nothing to stop it." Gracie glanced at Dirk. "I love you, but I'll protect my babies. Even if it's from their own father."

Dirk placed his hand over her rounding stomach and tugged her close. "How about if I protect you all?"

Gracie kissed his cheek. "That sounds like a plan to me."

Their love and devotion brought tears to Savannah's eyes. She glanced over to find Raff watching her. Or more like studying her as if she were a bug under a microscope.

"That story you told Luke's mom," he said. "Is it true? Or were you just trying to help Luke?""

When talking to Luke's mother, her past had just been a means to an end. But under Raff's intense gaze, she suddenly felt exposed and vulnerable. Like her skin had been stripped off and Raff now knew all her deepest, darkest secrets. And Savannah didn't like feeling vulnerable. She'd had enough of that as a kid.

She sent him a sly look. "Now what do you think, honey?"

Before he could answer, the waitress walked up to take their order. The conversation moved from Luke to Dirk and Gracie's new house. By the time their food arrived, Savannah had pulled out her phone and was showing them some of the décor ideas she had for their house.

Surprisingly, Raff seemed as interested in her ideas as they were. As he ate his hamburger and fries, he leaned closer to study the pictures she brought up on her phone. She got so excited about the painting she wanted Gracie to buy for the master bedroom that she missed the waitress asking if they wanted to order dessert. She was thoroughly disappointed when a big slice of chocolate cake was set down in front of Raff.

"So when do you move into the house?" he asked Dirk as he picked up his fork. Savannah's mouth watered as he dug into the gooey frosting and moist cake. He lifted the delectable bite . . . but not to his mouth. To Savannah's. Her eyes widened, and the happy, jumpy feeling returned in full force.

"Thank you," she said before she took the bite and closed her eyes in chocolate ecstasy. When she opened them, she discovered both Gracie and Dirk staring at her and Raff with stunned looks. "Raff knows how much I love chocolate," she explained.

They exchanged glances before Dirk answered Raff. "We're moving out of Ms. Marble's garage apartment this afternoon." Just the mention of Ms. Marble brought Savannah's thoughts back to Justin Bonner. She studied Dirk's features and wished she had a photograph of Justin so she could compare them. "The furniture we bought at the home décor shop in San Antonio comes first thing in the morning so we wanted to be there." Dirk glanced at Gracie. "You sure you'll be okay sleeping on an air mattress?"

Gracie laughed. "I can sleep on an air mattress for one night. I'm not a breakable piece of glass, Dirk. But I will miss Ms. Marble. She and I have gotten so close the last few months."

"You'll still be helping her with her baking."

"I know, but it won't be the same as living right over her garage. And I know she'll miss us too. I think she liked having us so close."

Dirk brushed her hair off her forehead. "Stop worrying. With the lack of apartments in town, I'm sure someone else will rent the space and keep her company."

"I could rent it." The words just popped out of Savannah's mouth. But now that she thought about it, it made sense. She'd seen the earlier picture of Justin in Ms. Marble's garage apartment. If she lived there, she could look for it and examine it more closely. And she wanted to examine it. She wouldn't be able to sleep until she knew the truth.

"I thought you were staying at Carly's," Raff said.

"I am, but their house is going to be overflowing when her parents get here next week." Gracie started to open her mouth, but Savannah held up a hand. "You have Granny Bon and Dirk's sisters coming. And Emery has her family coming. Me renting out Ms. Marble's room just makes sense. I'll still be able to help you decorate your house. And help Emery with the baby's room. And if I stay at Ms. Marble's, I won't have to bug anyone for a ride to the church for rehearsals. I can walk."

"I don't mind driving you." Raff nodded at the window with his half-smile on his face. "I'll have to drive Luke anyway." Savannah followed his gaze and saw Jennifer Slater's car driving past. When the car parked in front of the sheriff's office, Savannah couldn't help turning to Raff and giving him a hug.

"She brought him back!"

When Raff and Savannah got to the sheriff's office, Jennifer and Luke were standing by the car hugging. Or Jennifer was hugging. Luke was just standing there like an awkward teenager.

" . . . and you have to start school as soon as the holidays are over," Jennifer said. "And no more sucky grades." When she pulled away, Savannah could see the tears tracking down her cheeks. Savannah couldn't help the tears that filled her own eyes. She hadn't gotten a chance to say good-bye to her mama before she left, but if she had, she doubted that her mama would've cried for her. She had lost all her tears long before Savannah was born.

"I mean it, Lucas Marshall," Jennifer continued. "I'll contest this entire emancipation thing if you don't promise to get A's and B's."

Luke glanced over at Raff before he nodded. "Yes, ma'am."

Jennifer smoothed back a lock of his hair. "Okay, then. I'll talk to you soon." She gave him another hug, then turned and almost ran into Raff. She stopped and pointed a finger at him. "This is only on a trial basis. I'll be back in a week, and if things aren't to my liking, Luke is coming home. Do you hear me?"

Raff nodded. "Yes, ma'am."

"And the only reason I'm letting him stay with you is because of your girlfriend." She glanced at Savannah. "I figure if a kind-hearted woman like you loves Raff, he can't be as tough as he looks."

Savannah wiped the tears from her cheeks and sniffed. "Oh, we're not—"

Raff cut her off. "We'll watch out for your son. I give you my word."

"You better." Jennifer glanced at Luke one more time before she hurried to her car. Luke watched her go, and heart wrenching tears finally filled his eyes. Savannah started to move toward him to give him a hug, but Raff held her back and shook his head.

Luke watched his mom's car pull away, and then he wiped his eyes and turned to Raff. "I need to find a job. I won't be taking charity."

Raff nodded. "I wouldn't expect you to. But you'll need to get a daytime job. I have a feeling the pageant director will tan your hide if you miss one of her rehearsals."

Savannah swallowed back her tears. "You're darn tootin' I will. I can't have a pageant without a Joseph."

While Raff took Luke over to the diner to see about a job, Savannah headed to Ms. Marble's house to see about renting an apartment. Ms. Marble answered the door wearing an apron with a huge laughing Santa on the bib and elves on the pockets. Her usual hat was gone, and her hair shot out from her head in a puff of white. She smiled brightly when she saw Savannah.

"I'm glad you stopped by. I baked you some thank-you cookies for taking over for Joanna." She motioned her inside. "If I remember correctly, you have a weakness for chocolate."

"Yes, ma'am. But only give me a few. I've been eating way too many sweets while I've been in Bliss." She stepped inside. Ms. Marble's house looked like a curio shop. Every end table, shelf, and cabinet was filled with figurines and knick-knacks. It was cluttered, but also cozy. A cheery fire burned in the fireplace, and the air was scented with gingerbread.

Ms. Marble closed the door. "Overindulgence is what the holidays are all about. Diets are for New Year's resolutions."

"That's true, but I'm as horrible at keeping resolutions as I am at keeping secrets." It was an understatement. She was dying to call her friends and tell them what she'd found out about Lucy's lover, but she needed to wait until she had more proof. "I had lunch with Gracie and Dirk today, and they mentioned moving out of the room above your garage."

"I'm going to miss those two, but I'm happy they'll be able to celebrate the holidays in their new home." She held out a hand. "Let me take your coat." Her gaze narrowed on the sheepskin coat. "Although that doesn't look like it belongs to you."

Savannah didn't know why she blushed as she slipped off the coat. "Raff loaned it to me. I didn't bring one because I didn't think it would be as cold as it is."

Ms. Marble raised an almost invisible eyebrow as she took the coat. "Weather can be as unpredictable as men." She placed the coat on the back of a chair. "Come on into the kitchen and I'll make us some tea."

Savannah followed her into the kitchen. The table and counters were filled with all kinds of cookies. Gingerbread. Sugar. Thumbprint. Molasses. Chocolate-chocolate chip. Savannah felt like she'd died and gone to cookie heaven. She tried to ignore the tempting sights and smells and stay focused. "I was wondering if I could rent the room above the garage for the next week. Carly and Zane's house will be overflowing when both sets of parents arrive."

Ms. Marble filled a teakettle. "Of course you can. But you don't need to rent it. I appreciate you taking over for Joanna on such short notice." She set the kettle on the stove. "How is the pageant going?"

"Joseph quit the second night, but Luke took over."

Ms. Marble glanced at her. "Are we talking about

the boy Sheriff Kendall had in his jail?"

"That's him. Although he's not in jail any more. He's going to stay at Raff's—at least for the next few weeks."

A smile lit Ms. Marble's face. "That's exactly what that boy needs." Savannah assumed she was talking about Luke until she continued. "Raff has been on his own for too long. He needs responsibility."

Obviously, Ms. Marble didn't know Raff all that well. In the short time Savannah had known him, she'd figured out that he didn't like responsibility. "He's only planning on keeping Luke through the holidays. As soon as all the guests leave, Luke will go stay with Zane and Carly."

Ms. Marble snorted. "We'll just see about that." She finished making the tea, then brought a tray of steaming cups and a plate of cookies over to the table. Once she was seated, she turned her piercing blue eyes on Savannah. "So how are you doing? I heard about what your fiancé did."

Savannah should've said that she'd recovered from Miles desertion and moved on. But there was something about the cozy kitchen, the peppermint tea, and the scent of fresh baked cookies that made her start chattering like a magpie. As she sipped tea and munched on gingerbread cookies, she told Ms. Marble everything about how her perfect plan to get married and run a successful business had completely fallen apart.

Ms. Marble listened until she was finished, then she took a sip of tea and nodded. "I know all about perfect plans falling apart. Like you, I had a perfect plan. I was going to be a schoolteacher. I was going to live in Bliss. And I was going to marry the cutest cowboy to ever work the Arrington Ranch."

Justin. Savannah had to bite her lip to keep from saying the name.

"And I did become a teacher, marry that cute cowboy, and live in Bliss." Ms. Marble looked out the window as a flicker of pain crossed her face. "And life was perfect . . . until Justin died of a heart attack."

Savannah reached over and squeezed Ms. Marble's wrinkled hand. "I'm so sorry." She was even sorrier that Justin had been a cheater. Maybe that's what gave him the heart attack: Trying to keep up with two women.

"It was a sad time," Ms. Marble said. "We'd only been married a few years when he died. I was a widow at thirty."

Savannah blinked. "You married Justin in your late twenties? How much older were you than Lucy?"

Ms. Marble looked confused. "Lucy?"

Savannah tried to backpedal. "Did I say Lucy? I meant Justin."

"Justin was six years older than I was." Ms. Marble paused. "And I wasn't older than Lucy. Lucy was older than me."

If Ms. Marble was younger than Lucy, then that meant she couldn't have been married to Justin when Lucy was having sex with him. Lucy got pregnant when she was only fifteen. She'd died when she was around thirty. So that meant Ms. Marble had married Justin after Lucy had passed away. Savannah felt pure relief. Lucy wasn't a cheater. They had just been in love with the same man.

Savannah's eyes widened.

That's why Justin didn't marry Lucy.

He'd been in love with Ms. Marble!

"Dax recognized Billy Owens as soon as he rode into town. Billy was a cocky young gun who was out to prove he was the best. Dax had avoided him in Dallas, but there was no avoiding him in a town the size of Tender Heart."

CHAPTER FIFTEEN

❦

"**Y**OU KNOW THIS PLACE IS a shithole, right?"

For the hundredth time that day, Raff tamped down his anger. "It's better than sleeping in a barn—which could be an option, if you don't watch your mouth and show a little respect."

He pulled his truck up to the porch of his cabin and turned off the engine. As he hopped out, he couldn't help looking around. He had to admit that the kid was right. The place was in pretty bad shape. The porch roof sagged. The front steps were rotting. And the windows were so dirty you almost couldn't see through them.

Since he was rarely there, Raff hadn't done much to the cabin. It was just a place to sleep and eat when he stopped to drop off family heirlooms. As long as the roof didn't leak, he was good. When he and his father rebuilt the house, the cabin would no doubt go back to being a home for mice and birds. But if Luke's mom was coming in a week to check things out, maybe Raff should fix a few things. He headed to the barn.

Luke followed after him. "What are you doing?"

"We're going to fix the porch steps."

"I just got a job bussing tables at the diner. I don't need another job."

"Fixing the porch steps isn't a paying job. It's a job you do because it needs doing." Raff cringed. His father had used the exact same words when he'd wanted Raff to help around the ranch. It worked about as well as it had on him.

"No way. I'm not slave labor," Luke said belligerently.

"Suit yourself." He slid open the barn door and walked over to the pile of lumber his daddy had always kept in case he needed it. Raff had thought that was stupid, but he didn't think so now. He knelt and sorted through the wood for pieces that would work for the porch steps.

Luke came up behind him. "You're not going to make me help?"

"Nope."

"Good."

Raff picked out a couple of fairly decent two-by-fours and carried them back to the house, then he retrieved his toolbox from the truck. When he got to the porch, Luke was sitting on the rotting steps.

"Are you sure you know how to do this? This looks more complicated than a manger."

"I think I can manage." He took a measuring tape out of the toolbox and measured the steps. Then he marked off the measurements on the new pieces of wood before he grabbed a crowbar and started taking off the rotted steps. Luke leaned closer, and Raff had to bite back a smile. All guys were intrigued by demolition.

Raff held out the crowbar. "You want to try?"

Luke hesitated for just a second before he took the bar. He went after the rotted steps with a vengeance, but only ended up splintering the wood in one section.

"Start where the nails are." Raff instructed. "That's it. Right under there. Now get some leverage and push down." The nail creaked out of the wood beneath, and Luke grinned before he moved to the next nail. By the time he had all the boards off, he was grinning from ear to ear.

"That was fun."

"Tearing things up always is." Raff picked up his saw. "It's putting them back together that takes a little work."

Luke didn't say another word about slave labor as he helped Raff build the new steps. He had absorbed a lot while making the stable and manger for the Christmas play, and Raff only had to give him a few pointers. They finished the steps just as the sun was going down.

"We better clean up and eat something before we go to rehearsals. We don't want Savannah getting angry."

"She tries to act tough," Luke said. "But she never seems to get mad at anything. Even when the shepherds keep playing ninja with their staffs, or the horny wise men keep staring at her boobs, or the baby angels keep letting out screams that make you want to jump out of your skin. She just keeps smiling and never loses her cool. It's weird."

Raff had thought that too at one time. But now he didn't think it was weird as much as admirable. Savannah had a lot of admirable qualities. She still talked too much, but her chatter was the reason Luke was there and not with his asshole of a step-dad. Savannah had made Raff out to be a saint. She almost had him believing her. He'd even gotten a little choked up when she'd told the story about running away from her abusive father. But Savannah wasn't a runaway. She was a spoiled southern belle. A likable southern belle, though. He couldn't deny that.

"Where did you get that?"

Luke's words pulled him out of his thoughts, and he noticed the kid staring at the arrowhead that hung from the strip of leather around his wrist.

"I found it at Whispering Falls."

"Do you think I could find one?"

Raff nodded. "If you're willing to look hard enough." He handed Luke the toolbox while he cleaned up the lumber. "We'll go looking tomorrow morning before you have to head to the diner—after we clean the windows and the loft so you can sleep there instead of on the couch." Luke started to open his mouth, but Raff beat him to it. "I know. You're not slave labor."

Luke could eat about as well as he could sass. The kid ate three sloppy Joes, almost an entire bag of Fritos, and the last two cinnamon swirl muffins. At this rate, he'd eat Raff out of house and home. Raff's bank account could certainly use a hefty deposit. He waited until Luke had finished guzzling his glass of milk before he asked.

"Where's the gun?"

Luke lowered the glass. The belligerent look was back. "That's the only reason you helped me, isn't it? You want that stupid gun."

Raff could've argued the point, but he wasn't so sure he would've given the kid another thought if not for the gun. "Where is it?"

"I'm not telling. Not until I'm sure that my mom isn't going to make me go home. Then you'll get your stupid gun."

Irritated, Raff got up from the table and picked up his plate and glass. "Bring your dishes to the sink. I'm not slave labor either."

On the way to rehearsals, they swung by the Earhart Ranch to pick up Savannah, but Zane said Carly had dropped her off at Ms. Marble's apartment and she was going to walk to rehearsal. Luke sulked all the way into town. Raff felt pretty sulky himself, and it didn't have anything to do with the gun. He missed Savannah's chatter. And their off-key duets.

When they got to town, he spotted Savannah strutting down Main Street in her tight jeans, high-heeled boots, and his coat. Just like that, his sulky mood disappeared. Even Luke seemed happier as Raff pulled the truck next to the curb. He had to honk to get Savannah's attention. She jumped and placed a hand on her chest.

"You scared me to death," she said when Luke opened the door and got out to let her in.

"You shouldn't be walking at night if you're not going to pay attention to your surroundings," Raff said. "This might be a small town, but that doesn't mean everyone passing through are good people."

She settled in next to him, and he got a whiff

of fresh air and warm woman. "I guess I was just distracted."

That was an understatement. She barely talked at all on the drive to the church. And when he started singing along with the Christmas carols, she didn't join in once. It shouldn't have bothered him—she wasn't his concern—but it did. He remembered what Luke had said about the rehearsals and wondered if she was worried about having to deal with the ornery kids. When they arrived at the church, he couldn't help following her into the auditorium.

First, he pulled the shepherds aside and gave them a lecture about keeping their Kung Fu fighting to martial arts class. Then he pulled the wise men aside and warned them about being respectful. The babies he couldn't lecture. Savannah would have to deal with them on her own.

It only took him a little over an hour to finish sanding the stable and cutting a star out of plywood and painting it gold. He would attach the star to the top of the stable once he'd assembled all the pieces on the stage of the church for the dress rehearsal. For now, he stored the finished stable pieces against the wall of the gym and left the star on a table to finish drying. He was just cleaning up when Luke came racing in.

"Come quick! Savannah fell and broke her leg."

Raff dropped the hammer and ran after him. He found a group of crying angels, excited wise men, and scared shepherds. Raff pushed through the crowd of kids to discover Savannah sitting at the bottom of the carpeted steps that led to the stage. When she saw him, she looked more than relieved.

"Thank God you're here," she said. "You need to

call an ambulance."

He knelt next to her. "Where are you hurt?"

"My ankle. I broke my ankle." She lifted her right leg and wiggled her foot. His shoulders relaxed. If she could move it like that, it wasn't broken. "What are you waiting for?" she asked. "Call 911! And are you smiling? This isn't funny."

"It was kinda funny," one of the wise men said. "You should've seen her face when she stepped backwards off the stage. She screamed so loudly that Mary dropped the doll and the donkey stepped on it. Now Jesus has a squashed head." The other wise men laughed, and the shepherds and stable animals joined in. Even the angels stopped crying and giggled.

Savannah released an angry huff. "All of you should be ashamed of yourselves laughing over a woman breaking a leg and baby Jesus getting his head stepped on."

"You didn't break your leg," Raff said. "If you did, you wouldn't be able to move it and you'd be in a lot more pain."

"But it really hurts."

He carefully unzipped her boot and slipped it off. Her ankle didn't look broken, but it did look swollen. "You probably sprained it. We need to get some ice on it." He pulled out his phone. "I'll call Carly and see if she's still at the diner and can take over until the parents get here."

Carly was there in five minutes, but she didn't seem happy. Especially when Raff leaned down to pick up Savannah. "I'm sure she can walk, Raff. Can't you, Savannah?"

Savannah's arms tightened around Raff's neck.

"I can't walk, Carly Sue. I'm still not sure I didn't break a bone." Her eyes widened. "Or a rib, and it punctured a lung."

Carly rolled her eyes before she looked at Raff. "In case you haven't figured this out, she's overly dramatic." There was a warning in her brown eyes that he couldn't mistake. "She's also soft hearted. I hope you remember that."

He acknowledged the warning with a mere nod of his head before he carried Savannah out of the church. Once they were in his truck and on their way to Ms. Marble's, Savannah apologized for her friend.

"I'm sorry about that. Carly has always been a little too blunt and straightforward. She's also as protective as a mother lion to her cubs when it comes to her family and friends. After what happened with Miles, I guess she thinks that I'm going to rebound with the first man who shows me any kind of attention. Not that you've shown me attention . . . well, maybe a little." She glanced over at him. "You're much nicer than I thought you were."

He kept his eyes on the road. "I'm not nice. Nor am I rebound material."

"You are nice. But don't get all freaked out about me setting my sights on you. You aren't at all my type."

He wasn't sure why that would bother him. He should be glad that she wasn't setting her sights on him—all he needed was a dramatic redhead complicating his life. Except Savannah wasn't just dramatic. She *was* softhearted. And funny. And talented.

"And just what type is that?" he asked as he

pulled into Ms. Marble's driveway. "A type like the guy who left you at the altar?"

"He did not leave me at the altar." He shot a glance over at her, and she acquiesced. "Okay, he left me at the altar. But he had a good reason to get cold feet. His mother found out about the loan he gave me for my business. And I understand why she got so upset. I completely forgot what my Aunt Sally taught me—never mix business with pleasure. I shouldn't have taken the loan from Miles. If I hadn't, we would be married by now and living happily ever after."

Raff got out of the truck and slammed the door a little harder then he intended before he walked around to the passenger's side to get Savannah.

"What has you in a huff?" she asked as he carried her up the stairs.

He *was* in a huff, but he had no right to be. If Savannah wanted to live in a dream world, it wasn't his concern. And yet, he couldn't seem to stop himself from setting her straight.

"Even if you hadn't taken a loan, Miles wouldn't have married you," he said. "If he wanted to marry you, he would have. Men who really want to get married don't get cold feet or listen to their mothers."

He could tell by her tensing muscles that she didn't like hearing the truth. "And I suppose you're an expert on marriage."

"No, but I am a man. And if I loved a woman, I wouldn't let anything stand in the way of making her mine." He moved to the door. "Where's your key?"

In the porch light, her eyes were a turbulent violet. "Since you don't believe in marriage, I'm going to assume that making a woman yours would entail you tossing her over your shoulder and carrying her off like a Neanderthal to have sex in your cave. Miles isn't like that. He's a refined gentleman who cares about women's feelings—including his mama's."

The way she continued to defend her ex-fiancé pissed him off even more. "You mean he's a mama's boy who doesn't have enough gumption to tell her to stay the hell out of his business. Is that the kind of man you want to be married to? A wussy that needs to ask mommy for permission before he takes a piss?"

Her eyes widened. "Well, I certainly don't want a foulmouthed man who doesn't ask before he takes!"

"Are you sure about that?" He didn't know why he did what he did next. Maybe because he wanted to prove to her that she didn't want a mama's boy.

But as soon as he touched those soft strawberry lips, he realized his mistake. He didn't want to prove anything. He just wanted. He wanted Savannah. Every single delectable inch of her. And she seemed to want him too. Her fingers fisted in his hair, knocking his hat off, as her lips parted and allowed him full access to the wet heat of her mouth.

He growled low in his throat and released her legs, pinning her back against the door as he took a thorough taste. She tasted like sweet chocolate and addictive passion. And he couldn't get enough. He changed the angle of his head and deepened the kiss. She moaned into his mouth and hooked a leg around his hips, bumping her sweet center against the hard bulge beneath his fly.

It was like scratching the most intense itch. The more she rubbed against him, the more he needed to be rubbed. When he realized he was about to come from dry humping, he reached for the doorknob. Thankfully, it wasn't locked. He continued to suck all the heat from her mouth as he lifted her off her feet and pushed open the door with his boot. But he had only taken one step inside when a feline yowl had him stumbling back.

Savannah pulled away. "Miss Pitty!" She struggled out of his arms and then limped into the dark apartment to locate her injured cat. While she was gone, Raff pulled a Miles.

He took off like the wussy he was.

"It had only taken a smile to get Billy Owen's attention. But now that she had it, Melanie wondered if she'd made a big mistake."

CHAPTER SIXTEEN

&

IT WAS EXTREMELY DIFFICULT TO keep juicy tidbits of information to yourself. Especially when the juicy tidbit was about a love triangle between Ms. Marble, Lucy Arrington, and Justin Bonner. Savannah had spent hours studying the picture of Justin she'd found in the dresser drawer in the apartment above the garage, and there was no doubt in her mind that he was the father of Bonnie Blue. The thing that cinched it was his eyes. In the black and white photo in Mr. Sims's house she hadn't been able to see Justin's eye color. In the color picture in the apartment, she could.

Justin Bonner had the same exact grayish-blue eyes as Dirk.

While part of her thought Dirk should know about his great-grandfather, the other part didn't want to hurt Ms. Marble. Justin had been the love of her life. It would devastate her to find out about Lucy and Justin's affair and their baby. Which is why Savannah couldn't share her secret with her friends. The more people she told, the more likely the secret would get out.

To keep her lips zipped, Savannah tried to keep busy. She helped Gracie organize her house and get it decorated for Dirk's family's arrival. Then she helped Emery finish the baby's room and get the Christmas decorations down from the attic. They found a couple old wreaths that Emery didn't want. Savannah took them, cleaned them up, and added new ribbon and ornaments. The following morning, she walked into town and took one to the post office for their front door and one to the sheriff's office.

Sheriff Waylon Kendall was more than appreciative.

"Why that certainly spruces the place up," he said after he helped her hang the wreath on the front door. He glanced down at her foot. "I heard about your accident from one of the Nichols kids. How are you?"

"It was nothing serious. With a little ice and some ibuprofen, I was fine the next day." Her ankle had been fine, but her brain had been scrambled. Not by the fall, but by Raff's kiss.

Why did the man have to be the best kisser on both sides of the Mississippi? The things he could do with his lips and tongue could turn a saint into a sinner. And Savannah had wanted to pull Raff into her apartment and do some major sinning. If not for Miss Pitty, she knew she would have. While her mind knew that Raff was not the man for her, her body hadn't gotten the memo. She'd be so busy trying to save her business that she'd gone way too long without a man. It made sense that her libido would be awakened by the first man she spent any time with. And she had been spending a lot of time with Raff.

At least, she had before he'd kissed her the other night. Since the kiss, he hadn't been picking her up for rehearsals or driving her home. And that was probably a good thing.

"Well, I'm glad to hear you're okay." Waylon said. "How do you like staying at Ms. Marble's?"

Obviously, news traveled fast in a small town. "I love it. Especially the fresh baked goods. And it worked out well since the Arringtons are expecting so many visitors for the holidays."

He nodded. "Their family has certainly grown over the last few months." He paused. "I guess you're probably going to one of the ranches tonight for supper."

"I got numerous invitations, but I think my friends should have one night with their husbands before their families arrive. Since I don't have rehearsal tonight, I thought I'd grab something at the diner.

Waylon shoved his hands in his back pockets and rocked back on his heels in a shy manner that was cute and endearing. "Do you care for company? Maybe we could head over to the Watering Hole after for a little dancing."

She started to say no, but then stopped. Maybe going out with Waylon was just the distraction she needed to get her brain off Raff. "I'd love to go to dinner with you." She paused. "As friends." She didn't want the sweet sheriff to get the wrong idea.

He flashed a smile. "With the rash of weddings that have been going on around here, I can understand why you might be worried about me getting the wrong idea. And I promise I won't propose over dessert."

She laughed. "All right then. I'll see you tonight."

At dinner, Waylon was mannerly and kept the conversation going by talking about his family and his hunting dog that refused to hunt. After dinner, they walked to the Watering Hole. The bar was usually only crowded on Twofer Tuesdays. So Savannah was surprised that the parking lot was completely full of cars and trucks.

"Hank always throws a holiday bash in December," Waylon explained on their way into the bar. "First drink is on the house."

Inside was as crowded as the parking lot. People were crammed around the bar and the dance floor was filled with country swingers dancing to *Jingle Bell Rock*. Waylon lead her to a table in the corner, and Savannah couldn't help but notice all the glances he received from the women they passed. He usually wore a beige sheriff's shirt, jeans, and a tan hat. But tonight, he wore a snap down western shirt, jeans, and a black hat similar to Raff's. For some reason, it didn't look quite as good on him as it did on Raff.

"What would you like to drink?" he asked.

"I'll have a glass of merlot."

Waylon shook his head. "Hank buys cheap wine, so you might be better off with a margarita."

She laughed. "A margarita it is."

When he was gone, the man who worked at the post office came up and introduced himself. Fred thanked her for the wreath and said that numerous storeowners had asked where he'd gotten it and wanted to buy one for their businesses. While he was talking, Emmett and Joanna Daily walked up.

Joanna looked like she was feeling much better, but Emmett still kept a protective arm around her. Which Savannah thought was so sweet.

"I've seen those beautiful wreaths," Joanna said. "And I agree with Fred. I think they would look wonderful on every door on Main Street." She paused, and her eyes narrowed in thought.

Emmett groaned. "Here we go."

Joanna gave him a look before she continued. "The town council has a little extra money that we haven't spent for the year. If we paid you and bought your supplies, how quickly could you have the wreaths done?"

Savannah was a little taken back. "Umm . . . I guess that depends on how many you want."

"I think twenty should do to start." Joanna paused. "But the planters on the new lampposts need some sprucing up too. Could you make something to go in them?"

Savannah's mind fired with ideas for the planters. "Faux greenery and big, colored Christmas balls would look amazing. With maybe poinsettias on every other one. And I think twinkle lights in the trees is a must."

Joanna nodded. "That sounds perfect. I'll call you tomorrow with the exact number of wreaths and what we can afford to spend. But that's not the reason I came over. I wanted to thank you personally for taking over the pageant. I don't know what I would've done if you hadn't volunteered."

"You're very welcome." Savannah didn't think Joanna needed to know that Ms. Marble and Raff had bulldozed her into it. "It's been fun." It wasn't a lie. She was actually enjoying rehearsals and proud of how the play was coming along.

Joanna patted her arm. "Well, I'm glad to hear it." She looked at Emmett. "I think I've had enough fun for one evening."

Emmett smiled. "Yes, dear." But before he led her away, he glanced at the door. "Would you look at that? I don't think Raff has shown up for Hank's Christmas party in years."

Savannah almost fell off her stool as she leaned over so she could see the door. Sure enough, Raff stood there looking like the bad guy in an old western movie. His hat and western shirt were black and his jeans were dark enough to look black in the dimly lit bar. His gaze scanned the crowd, and Savannah ducked behind Emmett. She didn't know why she was hiding. Or why her heart suddenly felt like it was beating twice as fast as normal. Raff was a friend. And she needed to keep him as one. Mrs. Carlisle had texted her three times in the last few days asking about the desk.

"I think it's so nice you're here with Sheriff Waylon," Joanna said. "He's a mighty fine catch for a young woman."

"Oh, I'm not planning on catching anyone. I'm just here for a few weeks."

Emmett winked at her. "I think that's what your friends said too." He looked at Joanna. "Come on, Mama. Let's get you home. I'm craving some of those sugar cookies that Maybelline brought over."

When they were gone, Waylon showed up with their drinks. A margarita for her and a Dr. Pepper for him. "Just in case I get a call," he said as he took a sip of the soda.

Waylon was a good sheriff. The entire time they

conversed, he kept an eye on the crowd. Savannah didn't mind. She couldn't keep her gaze from the crowd either. Or maybe not the crowd as much as Raff. He had taken a seat at the end of the bar with his back to her and Waylon. For having grown up in the town, he didn't appear to be part of it. People didn't slap him on the back or engage him in conversation like they did with the other people who walked in the door. With Raff, they merely nodded a greeting before moving on.

Savannah couldn't help but wonder if their distance had to do with Raff's personality. He didn't exactly exude a warm fuzziness. Although not all the townsfolk were standoffish. Winnie Crawley squeezed right next to him at the bar. Savannah couldn't hear what she was saying, but her mouth appeared to be going a mile a minute. Since his back was to her, Savannah couldn't tell how he was reacting to Winnie's attention. But the tenseness in his shoulders said it wasn't good. She didn't know why his inattentiveness made her happy.

"Savannah?"

She turned to find Waylon looking at her. "I'm sorry. Did you ask me a question? It's hard to hear over the crowd and the music."

He placed his hand on the back of her chair and leaned closer. "I asked if you'd like to dance."

The song was a slow country ballad. Too slow to dance to with a man she wasn't interested in. "I better not. My ankle is still a little sore. In fact, I should probably get home and ice it." It was a pathetic excuse. Especially when she'd had no trouble walking all the way from the diner.

But Waylon only smiled and nodded. "Then let's

get you home." He waited for her to get up before he placed a hand on her back and guided her through the crowd. When they passed the bar, he called out a greeting to Raff. Raff must not have heard because he didn't turn around.

Waylon drove her home in his sheriff's SUV. It was kind of exciting to sit in the front seat of a police car. She wanted to ask to turn on the siren, but then thought it was a little too childish. When they reached Ms. Marble's, he opened her door and walked with her up the stairs. The wind had picked up, and when they reached her door, she shivered.

"I'm sorry," he said. "I didn't even realize you didn't have a coat. Let me get mine from the car."

"That's okay," she said. "I'll be inside in just a second." She was thankful when Waylon took the hint.

He took off his hat and nodded. "Well, it's been a nice evening."

"It has been. Thank you so much, Waylon." She leaned over and gave him a kiss on the cheek before she pulled out her key and unlocked the door.

Ms. Marble had offered to watch Miss Pitty while Savannah went to dinner. And since it was after ten o'clock, she decided to wait to get the cat until morning. She'd changed into a nightgown and was brushing her teeth when someone knocked on the door. Thinking it was Ms. Marble, she quickly rinsed and hurried to answer it.

Raff stood there with his hands braced on either side of the doorframe. His hat was tugged low, but she could still see his eyes as he gave her a thorough onceover. The heat of his stare felt like it burned right through the thin material of her nightgown.

She should've crossed her arms to cover her breasts, but her limbs were weighed down by the desire that flooded her body. All she could do was grip the doorknob as he finally lifted his gaze.

"Hey."

The word hung there, a puff of hot breath in the cold air, and she had to swallow hard before she could answer him back. "Hey."

His lips pressed together, making his scar more pronounced. "I thought I'd stop by to get my coat."

"Oh." She made no move to get his coat that hung on the hook by the door. She was too lost in the deep greens and soft browns of his eyes. They didn't blink as they stared back.

"So how was your date with Waylon?"

"It wasn't really a date."

He pushed off the doorframe. "With the way he was touching your back as you left the bar, it looked like a date to me."

"You saw me at the Watering Hole? But your back was turned to me."

"There's a mirror behind the bar, Savannah. I was watching you the entire time."

She suddenly felt breathless. "Why?"

There was a long stretch of silence before he spoke. "Because I couldn't seem to stop myself." He took a step closer. "I can't stop myself from watching you." He took another step. "I can't stop myself from thinking about you." He took another step until the toes of his boots touched her bare toes. "And I sure as hell can't stop myself from touching you." He pulled her into his arms, and his lips fastened onto hers in a slide of wet heat that made her knees weak and her head spin.

His hands slid through her hair and cradled her face as he walked her back into the room and kicked the door closed. In between deep kisses, he whispered against her lips.

"I don't want you going out with Waylon." He kissed the corner of her mouth. "I don't want him buying you drinks." He kissed the opposite corner. "Or putting his hand on the back of your chair." He pulled her bottom lip through his teeth, and then licked it better. "And I really don't want him touching you like this." He opened his mouth and kissed her so deeply she felt it all the way down to her panties.

When he pulled back, his eyes glittered with desire. "I want you, Savannah. And I don't want to share."

"Melanie woke with a start to find the shadow of a man standing over her bed. She reached for the derringer under her pillow, but stopped when she heard Dax's voice. 'You're playing with fire, Mellie. Billy's no good.' She rolled to her back and unbuttoned the top button of her nightgown. 'Maybe I want to get burned.'"

CHAPTER SEVENTEEN

(♆

OTHER MEN HAD TOLD SAVANNAH they wanted her, but never like Raff. There was a desperate edge in his voice and a hungry glimmer of need in his eyes. He didn't just want her. He had to have her. Like air. Or water. Or food. Savannah had never felt more beautiful. More desired. Or more needed. She wanted to fill that need. She wanted to give him breath. Quench his thirst. Ease his hunger.

She stared into his beautiful hazel eyes and slipped the straps of her nightgown off her shoulders. She shrugged, and the soft material slithered down her body and puddled at her feet.

His eyes lowered, and he released a low hiss between his teeth like steam from an iron. She expected him to touch her. Usually, men dove right in when she took off her top. But Raff didn't. He just stood there and looked until she grew self-conscious. Without a bra, her breasts were a little droopy. She started to cover them with her hands, but he stopped her.

"Uh-uh." He took her wrists and held her hands at her sides and continued to look his fill. She grew even more paranoid.

"I realize that I've put on a little weight. But that's not entirely my fault. Everyone indulges around the holidays, and Ms. Marble is the best baker on both sides of the Mississip—"

He pressed a finger to her lips and cut her off. "You're beautiful, Savannah. That's why I'm staring. Because I've never seen anything as beautiful as your body in my life."

She couldn't help the tears of gratitude that sprang to her eyes. "That's the sweetest thing any man has ever said to me," she whispered before she leaned in and kissed him. Lord, the man could kiss. His lips gave just enough sipping suction. His tongue just enough teasing sweeps. Somewhere between the gentle suction of his lips and hot sweeps of his tongue, his hand moved up to cradle her breast.

Her breasts had never felt small, but they felt small nestled in the warmth of his palm. He flicked his thumb over her nipple and desire spread through her like a fine wine. He continued to kiss and caress her until her breath grew heavy and uneven. Then he drew away and looked at her with eyes that were a combination of hot whiskey and molten green.

"One of us is overdressed," he said in a low, seductive voice that made her tummy feel airless. He took off his hat and sailed it onto the chair, then waited. She didn't know why her hands shook as she reached for the open collar of his shirt. She had removed a man's clothes before. But for some reason, this time felt different. His skin felt hot compared to the coolness of her fingers as she took the edges of his shirt. She tugged, and snaps popped until the shirt gapped open. She pushed it off his shoulders and sucked in her breath at the virtual candy store of hard muscle beneath.

She lifted her hand and tentatively brushed one pectoral. The muscle flexed beneath her fingers, and desire pooled inside her. She cupped the hardness in her palm, then flicked a fingernail over his nipple and watched as it tightened into a tiny nub. His chest rose and fell beneath her hand, and her breath matched his until all she could hear was their breathing. She spread her fingers wide and slid her hand down his stomach, strumming each rippled ab until she reached the waistband of his jeans.

She ran a nail back and forth along the edge. She knew the brand. Even when she hadn't liked him, she hadn't been able to keep her eyes off the way his butt filled out his jeans. "Wranglers," she said as she circled the button and traced the bulge beneath the fly.

He remained perfectly still and didn't make a sound. In fact, it seemed like he stopped breathing as she traced his thick, hard length. Wanting to feel him skin on skin, she flicked open the button and slid down the zipper. She slipped a hand inside the opening of his boxers and took his silken heat in her fist. She stroked him from base to tip and back again before he covered her hand and stopped her.

He removed her hand and swept her up in his

arms, carrying her to the bed. He laid her against the pillows, then removed the rest of his clothes.

Talk about beautiful. There didn't seem to be one imperfection on his body. Not one ounce of fat. Not one ugly mole or pimple. Even his tattoo was beautiful. The purple barbed wire heart amid the orange and red flames seemed to belong on the tanned muscled canvas of Raff's arm. She studied it as he walked toward the bed and felt a pang of sympathy for the man who had been so marked by his past.

But then he joined her on the bed, and she stopped thinking about the past. There was only the here and now, and the feel of Raff's hands and lips on her body. He touched her everywhere. His callused fingers glided over every square inch of skin, his warm lips sipped at every peak and valley until she burned with an all-consuming need.

"Raff," she pleaded. He brushed one more kiss over her hardened nipple before he focused his attention on the spot between her legs. His tongue flicked while his fingers played. The heat he built inside of her melted her bones to butter and had her nerves jumping for release.

He didn't give it to her. Right before she reached orgasm, he lifted his mouth. She opened her eyes to complain, but the words died in her throat. He knelt between her legs, his dark hair mussed from her fingers and his lips glistening from her wet heat. Every one of his muscles seemed to flex as he rolled a condom over his thick length. He glanced up, and their gazes locked and held. Something passed between them. Something Savannah couldn't name.

He lowered over her and thrust deep. So deep that she had to wonder if he could feel her heart-beat. Then he started to move in slow, steady thrusts. Once inside her, most men couldn't last long enough for her to reach orgasm. But Raff lasted. He lasted until the universe expanded. Until the stars collided. Until the world fell apart and came back together.

In his eyes, she saw it all. Because he never stopped looking at her. Not when she reached orgasm. And not when he quickly followed. His gaze remained locked with hers. It was only when they were both sated that he closed his eyes and slumped against her. He was heavy, but she liked the feel of his mus-cled body pressing into her softer one. She could've stayed right there for the rest of the night and slept quite contentedly if he hadn't suddenly lifted his head and glanced at the clock on the nightstand.

"Shit! I gotta go."

Without a "thank you" or "go to hell," he got up and walked into the bathroom. Savannah sat up and stared at the door. She was still staring at it when he came out and started grabbing his clothes from the floor.

"You're leaving?" she asked.

"I have to get home before Luke gets there. He went out with a couple kids he met in town and I told him to be back by eleven." He glanced at the digital clock again. "Which leaves me only a few minutes to get home." He zipped his jeans and buttoned them, then grabbed his shirt and boots. "I'll call you later." He headed for the door, but then stopped and turned around.

"Are you okay?"

Savannah tucked the sheet around her breasts and tried to keep the anger and hurt from her voice. "Of course. Why wouldn't I be okay? You need to get home for Luke. And even if you didn't, it's not like you owe me any explanation for racing off. I mean, we're not boyfriend and girlfriend." She flapped a hand. "This was just a . . . holiday fling."

His eyebrows lowered, and he squinted at her. "A holiday fling?"

"Exactly." She pinned on a smile.

He dropped his clothes and strode back over. He picked her up by her arms and gave her a kiss that curled her toes into the sheets. When he released her, Savannah melted right down to the mattress like a puddle of warm chocolate syrup.

"I'm sorry that I have to leave," he said. "I'd like nothing better than crawl right back in bed and spend all night making love to that gorgeous body of yours." He glanced down at her breasts and sighed heavily. "But Luke is my responsibility for the next couple weeks. And I can't ask the kid to have a curfew if I'm staying out all night." He smoothed back her hair. "But this wasn't just a fling. At least it wasn't for me. I like you, Savannah. I like you a lot. Okay?"

A feeling of happiness bubbled up inside of her. Which was silly. He hadn't declared his undying love. All he'd said was that he liked her. And yet, she couldn't stop the smile that bloomed on her face.

"Okay," she said. He gave her another kiss before he collected his clothes. He was almost out the door when she stopped him. "Just for the record, I like you too."

He turned and grinned his endearing half-grin.

"I'm glad to hear it. How would you like to come to the cabin for lunch tomorrow? Luke has to work at the diner all afternoon."

"Are we just talking about lunch, Mr. Arrington?" she teased.

"Lunch . . . with dessert." He winked before he grabbed his hat and walked out the door.

Savannah waited until she was sure he'd left before she flopped back on the pillows, drummed her feet against the mattress, and let out a squeal of delight. She loved Raff's dessert. She loved it better than she loved chocolate cake. Which was crazy.

Raff was the complete opposite of the men she was usually attracted to. And maybe that wasn't such a bad thing. Miles had turned out to be a complete jerk. As had every other man she'd gone out with. They might've dressed in expensive suits, come from wealthy families, and pretended to be southern gentlemen. But not one had come close to being as sincere and mannerly as Raff. Not one had offered her his coat or bought her a slice of chocolate cake or carried her up a flight of steep stairs. Not one had said her body was beautiful and sounded like he really meant it.

Raff might be a little rough around the edges. But he was a gentleman through and through. She smiled up at the ceiling. A gentleman who didn't like to share.

A knock sounded on the door, and her smile got bigger. Obviously, Raff had decided that more dessert was worth being a little late getting home. She jumped out of bed and pulled open the door to tease him. But it wasn't Raff. It was Ms. Marble dressed in a flowered flannel nightgown. She was holding Miss Pitty.

"Sweet Baby Jesus!" Savannah hid her body behind the door as her face flooded with embarrassment. "Umm . . . if you'll pardon me, I'll just close the door while I grab a robe." While she was putting on her robe, she tried to think up a good explanation for answering the door as naked as a jaybird. There wasn't one. So when she opened the door the second time, she pretended the first time hadn't happened.

"Hello, Ms. Marble." She smiled brightly. "Won't you come in?" She waited for her to step inside before she closed the door. "How was Miss Pitty? I hope she didn't give you any trouble."

Thankfully, Ms. Marble went along with her. "She was fine, but I think she missed you. She started meowing at the back door."

Savannah took the cat. "Did she wake you up? Shame, Miss Pitty. It is rude for guests to wake up their hosts."

One of Ms. Marble's invisible eyebrows lifted. "Actually, it was the headlights flashing in my bedroom window that woke me. The first I assumed belonged to Sheriff Kendall, but the second had me a little concerned."

Savannah fidgeted beneath Ms. Marble's piercing gaze. "I'm sorry to worry you, Ms. Marble. Raff just came by to . . ."

"I think I can figure out what Raff came by for, Savannah."

Her cheeks flushed with heat. "Yes, ma'am."

"And while I'm not one to tell people how to live their lives. I do feel the need to make a request." Savannah figured she was going to ask her to stop being slutty and asking men back to the apartment. She was surprised when that wasn't her request at all. "Raff has been through a lot. Please don't break his heart."

Savannah placed a hand on her chest. "It's not like that, Ms. Marble. Raff and I are just . . . friends."

Ms. Marble cleared her throat. "Yes, well, sometimes friendship can turn into other things."

"That's not going to happen in this case. I'm going to be leaving soon."

Ms. Marble studied her. "That's a shame. Joanna called me tonight and mentioned you were making wreaths for some of the businesses in town. And I've heard what a wonderful job you've done on Emery's baby room and Gracie and Dirk's house. This town could use your talents."

"Thank you, Ms. Marble. But I have a business in Atlanta. And I doubt that Bliss would support an interior design business."

Ms. Marble nodded. "You're probably right, but we're not all that far from Austin. And I think people of that growing city would love taking a trip to Bliss on the weekend to check out antiques."

"Antiques? I don't deal in antiques. I look for certain pieces for my decorating jobs, but that's about it. Now Raff, on the other hand, has an entire barn full of antiques that people would love to own." Savannah included. Thinking about the antiques in Raff's barn caused the last of her euphoric sexual haze to evaporate. She needed to remember why she came to Bliss in the first place. She'd come to save her business. And she couldn't let anything get in the way of that.

Not even delicious desserts.

"Making love to Melanie was a mistake. But it didn't feel like a mistake when he woke up with her in his arms. It felt like heaven."

CHAPTER EIGHTEEN

&

"**I** FOUND AN IMPERFECTION!"

Raff stopped nibbling his way up Savannah's leg and glanced at her. She was lying opposite him on the blankets they'd spread in front of the fire with her feet near his head. She was naked, her pale skin reflecting the firelight like smooth marble and her breasts hanging full and ripe like two sweet melons on the vine.

He wanted to touch them. To cradle their soft warmth in his palm. To take their rosy centers in his mouth and suck until they hardened against his tongue. But he restrained himself. He didn't want Savannah thinking that he was some boob-crazed idiot. Even if he was. Of course, he wasn't just crazy about her breasts. He was crazy about every inch of her.

He stroked the back of his hand over the soft skin of her thigh. "I have a lot of imperfections, Savannah."

"No, you don't. You have a body like a Greek god."

He couldn't help feeling an ego boost. He was

glad she liked his body. He liked hers too. More than he should. He was leaving soon. He had no business getting too attached. He leaned in and kissed a freckle above her knee. "What's this imperfection?"

She rolled to her side and tugged at his toe. "Your second toes are longer than your big toes."

He laughed. Something he'd been doing a lot of since he'd brought Savannah back to the cabin. "I have my father to thank for those. He gave me my toes and my somber personality. He isn't much of a smiler." He paused. "Of course, he doesn't have a lot to smile about. Neither does my mother."

She rested her head in her hand and studied him. "They have you. You're worth smiling about."

A stab of familiar pain pierced his heart. "For a rancher and a country girl, one child was like having one cow. It was nice, but not even close to a herd."

"Then why didn't your parents have more children?"

For some reason—maybe the soft, caring woman lying next to him—he spoke a truth he'd held inside for too long. "She did try. Again. And again. And again. And again." He sat up and rested his arms on his bent knees and stared into the fire. "She lost four babies after I was born."

Savannah sat up, her eyes pools of watery lavender. She gently touched the back of his hand. "I'm so sorry."

He took her hand. It was surprising how just touching her gave him the strength to continue. "I am too. It was hard seeing my mom and dad so sad after every loss."

"I'm sure you felt the loss too. I bet you were looking forward to having a little brother or sister."

"The first couple times, yes." He interlocked their fingers, tracing the smoothness of her nails with his thumb. "After that, I became terrified when she got sick in the mornings or showed any sign of being pregnant. I knew what was coming. It was a relief when they stopped trying." He paused. "Or at least, I thought they'd stopped trying. I found out differently the night of the fire." He hadn't intended to talk about the fire. He started to release her hand and pull away, but she closed her fingers around his.

"Tell me about it, Raff."

He shook his head. "It's in the past."

"Sometimes the past can't remain there if we want a future."

He hadn't really thought about his future. Maybe because it always looked so dark. Now it seemed to be filled with lavender blue light. A light that beckoned to him. He took a deep breath and released it before he started to talk.

"My mom called me a few weeks before Christmas wanting to make sure I came home for the holidays. She said that she and my father had a surprise for me. I was thinking she was trying to fix me up with another woman she thought would make a perfect wife. But her surprise wasn't a woman. The surprise was a baby. She was pregnant."

He turned Savannah's hand over and traced along the lifeline of her palm. "My mom was forty-nine. I thought she was too old to have kids. Too old to want to go through the pain again. I sure as hell didn't want to watch her go through it again. Which is why I didn't take the news well.

I yelled at them and called them both all kinds of fools. Then after they went to bed, I got drunk off my ass. My mom had these angels that she put on our Christmas tree every year. One angel for each child she'd lost. As I was sitting there drowning my sorrows, those angels seemed to be mocking me."

Savannah's hand tightened on his as if she knew what he was going to say next.

He swallowed hard. "I don't know how it happened. One second, I was sitting there sulking, and the next, I was trying to shove the entire tree into the fire. When it went up like a torch, I realized what I'd done. I tried to put it out, but it was too late. I got my parents out and called 911. But the firemen didn't get there in time to save the house. I attacked the first fireman who showed up at the scene. As if it was his fault my parents' house had burned to the ground. Waylon was a deputy at the time, he was the one who pulled me off, hand-cuffed me, and took me to jail. I should've been charged with assault and arson. But I'd gone to school with the fireman so he didn't press charges, and the judge was a friend of the family and took pity on me." He paused. "The insurance company had no pity once the investigators discovered it wasn't an accident. They refused to pay a dime."

"Oh, Raff," Savannah pressed her wet cheek to his chest. "I'm so sorry."

He released his breath. "To this day, I don't understand why my parents continued the madness. Why my mother couldn't be satisfied with one child. Why my father didn't talk her into adopting or just use a damned condom after the first two miscarriages."

She hugged him closer. Cocooned in her arms, the pain he'd carried around with him seemed to lessen. Or maybe it had more to do with sharing his pain with someone else. Someone who understood because she carried pain of her own.

"Sometimes it's hard to understand why people do the things they do," she said. "I can't understand why my mother hasn't left my abusive father. Why would she want to continue to live with a man who turns into such a beast when he drinks?"

Raff froze and stared down at her bent head. "You weren't lying. You did have an abusive father like Luke."

She kept her head bent, and her shoulders lifted in a weak shrug. "Except I was my daddy's flesh and blood child. But that didn't stop him from beating me with anything he could get his hands on—when he could catch me. The last time, I made sure he would never catch me again."

The truth of Savannah's abusive childhood completely blindsided Raff. For so long, he'd thought of her as a spoiled little southern belle who got everything she wanted. But she hadn't been spoiled at all. Disbelief and sympathy mixed with a whole lot of anger. When he spoke, it was hard to keep that anger from his voice.

"Where does your father live?"

"Just outside of Shreveport, Louisiana. I lied about being from Atlanta because, like you, I wanted to forget my past. But I need to take my own advice and accept who I am and where I came from so I can move on."

She'd moved on much better than he had—especially after everything she'd been through. He hadn't understood how Luke's stepdad could beat him. He sure as hell didn't understand how a father could hit his little girl. "I want his address, Savannah. Number and street."

She lifted her head and stared at him. "Why would you need—?" Her eyes widened. "You're going to go kick his bottom, aren't you?"

"His ass. I'm going to go kick his ass. Now what's his address?"

A smile lit her face, and she cupped his face in her hands. "That's so sweet of you. But if I learned anything from my aunts, it was not to waste your time and thoughts on someone who's not worth it. And my daddy isn't worth it. He's just an angry drunk with no love in his heart. Last time I talked with my mama, she said he was in ill health and could barely walk to the mailbox without gasping for breath—no doubt from all the cigarettes he smokes."

"You still talk to your mother?"

She released his face and nodded sadly. "I call her at least once a month, but I've stopped trying to get her to leave and just accepted who she is."

"What about your brothers?"

"We talk occasionally. They're older than me by twelve and thirteen years. So we've never been close. They always referred to me as 'the mistake.'"

It sounded like her brothers needed their asses kicked as much as her father. And if Raff ever met them, he'd be happy to do the kicking. "What about your aunts? Why didn't they get you out of the bad situation sooner? They sound like amazing women. They should've seen what was happening."

She lowered her eyes and traced a finger along

the flames of the tattoo on his arm. "Well, actually, they weren't really my aunts. They were just some very sweet old ladies who lived at the retirement community I worked at after I ran away. They took me under their wings. It was their love and support that made me believe in myself. Aunt Sally was the one who pointed out my talent for design and pushed me to go to college. Aunt Rue talked her daughter into renting me a room at her house in LA when I got accepted at college. Aunt Bessy and Aunt Lily helped me with my first year of tuition."

She proceeded to talk about her adopted aunts in glowing terms. As she talked, he started to get the full picture of the woman he held in his arms. She wasn't a frivolous, superficial southern belle. She was a loving, determined survivor.

Raff's life hadn't been perfect, but it had been better than hers. He had a mother and father who loved him and had never given him more than a stern lecture. Yes, there were some painful memories, but there were so many good ones too. Woodworking in the barn with his father. Baking in their cozy kitchen with his mom. Swimming at Whispering Falls with his cousins. And living on the ranch and riding horses and wrangling cattle. How had he forgotten all those good memories? How had he let them be buried beneath the bad?

Savannah's cool fingers on his forehead brought him out of his thoughts. "If you keep those frowns up, you're going to need Botox." She caressed his forehead, her eyes compassionate. "I'm sorry I brought up the fire. But regardless of what happened, it was an accident, Raff. I know you never intended to burn down your parents' house and all their belong—" She cut off as her eyes widened. "That's why you're collecting all the antiques in the barn. You're trying to replace what got lost in the fire."

Before he could feel like too much of a sentimental fool, she flung her arms around him. "Oh, Raff, that is the sweetest thing ever." When she drew back, her eyes were glistening with tears. "That's why you're a junkman."

He started to correct her, but then laughed. "Yes, that's why I'm a junkman."

"So when are you going to surprise them with what you bought?" Her eyes sparkled. "This Christmas?"

"Actually, I was. But it doesn't look like that's going to happen."

"Why not?"

"Because the gun I was going to sell to get the money to rebuild their house is the same gun Luke stole."

Her face fell for only a second before she got a stubborn look. "Then we're just going to have to make sure his mother lets him stay so he'll tell us where the gun is." She glanced around. "And I can't see her being real happy to have her son living here."

"Are you saying my cabin's a dump?" he teased.

"Not a dump. Just in need of a little house TLC. Something I happen to be an expert on." She sent him a sassy look. Although, with the flicker of the firelight dancing over her naked body, she didn't look sassy as much as breathtakingly beautiful.

He reached out and ran the backs of his fingers over the soft fullness of one breast. "Speaking of

TLC ..."

They gave each other a lot of tender loving care before they got dressed and ate lunch. He had made chili in the crockpot, but she insisted on a peanut butter and jelly sandwich. She enjoyed it like it was a five-star steak dinner, and once she was finished, she wasted no time making the cabin presentable.

She made a list of things she wanted to keep in the house and things she wanted to take to the barn and exchange for other furniture. Almost everything went in the "To Go" list. The only things she wanted to keep were the couch, overstuffed chair, and bed. Once they carried the furniture to the barn, she selected the furniture she wanted to take back to the cabin. He noticed her gaze drifting to Lucy's desk, but she didn't ask to buy it again. Nor did she choose it for the cabin. Instead, she chose sturdy end tables, a bed and dresser for Luke's loft, and the harvest table and benches.

"Where did you get this dining table?" she asked as she examined the reclaimed wood top. "The legs look new, but this top is definitely older."

He cleared his throat and felt a little embarrassed. "I made it. It's similar to the one my father made—although not even close to being as good."

She turned to him, and a smile broke over her face. A smile that made him feel like making a table was the best thing a man could do. "Why, you're more gifted than I thought, Raff Arrington. If I didn't think the table would look so amazing in your cabin, I'd try and talk you into selling it to me for my shop. Now show me those big muscles and help me carry this into the house."

They spent the next couple hours arranging furniture. He had to admit that she was good at her business. When they were finished, the cabin didn't look like an old shack that had been left to decay. It looked like a home.

"It's better," she said. "But I'm not finished yet. We need to order a new mattress for Luke's bed in the loft, bedding, and towels that don't look like they've been used to wash your truck. Some dishes and placemats, and some candles for the mantel." She paused as she studied the mantel. "In fact, Christmas greenery might look even better." She pointed at the corner next to the fireplace. "And a Christmas tree right there." She turned to him. There was understanding in her eyes, but no sympathy. "Not a real one—I hear those are major fire hazards—but an artificial one. What do you think?"

He waited for the bad the memories to wash over him, but they got lost in a pair of bluebonnet eyes. "I think that's a good idea." He held out a hand. "Do you know what else is a good idea?"

She allowed him to pull her into his arms. "I think I can guess."

"Smart woman." He carried her into the bedroom.

They were late picking up Luke from the diner, but the kid didn't seem to mind. Ms. Marble had delivered the baked goods for the following day, and Luke was her taste tester. The kid was so filled with gingerbread, pumpkin pie, and red velvet cake that he was on a sugar high. Gone was the belligerent teenager, and in his place was an excited chatterbox who was actually a pleasure to be around.

"Carly taught me how to make her granola pancakes," he said as soon as he hopped in the truck next to Savannah. "And she let me take Old Man Sims's order because she said my voice is louder than the waitress's. I hope it didn't hurt Kelly's feelings. She's nice."

Savannah winked at Raff as he pulled away from the curb. "She's pretty too. From what Carly said, she's a senior this year at the high school. It will be nice to know someone when you start in January."

There was a long pause before Luke answered. "Yeah, I guess that would be cool."

Since Raff didn't want the day to end, he drove to the Walmart Supercenter in Fredericksburg and let her pick out everything she thought the cabin needed. It was a mistake. Savannah was a world-class shopper. In record time, she filled a shopping cart with bedding, towels, and kitchenware, and then she handed it off to Luke and grabbed another cart and hit the Christmas section.

That's when things really got out of control. While he and Luke watched in amazement, she filled the basket with rolls of ribbons, boxes of ornaments, strings of lights, loops of garland, and more Christmas crap than Raff's mother used to store in their attic. Then she used her southern sweetness to charm a male salesclerk into bringing a freight cart and loading an artificial tree and the store's entire stock of wreaths.

"Hold up there," Raff said. "I don't think we need this many wreaths for one cabin."

She flapped a hand. "These aren't for the cabin, silly. They're for decorating all the businesses in Bliss. We'll just need one for our door."

A warm feeling settled in his stomach at the word "*our.*" A feeling that he tried to ignore as they finished buying out the Christmas section and headed back to the cabin. But the feeling burned even brighter on the way home when he started singing Christmas carols and both Savannah and Luke joined in. The kid sang as badly as they did.

When they got to the cabin, Luke and Raff put up the pre-lit tree in the corner while Savannah draped lights and garland over the mantel. They decorated the tree together, although Savannah came along afterwards and repositioned all of Luke and Raff's ornaments to her liking. When the tree was finished, Raff served up the chili he'd made that morning and they sat down at the harvest table to eat and admire the tree.

"It looks pretty awesome." Luke spoke between shoveling in bites.

"Don't talk with your mouth full, young man," Savannah scolded. "But you're right." She sighed as she looked at the glittering tree with its gold and red ornaments. "It is pretty awesome." She glanced over at Raff and smiled. "What do you think?"

Sitting there at a table he'd built with two people who had each touched his heart in some way, Raff had to agree. "Awesome."

"Melanie was smiling as she walked up the stairs of the boardinghouse with the tray of coffee and breakfast rolls. The smile faded when she opened the door of her room to see the window open and Dax gone."

CHAPTER NINETEEN

"I DIDN'T FIND A THING IN Mr. Sims's house." Gracie munched on her third slice of pumpkin bread. Since finding out about the triplets, she'd tripled her eating. She now ate as much as Savannah. Not that Savannah had eaten all that much at Carly and Zane's Christmas gathering. Her tummy was too full with giddy happiness to eat.

She looked through the doorway of the kitchen into the living room where Raff was laughing at something his cousin Becky had just said. With his dark hair, chiseled features, phenomenal body, and sexy tattoo, he was handsomer than all the Arrington men put together.

And hotter. Much hotter.

For the last four days, they'd spent every afternoon at the cabin making love, and she still hadn't gotten her fill of Raff. Maybe because being with him wasn't just about the sex. She liked his company. He was a good listener. And Lord knew, she was a good talker. But they didn't have to talk.

They could sing Christmas carols at the top of their lungs or just remain silent as she worked on the wreaths for the businesses in town and he worked on a piece of furniture. Although lately he'd been spending a lot of time looking at cows on his laptop.

"Are you listening, Savannah?" Emery asked.

Savannah pulled her gaze away from Raff. "Excuse me?"

"I asked if you saw anything at Mr. Sims's house that would connect him with the lost chapters of the final book."

Savannah bit her lip. "No, I didn't see a thing that had to do with the lost chapters."

Emery nodded. "Then I think we need to start looking at the other candidates Gracie and Savannah came up with for Lucy's lover."

"But what if he's dead?" Savannah asked, as nonchalantly as possible. "If he's dead, he couldn't be hiding the chapters."

"It's definitely a possibility. But even if he's dead, we need to find out who he is so we can search the places he lived or might've met Lucy for other chapters. Whoever is hiding the chapters knew Lucy well enough to know she had a lover."

Emery was right. If Justin had been Lucy's lover, then it made sense that whoever was hiding the chapters would hide them in places connected with Justin. Had Justin lived in Ms. Marble's house? It was certainly something to look into.

"I think we've hit a wall on where else to look," Carly said as she arranged appetizers on a platter. "I'm starting to think it's going to be another fifty years before we find the rest of the book."

"Don't even think it," Gracie said. "We'll find it."

"Find what?" Dirk walked into the kitchen. When all the women looked at him, his eyes twinkled. "Still looking for that book, huh? I don't know how y'all are going to keep entertained once you find it." He took a bacon-wrapped scallop off the tray Carly was arranging and popped it into his mouth. "You ready to go, Gracie? Granny Bon and the girls come in tomorrow. And believe me, we're going to need to be rested up for a visit from my three sisters." He placed a hand on her stomach. "Let's hope these triplets aren't as ornery."

"I hope they're just as ornery as you." Gracie kissed him on the cheek. "I'm ready. Let me just say goodbye to everyone." She hugged Carly, Emery, and Savannah before she and Dirk headed to the living room. Again Savannah's gaze found Raff in the crowd, but this time he happened to be looking right at her. His hazel eyes were direct . . . and heated. A warm flush ran through her body, and she had to fight back the strong desire to walk straight into his arms and kiss him senseless.

"Okay, what's going on?"

Savannah pulled her gaze away from Raff and looked at Carly. "What are you talking about, Carly Sue?"

"I'm talking about you staring at Raff like he's a succulent lobster you can't wait to dip in butter and devour. I'm talking about him becoming a mother hen after you fell off the stage and twisted your ankle. I'm talking about him feeding you chocolate cake every time you're in the diner like you're an undernourished toddler."

Obviously, Carly had been paying closer attention to her and Raff than she'd thought. "He's just a nice man who doesn't mind sharing his desserts. A caring man who was just worried about me spraining my ankle. And I was not staring at him just now. I was looking at the amazing job you did decorating the Christmas tree."

Carly rolled her eyes. "The tree is in the other corner, Savannah. And I did a horrific job of decorating it. Mainly because Zane kept distracting me with kisses. Sort of like Raff is distracting you." She glanced at Emery. "I told you we needed to do an intervention." When Emery nodded, Carly pulled Savannah out of the kitchen and down the hallway into her and Zane's bedroom. Emery followed and closed the door.

Carly walked Savannah over to the bed and pointed. "Sit."

"I am not a dog, Carly Sue."

"Fine. Don't sit, but you are going to tell us what's going on between you and Raff." Savannah started to open her mouth, but Carly held up a hand. "Don't you dare say nothing. Emery and I know you're having sex with him."

Savannah gasped. "Ms. Marble! I never thought that sweet old woman would be a gossip."

"Ms. Marble?" Emery moved into the room. "Ms. Marble didn't tell us anything."

"Then how did you know Raff and I were having sex?"

Carly flopped down on the bed. "It wasn't hard to figure out with the moon eyes you've been giving each other all night. And please don't tell me that Ms. Marble caught you having sex, because that's just gross."

"She did not catch us having sex. She came calling after Raff left and I thought it was him and answered the door nekked."

"*Nekked* is not a word. It's nay-ked."

"Tomay-to. Tomoh-to."

Emery took a seat on the bed next to Savannah. Her eyes were concerned. "You and Raff, Savannah? I thought you didn't like him."

Savannah was glad the truth was out. Keeping secrets from her best friends was absolute hell. She slipped off her high heels and crossed her legs on the bed.

"I didn't at first. He was way too bossy and grumpy. But then I got to know him, and he's not as rough around the edges as I thought. In fact, I think all that grumpiness is just there to protect his sweet heart. You should see him with Luke. He's so kind and patient. You just know that he's going to make the best daddy in the world."

Carly's eyes widened. "Daddy?"

"Just because he has a tattoo, Carly, doesn't mean he won't be a good father." She paused as an image popped into her head of Raff cradling a precious little baby in his tattooed, muscular arm. Her heart turned to goo.

"That look on your face is scaring me, Savannah," Emery said. "You certainly can't be thinking about him as a father for your children."

Savannah laughed, but she had to admit that it sounded forced even to her ears. "Of course not. I wasn't thinking about him fathering my children, silly. I was just saying that he would make a really good daddy for someone's children." She didn't know why she suddenly felt sick to her stomach at

just the thought of Raff making babies with someone else.

Carly flopped back on the pillows and covered
her face with her hand. "She's doing it again. She's
planning a happily-ever-after with some guy she
doesn't even know." She lowered her hand and
looked at Savannah. "Didn't you learn anything
from Asshole Miles? You knew him for a month
and started planning a life with him. And look how
that turned out."

"Stop being so harsh, Carly," Emery said. She
turned to Savannah. "What Carly is trying to say is
that we're worried about you. We don't want you
to get hurt again."

"There's no need to worry, Em. I'm not falling
for Raff. We're just friends who . . . made love a
few times."

"Sex!" Carly sat up. "You've had sex. Making
love is what you do with someone you are in love
with. Someone you've known longer than a few
weeks."

She couldn't argue the point. Love took longer
than a few weeks. Didn't it? "Fine. We had sex."
But even as she said the word, it didn't sound right.
She'd had sex before with other men. She'd even
had sex with Miles. But what she did with Raff
was nothing like those times. It was different. It
was special.

"Okay," Emery said. "As long as you know that
whatever's between you and Raff isn't forever.
From what Cole says, Raff is leaving as soon as the
holidays are over. And so are you."

Savannah knew that. She'd always known that.
She just didn't know why it suddenly made her

feel so sad. Maybe because in the last few days she'd stopped thinking about leaving. She'd stopped thinking about her little shop in Atlanta. She'd even stopped answering Mrs. Carlisle's texts.

She walked to the window and looked out. After growing up in the country, she'd never thought she'd want to go back. But while she hadn't missed her family, the country girl inside her had missed seeing the horizon without a cluster of buildings getting in her way. And driving down a bumpy dirt road with miles and miles of countryside stretched out in front of her. And walking down Main Street and having people smile and wave at her.

When she left Bliss, she would miss eating at the diner where she always knew what was on the menu and sitting in Ms. Marble's warm kitchen with a gingerbread cookie and a cup of hot tea. She'd miss seeing her friends every day and seeing a vintage Chevy truck pull up in front of her apartment with a handsome cowboy inside.

A thought struck her, and she pressed her hands to the giddy feeling in her stomach. "What if I didn't leave? What if I stayed right here in Bliss and opened up an antique store?" There was complete silence, and Savannah turned around and stared at her friends. "You don't want me to stay in Bliss?"

Emery jumped up and walked over to her. "Of course that's not it. We would love for you to live in Bliss. We just don't want you moving here because of Raff."

"I know y'all are concerned about me. And I understand. I kind of fell apart after Miles left me at the altar. But Raff isn't like Miles."

"No, he's not." Carly got up from the bed. "Miles

was a pussycat, an asshole pussycat, but still a pussy-cat. Raff is a bad boy with issues. And believe me, I know a bad boy with issues when I see one. That's all I dated before Zane."

"Why does everyone think Raff is a bad boy? Maybe he was when he was younger, but that's because everyone put pressure on him to be a perfect Arrington. But he's worked through those issues."

Carly snorted. "Which is why he's a nomad who roams all over the countryside buying junk that he doesn't sell. The guy is a real gem."

Anger welled up inside of Savannah. Anger she couldn't control. "Shut the fuck up, Carly Sue! You don't know anything about Raff or what he's been through. I let you talk about Miles because . . . well, because deep in my heart I knew you were right. I knew the man was a jerk. But Raff is a good, kind-hearted man who has had some tough times. And I will not let you say anything disparaging about him. Do you understand me?"

Carly looked confused. "Did you just say fuck?"

"I did, but only because you pushed me beyond my limits."

Carly glanced over at Emery. "It's too late. She's already headed for heartbreak. She never once stood up for Miles like she did just now for Raff. Not one time. Which makes me believe that she's actually fallen in love with this guy."

Savannah was so stunned it took her a moment to speak. "No, Carly Sue, I don't love Raff. I mean, I love how precious he is with Luke. And how he sings Christmas songs with the radio, even when he can't carry a tune to save his sweet soul. And the way he kisses. Lord, the man is the best kisser on both sides of the Mississippi. And I love the way he runs his hands over wood after he's finished sanding it like it's a woman's skin. And I love the way he—"

She cut off when she noticed the tears in Emery's eyes. "What? I just was telling you why I love—" Her eyes widened "Sweet Baby Jesus," she breathed. "I love Raff."

Carly heaved a sigh. "No shit."

The epiphany should've scared Savannah. Raff was nothing like the man she envisioned herself marrying. He wasn't a polished, soft-spoken businessman. He was a tattooed, gruff junkman . . . and she loved him. She loved his tattoo. She loved his gruffness. And she loved that he'd driven around the country for the last two years trying to find family heirlooms to replace the ones he thought he'd taken from his parents.

Her dream had once been to own a successful business in a big city and marry a gentleman who would buy her a big house and a big SUV to drive their two children to school in. But now that dream didn't seem appealing at all. It seemed boring and cookie-cutter. She didn't need a big city. Or a big house. Or an SUV. Or even a gentleman. What she needed was a gentle man. A man who would give her his coat when she was cold. Feed her when she was hungry. And hold her when she was weak.

A man who would never leave her like Miles had.

"Dax rode out of Tender Heart without a backwards glance. If he wanted Melanie to be happy, he needed to let her go."

CHAPTER TWENTY

Ⅽ

"HEY, LUKE," RAFF SAID. "HAVE you seen Savannah?"

Luke swallowed the bite of sugar cookie he was eating. "She went that way with Carly and Emery." He pointed down the hallway. "Why? We're not going yet, are we? I haven't even gotten to the chocolate cake."

"No. I just wanted to talk with her for a second." Or not talk as much as sneak her into an empty room for a few stolen kisses. The sexy black dress and heels she had on were driving him crazy. And had been all night. Of course, everything she wore drove him crazy. Except his sheepskin coat. When she was all snuggled up in his jacket, he didn't feel crazy as much as content—as if all was right in the world. It had been a long time since he'd felt like things were right in his world.

"Hey, you two," Zane walked up and thumped Luke on the back. "How are you enjoying the party, Luke?"

"It's great. Especially the food." Luke finished off the cookie and picked up another from the plate he held.

"He has a bottomless pit of a stomach, like you," Raff teased his cousin.

Zane laughed. "Then he's come to the right place. Carly knows how to fill an empty stomach. Of course, Luke probably already knows that. How do you like working at the diner?"

"I like it a lot. Carly's a cool boss. In the morning before the lunch rush, she's been teaching me how to be her sous chef." Luke's face fell. "Something I won't be able to do after school starts."

"I'm sure there will be plenty of time for Carly to teach you to be a sous chef when you move here to the Earhart Ranch," Zane said.

Luke lowered the cookie. "I'm not moving here. I'm living with Raff."

Raff cringed. He'd thought Luke's mother had talked to him about moving in with Zane. But obviously that wasn't the case. And Raff shouldn't have left it to Jennifer. He should've talked with Luke. He should've brought him to the ranch sooner and showed him around so Luke could get comfortable with the idea. Instead, he'd been chasing after Savannah like a dog in heat. He tried to salvage the situation.

"Didn't Shep just sire some puppies, Zane?" he asked. "Do you mind if I take Luke out to the barn to see them?"

Before Zane could answer, Luke turned to Raff with hurt written all over his face. "You want me to live here?"

Part of Raff wanted to deny it. He had grown to care about Luke. He liked having him around. He liked hearing him snoring up in the loft at night and fixing him breakfast in the morning. He liked teaching him woodworking and how to fix things around the cabin. He had even thought about borrowing a horse from Zane or Cole and teaching him to ride. But the other part of him, the logical part, knew that he couldn't take on the responsibility of a teenager. His life was too unstable. He was too unstable.

"It only makes sense, Luke," he said. "Especially with me traveling all the time. The Earhart Ranch is a great place for a boy to live. Much better than my cabin. You'll have your own room instead of a cramped loft. Your own bathroom that you don't have to share. Horses and dirt bikes to ride whenever you want. And Carly to make you whatever food you want to eat. She and Zane will do a much better job of raising you than I can."

Luke's voice held a desperate edge that ate a hole right through Raff's chest. "You don't have to raise me. I'm a man, and I can do my share. I could keep an eye on things while you're gone. Clean the cabin. Weed the yard. Raise any animals we got. I've seen you looking at cattle online. If you bought some, I could take care of them while you're gone. And then when you get back we could hang out like we've been doing." He paused and swallowed hard. "I like hanging out with you."

Raff felt like the kid was physically punching him. "I'm glad you like hanging out with me. I like hanging out with you too. And I promise we'll continue to hang out together. Every time I come to town, I'll stop by to visit."

For a long, heart-crushing moment, Luke stared at him. "What about the gun? If you don't let me live with you, I won't give you the gun."

"Me helping you has nothing to do with the gun, Luke." He put a hand on Luke's shoulder. "I care about you. That's why I want the best for you."

Luke jerked away. "You don't care about me. If you cared about me, you'd keep me." He looked at Zane. "Can I move in now?"

Zane glanced at Raff. Raff wanted to insist that the kid come home with him, but he knew that would only postpone the pain . . . for both of them. "If it's okay with you, Zane, it's good with me."

Zane nodded. "Sure. Becky and Mason got their water pipe fixed so Luke can have their room."

"Great." Luke gave Raff one more belligerent look before he turned and walked off.

Raff should be happy. With Luke gone, he was back to having no responsibilities. He could go where he wanted to go and have Savannah as an overnight guest. But he didn't feel happy. He felt like he was losing something he wasn't ready to give up. Which was selfish. It would be better for Luke if he moved in now and got used to living at the Earhart Ranch.

Zane placed a hand on Raff's shoulder. "Come into my study, and I'll pour you something stronger than Carly's holiday punch."

Once inside the study, Raff sat down on the couch in front of the fire and stared into the flames until Zane handed him a glass of amber liquid. Not caring what it was, Raff took a long drink.

"I'm sorry," Zane said as he took a chair behind the desk. "I thought Luke knew."

"It's my fault. I should've told him sooner. I just thought his mom had explained that he'd eventually be moving in with you." Raff took another drink, in the hopes it would ease the ache in his stomach. Or maybe it was his heart that hurt. He couldn't tell. "He'll be okay once he realizes what a great place the Earhart Ranch is to live."

"Maybe he's not looking for a great place to live. Maybe he's looking for a home."

Raff turned and looked at his cousin. "You actually think the kid would be better off with me than with you?"

"I'll admit that I didn't at first, but I do now." Zane studied Raff. "You've changed. You aren't nearly as hotheaded as you used to be. You're great with Luke. Carly says that you're all he talks about when he's working at the diner. You and Savannah."

"That's all Savannah. She can make anyone feel comfortable."

Zane tipped his head. "Maybe. Or maybe you're a better man than you think." He sipped his drink. "So what gun does Luke have?"

Raff had kept the gun a secret from his cousins for one reason and one reason only. He didn't want them talking him out of selling it. But now that the gun was gone and he didn't have a clue where it was, there was no reason to keep it a secret any longer. "Gus's 1872 Winchester."

Zane choked and spewed bourbon out of his mouth. "Holy shit." He wiped off his chin. "I didn't think you were talking about that Winchester. Where the hell did you find it?"

"I tracked it down."

"You must have done some major tracking. That gun has been missing longer than the final Tender

Heart book. Are you sure it's the same gun?"

"It has the Arrington brand on the stock," Raff said. "That's how I found it. I had a picture of Gus holding the gun enlarged, and I put it on the Internet. A truck driver contacted me and said he had it. I guess he found it at garage sale. I made him an offer and he took it. But before I'd even gone to pick it up, a gun dealer from Austin contacted me and offered me a hundred and fifty thousand dollars for it."

Zane whistled through his teeth. "Damn, for a gun?"

"I guess he's a Tender Heart fan and recognized the brand."

Zane stared at him. "Tell me you aren't planning on selling our great-granddaddy's Winchester."

"I was planning on it," Raff said. "I was planning on selling it and using the money to rebuild the house. But now I'm not sure Luke will ever tell me where it is." He wanted to be mad at Luke, but he wasn't. He didn't care about the gun as much as he cared about hurting Luke. He finished off his drink, and then stared into the flames until Zane spoke.

"Why do you have to be so damned stubborn? Why can't you just admit that you care about Luke and want the kid to stay with you?"

Raff got up and moved closer to the fire. "Because I'm not staying. I don't want to stay. I'm not you and Cole. I'm not someone who can live up to the town's image of a perfect Arrington. And I never will be."

"That's what I thought."

Raff turned to see Carly standing in the doorway. She did not look happy. She looked pissed. Zane immediately got to his feet.

"Now don't be angry, honey. I know I shouldn't have eaten all the little stuffed mushrooms you made, but those were the best things I've ever put in my mouth."

"I'm not angry at you for eating appetizers. I'm mad at Raff for screwing over my friend."

Zane glanced at Raff. "What is she talking about?"

Carly stepped further in the room and closed the door. "What I'm talking about is Raff seducing Savannah." She walked over and poked Raff in the chest. For a little blond pixie of a woman, she had a strong poke. "And don't act all wide-eyed and innocent. You knew she was vulnerable after Miles left her at the altar. You knew she would be an easy mark for your alpha bad-boy good looks. Especially after her pantywaist of a fiancé."

"Now, Carly"—Zane walked around his desk—"I'm sure Raff wouldn't do anything to hurt Savannah."

She turned on her husband. "He already did. He made Savannah fall in love with him!"

Raff had thought he felt beat up over Luke. Now he didn't feel like he'd been punched as much as broadsided by a train. Savannah was in love with him? She loved him? As blindsided as he felt, he also felt something else. A warm glow started in his stomach and spread through his entire body as Carly continued to rant.

"And that wouldn't be so bad if he returned her affections, but I just heard him telling you that he has no intention of staying here in Bliss."

"But, sweetheart," Zane said, "I didn't think Savannah was staying in Bliss either."

"She wasn't, but she is now." She looked back at Raff. "She's in my bedroom right now taking about a wedding in the little white chapel and how she can't wait to cuddle a precious baby boy with your dark hair and hazel eyes."

The warm glow was doused like it had been hit with a bucket of ice water. He pictured Savannah pregnant . . . then he pictured her beautiful eyes filled with the same haunted look his mother had had every time she'd come home empty-handed from the hospital. Suddenly, he felt as if all the oxygen had been sucked out of his lungs. And he knew he couldn't do it. He couldn't go through what his father had. He couldn't survive watching a woman he loved suffer like his mother. And he did love Savannah. He loved her enough to let her go.

Without a word, he walked out of the study. He didn't try to find Savannah or look for Luke to say goodbye. He just grabbed his hat from the hook by the door and left. On the porch, he took big gulps of air. It didn't help the twisting pain in his gut. In fact, the scent of the smoke from Zane's chimneys tightened his insides even more. He headed to his truck. He was just reaching for the door handle when Savannah called his name.

"Raff!"

He tried to ignore her, but Savannah was not a woman you could ignore. Before he could open his truck door she was there, filling his vision with big bluebonnet eyes that confirmed everything that Carly had said. The love he saw had him cringing in pain. She instantly became concerned.

"Are you okay?"

He looked away and stared at a star that hovered over the horizon. "I have to go."

"Okay. Let me just run inside and get Luke."

The knot in his stomach became almost unbearable. "Luke's not coming with me. He's staying here with Zane."

"I don't understand. Why would he stay here?"

He kept his gaze pinned on the star, desperately wishing that this torture would end soon. "He decided to move in with Zane early."

"But why? Why would he do that? Why would you let him? And why won't you look at me?"

His control snapped, and he slammed a hand on the roof of his truck before he turned to her. "Because it's for the best! Luke was never going to stay with me forever. That wasn't the plan. The plan was to get my gun and leave him with Zane. And I'm sick of people looking at me like I have some responsibility to the kid. I'm not his father. And I don't want to be his father. I never want to be a father!"

Savannah took a step back as if he'd hit her, her eyes deep pools of hurt. "So you only took him in to get the gun?"

The knot in his stomach tightened so much that he was either going to throw up or pass out. He needed to put an end to this and get out of there. And the only way he could see to do that was to be brutally honest.

"What did you expect, Savannah? Did you expect me to be a hero like the ones in your Tender Heart books? Did you expect me to save the day in the last twenty pages? Well, sorry to disappoint you. But I'm no hero. I'm the villain. The one who scares the townsfolk, doesn't save the ranch, and leaves the heroine high and dry." He thumped his chest. "I'm that guy."

Tears welled in her eyes. "You're leaving me."

He knew she wasn't talking about leaving her at the party. He knew she was talking about leaving her for good. Leaving her the same way Miles had left her. He swallowed hard. "I was always leaving, Savannah. You knew that."

"I just thought . . ." She let the sentence trail off. But he knew what she was going to say. She'd thought that he'd changed his mind and decided to stay. He did want to stay. He wanted to stay and be the hero. A hero who would be a good mentor to Luke. A hero who would love Savannah enough to leave the past behind and give her the husband and children she'd dreamed of.

But he wasn't strong enough. He never had been.

"Goodbye, Savannah."

"Melanie finally accepted the truth. She'd lost Dax."

CHAPTER TWENTY-ONE

Ⓒ

SAVANNAH HAD THOUGHT SHE'D BEEN brokenhearted when Miles ended their relationship, but now she knew what a broken heart felt like. Her heart ached like it was being squeezed in a giant fist. When Miles left her, she'd cried buckets. With Raff, she didn't shed a tear. It was like everything inside her was all dried up. She felt empty and lost. But she refused to show it. She wasn't about to ruin her friends' holiday by moping around. Especially when they had warned her.

So she put on a brave front and acted like everything was hunky dory. She helped with all the family dinner parties and gatherings. She finished the wreaths for the businesses on Main Street and made ornament and poinsettia arrangements for the hanging streetlamp planters. And she went to Christmas pageant rehearsals every night. Even though every time she looked at Luke, she was reminded of Raff.

She was surprised that the teenager had continued to come. But even after he'd gone to live with Zane and Carly, Luke showed up for every rehearsal. His mother had come to visit and seemed satisfied that her son was being well cared for, and Becky's lawyer husband Mason was helping Luke with the emancipation. Savannah thought that would make Luke happy, but on the night of the dress rehearsal, she found him sitting alone in a pew looking as sad as she felt.

"Your costume looks great," she said as she took a seat next to him. "You make a very handsome Joseph."

He shrugged his shoulders. "It's just a couple bed sheets and a rope." He leaned down and pulled the Tender Heart chapter out of his backpack. As he handed it to her, his eyes glittered with unshed tears. "I should've given him the stupid gun. If I had, he might've kept me."

Luke's sadness finally broke through Savannah's depression. How dare Raff make this sweet boy believe that a gun meant more to him than Luke did? Suddenly, she wasn't just angry—she was pissed.

She gave Luke a tight hug. "Don't you give that man another thought. Do you hear me? He's not worth it. We're not going to let a bad boy with issues ruin our holidays. Come on, honey. Let's get ready to welcome Sweet Baby Jesus."

The dress rehearsal went as well as could be expected. A wise man forgot his lines. A shepherd misplaced his staff. The donkey got into a fight with a camel over some tail pulling. And the star fell off the peak of the stable and almost took out an angel. Savannah felt responsible, given that she had superglued the star on. But she'd had no choice. Raff had left town, leaving Emmett to put the stable together and Savannah to glue on the star herself.

Savannah was glad Raff had left. She didn't think she could control her anger if she'd run into him. But it wasn't anger that filled her when she got home after dress rehearsals to find Lucy's childhood desk sitting on the landing outside her apartment door. As soon as she saw the desk, she burst into tears. It was the first time she'd cried since he'd dumped her, and she swore it would be the last. She was through allowing men to manipulate her emotions. And she was through looking for the right man to give her a happily-ever-after. She would make her own happiness.

But when she called up Mrs. Carlisle to tell her about the desk and got the interior decorating job, she didn't feel happy. She felt miserable. She couldn't stand the thought of Lucy's childhood desk being anywhere but Bliss. The following morning, she called Mrs. Carlisle back and told her that she'd made a mistake, she couldn't get the desk after all. Mrs. Carlisle was thoroughly disappointed and not very nice about telling Savannah she could no longer use her as a designer.

Savannah should've been upset. Without the Carlisle job, she would lose her business. But she wasn't upset. She felt relieved. Like a huge weight had been lifted off her shoulders. That morning when she went into town to deliver the wreaths, the empty building two doors down from the diner caught her eye. It had big picture windows that would be perfect for displaying furniture and home décor accessories. And beneath the windows, Savannah could just picture cute window boxes filled with flowers.

A flicker of excitement settled in the pit of her stomach. Could she do it? Could she really open an antique store in a small town like Bliss and make it work? Why couldn't she? Bliss might be small, but Austin was just an hour away and Houston and San Antonio not much further. And city people loved to take trips to the country to go antiquing. Or just browse quaint little decorating shops for unique things to take back to the city.

Savannah smiled. She could make it work. She knew she could make it work.

A honk drew her attention away from the store-front. Ms. Marble pulled her big ol' car up next to the curb and rolled down the window. She wore her usual bonnet. This one was festooned with candy cane striped ribbon. "I'm headed out to the little white chapel to deliver some candles for the Christmas Eve service. You want to come with me?"

Savannah never could pass up a chance to go to the little white chapel. Plus, she wanted to go over her idea with Ms. Marble. She chattered the entire drive out to Arrington land about wanting to turn the vacant building into an antique and home décor shop. Ms. Marble seemed thrilled with the idea.

"That building belongs to Zane Arrington," she said as they pulled up to the copse of trees that surrounded the white chapel. "I'm sure you could get it for a song. And Raff can help you fill it with antiques." She winked. "I saw him delivering the desk yesterday. You must be special if he's willing to give you his great-aunt's desk."

Savannah's happiness fizzled. "I'm not special

to Raff. It was more of a guilt gift before he left town."

"That boy will be back. He doesn't realize it yet, but this is where he belongs."

She stared out the windshield. "I don't care if he does come back. I'm done with men." She could feel Ms. Marble studying her with her intense blue eyes.

"I said that once myself, but thankfully God didn't hold me to it." She picked up the bouquet of pink roses that sat on the seat between them. "Would you mind taking these to Lucy's grave while I take the candles into the chapel?"

In the last few days, Savannah hadn't given much thought to the love triangle between Ms. Marble, Justin Bonner, and Lucy. Now she had to wonder if the roses Ms. Marble left on Lucy's grave were a guilt gift. Maybe Ms. Marble knew she had taken Justin away from Lucy.

"Of course," she said as she took the bouquet.

Before she got out, Ms. Marble pulled one pink rose from the bouquet. "And place this on Justin Bonner's grave."

Savannah stared at her in shock. "Your first husband is buried in the Arrington cemetery?"

Ms. Marble smiled. "The Arringtons often allowed their employees to be buried here if that was their wish. And it was Justin's wish."

Savannah was confused. Why would Justin have asked to be buried in the same cemetery as Lucy if he loved Ms. Marble enough to marry her? And why did Ms. Marble allow her husband to be buried here? The questions continued to circle as she got out of the car and made her way to the cemetery.

The cemetery was behind the chapel. As she stepped through the gate, a gust of cold wind had her wishing she'd brought Raff's coat. Although it was better to be cold than wear a jerk's coat.

Savannah had been to Lucy's grave numerous times and knew exactly where it was located. The gravestone was in the shape of an open book with the inscription *Lucy Arrington, a Tender Heart*. She carefully rested the bouquet of roses at the base of the stone before she went in search of Justin Bonner's. She was shocked to find it so close to Lucy's. Only a small evergreen shrub divided the two headstones. It was a simple gray marble headstone, inscribed with the words: Justin Bonner. Cowboy. Soldier. Husband. Father.

Savannah stared at the last word. Father? But Ms. Marble said that they hadn't had children. Had Justin been married before and had children? Or was this referring to Bonnie Blue? If that were the case, then Ms. Marble must have known about her husband's affair with Lucy.

As she was digesting this, the wind blew a petal off the pink rose she held. It fluttered through the air, and then got caught in the shrub between the two graves. Through the waxy leaves of the bush, Savannah caught the glimmer of something shiny. She knelt on the ground and reached under the bush until her fingers brushed something hard and cold.

She pulled out a metal box with a latch.

Inside was not one, but sixteen chapters of the final Tender Heart book.

"I knew when you asked about Lucy while we

were talking about Justin that you had figured things out."

Savannah almost jumped out of her skin at the softly spoken words. She glanced up to see Ms. Marble standing there holding her hat so it wouldn't be blown off in the wind.

"You?" Savannah said. "You're the one who's been hiding the chapters?"

Ms. Marble nodded before she moved over to a stone bench and sat down. "I expect you have a few questions."

A few? Try a thousand. There were so many Savannah didn't know where to start. She glanced at the gravestones. "You knew. You knew about Justin and Lucy. You knew about the baby."

Ms. Marble took off her hat and set it on the bench next to her. "I didn't know about their affair until after I married Justin."

"He loved you. That's why he didn't marry Lucy. That's why he didn't claim Bonnie Blue."

"I wish that were the case, but Justin always loved Lucy. I was just a substitute. Just a woman he turned to after her death."

"But I don't understand. If he loved her, why didn't he marry her and claim Bonnie Blue as his own?"

"Because he didn't know about Bonnie Blue. Before she knew she was pregnant, Justin and Lucy got in an argument. Lucy wanted him to marry her and work the Arrington Ranch with her family. Justin didn't want to be under her family's thumb. He wanted his own spread. So he left and took a job in the oil fields. His plan was to return and buy land with the money he'd made, then ask

Lucy to marry him. But by the time he returned, Lucy had had the baby and Bonnie Blue was gone. She blamed him for leaving and he blamed her for giving away their child. He tried to find Bonnie, and when he couldn't, he joined the army. Lucy became a reclusive writer."

It was the saddest love story Savannah had ever heard, and she couldn't keep the tears from her eyes. "And Justin never came back again before she died?"

Ms. Marble shook her head. "It was something he regretted until the day he died. Every day after her funeral, he brought pink roses to her grave and sat here until the sun went down. It broke my heart." Tears rolled down her wrinkled cheeks. "You see, I loved Justin all my life just like Lucy did. It was hard not to. He was handsome and charming and the perfect cowboy hero. And when he finally started coming out of his grief, I was right there to comfort him. We married only months later."

"And the book? How did you get the final Tender Heart book?"

"Lucy gave it to me before she died. That's when she told me about the baby. She didn't tell me who the father was. She knew I had always been in love with Justin, and I think she didn't want to hurt me. When she gave me the book, she made me promise to find Bonnie Blue and give it to her."

Ms. Marble stared at Savannah with tears brimming her aged eyes. "I planned to do just that for my friend, but then Justin came back. And when I saw his heartbreak, I figured everything out. I was angry at Lucy for not confiding in me." She paused. "Then after Justin and I got married, I was angry that Lucy had been able to give Justin a child when I couldn't. So I didn't look for Bonnie, and I didn't tell anyone about the book. Not even Justin. I think I was scared if he knew, he'd start searching for Bonnie again. And if he found her, he would love her more than he loved me."

She shook her head. "It was foolishness. Pure foolishness. And once Justin died and I married David, David helped me figure that out. I started searching in earnest for Bonnie and didn't give up until a year ago. At that time, I decided it was time to break my promise and give the Tender Heart fans their final book. I couldn't give it to Bonnie Blue, but I could give it to the younger Arringtons. They deserved to get the royalties from one of Lucy's books."

"But why the treasure hunt? Why didn't you just give it to them?"

"I guess I didn't want them to hate me. I could've just hidden the entire book in one place, but I thought they needed to learn about their great-aunt. Where she plotted. Where she found inspiration. Where she fell in love. Of course, if you girls hadn't shown up, it could've taken a while. And Justin and Lucy's grandson arriving certainly threw a surprise curve."

"You recognized Dirk?"

"From the moment he stepped into town. He looks just like Justin."

"So why didn't you give him the book?"

Ms. Marble lifted an eyebrow. "Would you have given the final book to a drifter? It took me a while to be sure that I could trust him. Plus, Lucy had made me promise to only give it to Bonnie

Blue. So I waited. I figured Bonnie would show up eventually. Once she did, I told her the full story." She smiled and shook her head. "She's just like Lucy. Stubborn. She said she didn't want the book. She had plenty of money and was quite happy in her little house in Waco. She felt like the book belonged to the Arringtons. And since the treasure hunt had led to so many happy endings, why not continue it for a little while longer? We both agree that Lucy has been sitting up in heaven having a grand old time using chapters of her books to matchmake. How else would they have led to so many happily-ever-afters?"

It did seem like more than a fluke that all the Arrington cousins had found the loves of their lives and married in such a short time.

"Everyone but Raff," Savannah said, more to herself than to Ms. Marble.

"And who says he can't?" Ms. Marble's intense blue eyes stared right through her. "Maybe there's one more chapter before the book ends. And I'm not talking about Lucy's ending. I'm talking about yours. Everyone has a chance to write their own endings. You can wait like Lucy and Justin and let fate write yours for you, or you can write it yourself. Raff loves you. I've been in his barn. I've seen the stockpile of heirlooms he's hoarding to alleviate his guilt. He wouldn't have given you Lucy's desk if he didn't love you."

"Then why did he leave? If he really loves me, he wouldn't have run off."

"If I've learned anything in my life, it's that love isn't perfect. Or maybe love is perfect, it's people that aren't. Don't be like Lucy. When Justin refused to go along with her plan, she convinced herself that he didn't love her. If she had just given him a chance, Lucy and Justin's story might've ended differently." Ms. Marble stood and placed her hat back on. It was strange, but the wind had completely died. "Now if you'll give me a few minutes, I need to chat with my best friend."

Savannah left the cemetery with the chapters clutched to her chest and her mind focused on Ms. Marble's words. Was she right? Did Raff love her?

She stopped in front of the little white chapel and stared up at the steeple that speared the blue Texas sky. The last time she'd been there she'd made a wish for a happily-ever-after with Miles. But she now realized she would never have been happy with Miles. She'd thought his money would give her security. But security wasn't about money. It was about feeling safe. And Savannah had never felt as safe in a high-rise apartment as she felt in Raff's rundown cabin. She never felt as warm and cozy in her designer clothes as she felt in his sheepskin jacket. And she never felt as loved in a big city as she felt in this small town.

She closed her eyes and made another wish. But this one didn't have to do with marrying a southern man with money. This one had to do with marrying a junkman.

"Dax had gone only a mile outside of Tender Heart when the truth hit him. What was he running from? He couldn't change the massacre that took place in that small Sioux village. He'd tried to stop it and failed. But what he could change was his future. And he'd have no future without Melanie."

CHAPTER TWENTY-TWO

RAFF HADN'T KNOWN WHERE HE was headed when he left Bliss. All he knew was that he couldn't stay in the cabin another second without going crazy. He had thought that Savannah's decorating had made the cabin feel like a home, but after days of staying in the cabin alone, he realized that it wasn't the furniture or the new bedding and towels or the Christmas decorations that had made the house homey. It was Savannah and Luke. And now that they were gone, it just felt empty. As empty as he felt.

He tried to fill up that emptiness by getting as far away from Bliss as he could. But the more miles he drove away from the town, the more empty he felt. When he crossed the Texas-Oklahoma border, he finally realized where he was headed.

His parents' house had once belonged to his grandmother. He could remember coming to visit every Thanksgiving when he was a kid. So there was something comforting about pulling into the gravel driveway.

The last time he'd been there, he'd helped his dad paint the two-story farmhouse a cheery yellow with white trim. His mother had wanted the door painted a bright cranberry red. He'd thought it was a little too wild at the time, but now he had to admit that it looked good with the festive wreath and the multi-colored Christmas lights draped over the frame.

Since it was after dark, there were lights on. Through the window, he could see his mother puttering around in the kitchen. She was no doubt baking some holiday treat. She loved to bake as much as Ms. Marble did. Luke would've loved her.

The thought of Luke made Raff feel like crap all over again. He wondered if he should've come to see his parents after all. They didn't need him ruining their holidays with his depression. But before he could back out of the driveway, his father came out the front door.

He tugged on his cowboy hat and buttoned up his jacket before walking down the steps of the porch. At first, Raff thought his dad hadn't seen the truck in the dark. But then his father turned in his direction and lifted his hand. The greeting was so like his father. While Zane and Cole's dads were outspoken and gregarious, Raff's was soft-spoken and introverted. Raff's father didn't hug him when he got out of the truck. He just stood there.

"You forget your coat?"

Just the mention of his coat brought up images of Savannah cuddled up in the wooly sheepskin. Although she probably wasn't cuddled up in it now. She'd probably burned it.

"I loaned it to a woman."

His dad nodded. "Can't let women get cold." He turned and headed toward the shed. Raff followed. The shed was much smaller than the Tender Heart Ranch's barn. When Raff had first seen his dad working in it, he'd been more motivated than ever to get the house built and his father back on the ranch where he belonged. But now, the shed didn't seem so bad. It wasn't nearly as cold as the barn, and his father had filled it with saws and lathes and sanders. Some Raff had purchased for him for birthdays, Father's Days, and Christmases. This year, he hadn't gotten his father anything for Christmas. He added that to the growing list of things to feel bad about.

As he closed the door behind him, the family Australian shepherd, Sarah, came up to greet him with tag wagging. Two fat puppies followed in her wake. Again he thought of Luke. Had Zane given him a puppy? He hoped so. The kid could use a furry friend.

"Sarah had pups?" He bent down to scratch Sarah's ears, and the puppies nosed their way in between his legs for their turn at attention.

"She had eight. One died at birth, and I sold all but one. The bigger one the neighbor bought for his son, but he won't pick him up until Christmas Eve. Christmas present. That just leaves the runt."

Raff stared down at the smaller puppy with the black spot around one eye as his father hung up his coat and hat. "We weren't expecting you until New Year's," his father said.

He finished scratching the dogs and stood. "I

thought I'd come a little early."

His dad picked up two pieces of sandpaper. He handed Raff one before he sat down on a low stool next to a rocking horse and started sanding. Raff sat down on the floor on the other side, but it wasn't easy to sand with the two puppies clambering over his crossed legs and nipping at the sandpaper. When he ignored their antics, they finally settled down in his lap.

"So this woman you loaned your coat to, is she special?" his father asked.

This time an entire plethora of images ran through his brain. Savannah smiling at toddler angels as they wiped their snotty noses on her sweater. Laughing at something Luke said as they decorated the tree. Singing Christmas carols at the top of her lungs. Closing her eyes and humming in ecstasy over a bite of chocolate cake . . . or when Raff slid deep inside her.

His throat tightened with emotion so he couldn't tell his father how special Savannah was. All he could do was nod.

The wisp of sandpaper against wood continued before his father asked the one question he didn't want him to ask. "You gonna marry her?"

Raff stopped sanding and picked up the sleeping puppies and carried them over to their mama. Once they were snuggled close to Sarah, he stepped to the window and stared at the house. His mother was still in the kitchen. She appeared to be singing. She had always been singing when he was a kid—unless she was grieving.

"I don't think I can get married," he said. "If something happened . . ." He let the sentence drift off. "I just don't think I could deal with being a husband. I'm not strong enough."

The sanding stopped behind him, and a second later, he felt his dad's hand on his shoulder. His father wasn't nearly as big as Raff, but he'd always seemed bigger. Calmer. So much more in control. Which was why Raff was surprised when he turned and saw the tears tracking down his father's cheeks.

"Dad?"

His father's hand tightened on his shoulder as he stared out the window at the house. "I'm not strong, son. Every time we lost a child, I wept like a baby and beat that punching bag in the barn until my hands bled." And here Raff had thought the bag had been for his temper. It surprised him that his dad had needed it more than he had.

"Then why didn't you stop trying?" he asked. "Why did you keep getting Mom pregnant?"

His father released a quivery breath. "I guess it's a little like you giving that woman your coat. When someone you care about needs something, you want to try and fill that need. And your mama wanted another baby. She wanted one badly."

Raff voiced his worst fear. "Wasn't I enough?"

His father turned to him with a shocked look. "Is that what you think? You think we kept trying for kids because you weren't enough?"

"Or maybe I was too much. I was a spoiled brat, Dad. You can't deny it."

"You were strong-willed and hot-tempered— both Arrington traits. And you're wrong, son. Your mother didn't want another child because you weren't enough. She wanted another child as much for you as for herself. She wanted you to have a younger sibling to play with and cherish like Zane and Cole cherished their sisters."

"I didn't want a sibling. I wanted a happy father and mother." His father's shoulders wilted, and Raff tried to take the harsh words back. "I'm sorry, Dad. I shouldn't have said that. I had a happy childhood. I just felt so helpless every time Mom lost a baby. And what made it even worse is neither one of you would talk about it with me. You acted like I was too young to know what was going on. But I knew."

"You're right," his father said. "We should've let you share in our grief and taught you that grief is just a small part of life. Because for all the grief your mama and I have gone through, we've gone through so much more happiness. We've been blessed." He squeezed Raff's shoulder, his eyes still gleaming with tears. "And you're one of our biggest blessings. I pray you don't have go through with your wife what your mother and I went through, but you'll have to go through something, son. Life is filled with hard times and good times. You can't have one without the other."

Raff's own eyes burned with tears. "But what if I'm not strong enough?"

His father pulled him in for a tight hug before he drew back. "You'll be strong enough. Love makes you strong enough." He nodded at the rocking horse. "Now, you want help me finish sanding so I can paint it and have it ready for Christmas morning?"

Raff blinked back his tears and took the sandpaper his father offered. As they worked, he thought about his father's words. After his childhood, Raff had wanted to live a pain-free life. That's why he'd left Bliss right after high school. Why he'd never formed any lasting attachments. He'd thought that if he had no responsibilities or attachments, he couldn't get hurt. And he'd been right. If he had never gotten close to Luke and Savannah, he wouldn't be sitting there with a dull ache in his heart. He'd be on a highway somewhere with no pain. But he wouldn't have experienced the joyful times with Luke and Savannah either. And he wanted to experience that joy again.

Once the horse was painted, he and his father rinsed the brushes at the sink, and then headed to the house. As soon as they stepped in the door, his mother released a gasp.

"Raff!" She wiped her hands on a dish towel and hurried over to give him a tight hug. "You should've told me you were coming. I would've made you pecan pie."

He held her close for a long moment, absorbing her love before he drew back and sniffed the spicy scent in the air. "Pumpkin will do just fine."

They ate pumpkin pie by the fire and caught up. His mother was much more talkative than his father. She wanted to know everything that was going on with her friends back in Bliss and if more chapters of the final Tender Heart book had been found. She was surprised to find out that the most recent chapters had been found in the Tender Heart barn. And not at all surprised that Raff had hunted down Lucy's furniture.

"You've always loved your Arrington heritage, Raff." She smiled. "So what are you going to do with the furniture?"

He hesitated for only a moment before he sprung his surprise. "I'm going to fill your new house with it." He glanced at his father and smiled. "The one Daddy and I are going to build—just as soon as I get the money together to buy the materials. It's my way of replacing the things I took from you."

His parents exchanged surprised looks before his mother's eyes filled with tears and she hugged him. "Oh Raff, that is about the sweetest Christmas gift anyone has ever given me." She pulled back and looked at him. "But you didn't take anything from us the night of the fire. In fact, you gave us something. You gave us a new start on life."

He looked at his father. "What do you mean? I burned down your house and forced you to leave."

"You didn't force us to leave, son," his father said. "You gave us an excuse to leave. One I'd needed for a long time. I was never much of a rancher. I love working with wood much more than I like working with animals. You are the one who loves ranching. The one who has patience with animals and can rope and ride better than all your cousins put together." He glanced at his wife before looking back at Raff and smiling. "That's why we've decided to give you the Tender Heart Ranch."

Raff was stunned. "You don't want to live in Bliss? But it's your heritage."

"I don't need to live in Texas to be proud of my heritage, son."

"But what about all the family heirlooms I bought?" And spent two years looking for.

"Why don't you give them back to the Tender Heart fans?" his mother said. "You could start a museum. Cole has more than a few things of Lucy's, and if you had the people of the town donate their heirlooms from the mail-order brides, you'd have plenty. I know people would flock to see things that inspired the Tender Heart series and it would bring a lot of revenue to the town."

Raff didn't know what to say. He'd spent the last two years of his life trying to make up for what he'd taken from his parents, and it turned out that he hadn't taken anything at all. He should be ticked off that he'd wasted all that time and money, but he wasn't. He just felt relief that years of guilt had been lifted from his shoulders. He laughed. He laughed so hard that his mother joined in. Even his father chuckled before he got up from his chair.

"Whelp, I'm headed to bed."

His mother wiped the tears of laughter from her eyes. "It is getting late, and you-know-who will be waking us up bright and early."

Raff stood. "I'll just go get my duffel from the truck."

When he returned, his mother was in the guest room folding back the sheet and bedspread on the bed. Raff set his duffel on the dresser before he asked, "Can I go see him? I promise not to wake him up."

She smiled and nodded. "You don't have to worry about waking him. He sleeps like the dead. Just like you do."

He took off his boots anyway before he headed to the room next to his. It was dark, but the Winnie the Pooh nightlight gave enough light for Raff to see the sleeping little boy in the crib.

Rolland slept on his back with his arms over

his head and his fuzzy blanket twisted around his legs. He looked like he'd gained more than a few pounds since Raff had seen him last. His cheeks were full and rosy. His arms plump and dimpled. His hair was dark like Raff's, but still baby-thin. And his eyes, when they were open, were a deep Arrington blue.

Raff leaned over the crib and brushed a strand back from his forehead, awed by the silkiness of his hair and the softness of his skin. As he stood there looking down at the innocent perfection of his baby brother, Raff suddenly realized he was glad his parents had kept trying. There are things in life well worth the pain.

He straightened the blanket around his brother's chubby body before he turned and walked out of the room. His mother was waiting in the hallway with fresh towels. He walked straight to her and pulled her into his arms, pressing his face into her shirt that smelled of pumpkin pie spices.

"I love you," he said.

"I love you too." She squeezed him close before she drew back and studied him with concerned eyes. "What's going on, Raff? What happened?"

He didn't even try to blink back the tears. "I fell in love."

They went back to the living room. By the light of the Christmas tree and the glowing embers of the fire, Raff told her what had been going on in his life for the last few weeks. He left nothing out. He told her about Savannah. And Luke. And his fear. When he was finished, she didn't hug him or sympathize. She merely took his face in her cool hands and gave him an order as if he were ten years old again.

"You need to get some rest. You have a long way to travel tomorrow."

Raff looked into his mother's loving hazel eyes and realized she was right. He went to bed, but he didn't get much sleep. His mind was too full of what he was going to do when he got to Bliss.

In the morning, his mother insisted he eat a good breakfast before she hugged him tight and handed him Rolland for a slobbery kiss. Before he left, he went with his father to the shed and got the runt of Sarah's litter with the black spot around one eye. His father packed him a bag with puppy food, a container of water, and a leash before walking him out.

He didn't give him a hug. Just a hard thump on the back. "I think it's going to be a good Christmas."

Raff certainly hoped so.

"Melanie ran out of the stage depot when she heard about the gunfight. But when she arrived in the middle of the street, Billy was gone and only Dax was standing there looking completely unharmed. 'What happened?' she asked. He smiled a smile that made her knees weak. 'I told him that he'd have to find someone else to prove he was the fastest gun.' He pulled her into his arms. 'I'm just an old married man.'"

CHAPTER TWENTY-THREE

☾

"IT'S ALL HERE," EMERY BREATHED the words like a reverent prayer.

Savannah understood why. The dream of finding the final book of the Tender Heart series had been realized. The entire book sat in the middle of the desk in Emery and Cole's bedroom. The same desk that Lucy Arrington had written it on. Emery, Carly, Gracie, Becky, and Savannah stood around the desk, staring at it like it was the Holy Grail.

"I can't believe it was Ms. Marble who had it all along," Carly said. "She's been working for me all these months and I didn't have a clue."

Becky turned to Gracie. "I can't believe Granny Bon didn't tell you and Dirk after Ms. Marble told her."

"She did tell him." When everyone looked at her, Gracie scowled with annoyance. "My rascally husband thought we were having such a good time searching for the book he didn't want to ruin it for us."

"I knew he was looking a little too mischievous lately," Carly said. "So I guess he wasn't mad at Ms. Marble for keeping the secret about Justin being his great-grandfather?"

"Dirk understands keeping secrets because of an oath. His oath to his grandmother was why he didn't tell anyone who he was when he first came to Bliss. Besides, he loves Ms. Marble as much as he loves Bonnie Blue."

Savannah loved her too. "She's a sweet woman who's been through a lot. I don't think anyone should be upset with her. She was a good friend to Lucy. And if she had just handed over the book to the Arringtons, not one of you would be standing here happily wed."

They glanced at each other and smiled. "She does have a point," Emery said. She looked over at Savannah, and her eyes grew sad. "Cole told me about Raff leaving town. Why didn't you say anything?"

"Because I didn't want everyone worried about me. And I still don't. If Raff loves me, he'll be back. If he doesn't, I'll deal with it. I don't need a man to make me happy."

Carly looked surprised for only a second before she gave Savannah a tight squeeze. "I didn't think it would ever happen, but our little Savannah has finally grown up."

Savannah swatted her. "Behave yourself, Carly Sue." She looked at the book. "So what do we do with the book now that we've found it?"

"We publish it," Emery said, "and give it to all the Tender Heart fans who have been waiting for their happy ending for such a long time."

"And hopefully make boatloads of money for the Arringtons in the process," Becky said. "But I do think that once you authenticate it, the rest of us should get to read it."

As much as Savannah wanted to know what happened to Dax, she shook her head. "I think we should wait until it's published. Then I think we should all go to the little white chapel and spend the entire day reading it together."

Emery smiled. "I think that's a perfect idea. Besides, right now we have a Christmas pageant to go to."

❦

The Christmas pageant was standing room only. Everyone in Bliss was there, along with all their friends and relatives within a hundred-mile radius. Savannah had to admit she was a little nervous as she hustled around backstage, straightening halos and donkey ears and making sure everyone was lined up in the correct order.

"Remember, if you forget your lines, don't panic," she said. "I'll be sitting right off stage. Just look at me and I'll start you out with the first few words."

"What if we forget all the words?" the Angel of the Lord asked.

Her eyes widened in panic. "You didn't forget all your lines, did you?"

"'Fear not, I bring you good tidings of great joy.'" He grinned.

Savannah swatted his halo. "This is not the time for teasin'." She glanced around. "Now where is the third wise man?"

Mary appeared. "I saw him heading to the bathroom."

Savannah stared in shock at the girl's makeup. She looked like a jezebel instead of a virgin. "Uhh . . . honey. Is there a reason you put on fake eyelashes?"

Mary batted them. "My big sister put them on. She works at the makeup counter at Walgreens. She did all my makeup. She said that stage actresses need to accentuate their features so people in the audience can see their expressions." She widened her eyes until her eyelashes touched her darkly penciled eyebrows, then clutched her stomach. "Joseph! The time is near. We must find shelter."

At least she had her lines down cold. "That's great, honey. But maybe you should wipe off the lipstick. They probably didn't have Cherry Tart red in Jesus's time."

Mary's forehead knitted in confusion. "Are you sure? Because I saw a movie about Cleopatra and she wore red lipstick just like yours."

Savannah pulled the package of baby wipes that she'd taken to carrying for angel drool from her back pocket and handed one to Mary. "We'll Google it later. For now, get in line." She glanced at Joseph. Luke was no longer trying to hide his depression. He stood behind the shepherds, holding Miss Pitty and looking like he'd lost his best friend.

"Everything okay, Luke?" she asked.

"I thought he'd come back."

She'd thought the same thing. She had truly

believed that Raff would be back by now. If not
for her, then for Luke. But he hadn't shown up. She
tried to think of something to say that would make
Luke feel better, but she couldn't think of a thing.
So she just hugged him until Miss Pitty squirmed
between them. "I know. I miss him too."

Joanna came hurrying backstage. She'd recovered
completely from her surgery. She looked cheerful
in her holiday sweater with a family of snowmen
on the front. "It's time to start."

Savannah took Miss Pitty from Luke and glanced
around. "We're missing a wise man. Could you
have Emmett check the men's bathroom?"

Only a few seconds later, Joanna returned, not
looking so cheerful. "I'm afraid the young man has
stage fright—either that or the same flu that kept
Jason Bennett from being Joseph. Emmett says he's
throwing up like crazy."

Savannah wanted to puke herself. "Okay, we'll
just have to have two wise men. They'll split
his lines between them." She hurried to tell the
other two boys. Since she worried they wouldn't
remember their new lines, she had them cut and
taped them to the side of their frankincense and
myrrh mason jars. Then she sent them to the lobby
to wait for their grand entrance. Once they were
gone, she headed back to Joanna. "We're ready."

Joanna hurried off to tell the lighting and sound
volunteers. A few moments later, the lights went
down and the auditorium grew so quiet you could
hear a pin drop . . . or Mary holler.

"I'm blind!"

Savannah hurried to where Mary was holding
her eye. "What happened?"

"I accidentally rubbed my eye and an eyelash got in it."

Savannah tried not to hyperventilate. "It's okay." She didn't know if she was talking to Mary or herself. She handed the cat to the donkey, who looked thrilled to have the furry pet to strangle. "Let me see if I can get it out. It's really not a big deal, honey."

"Not a big deal?" Mary stared at her with one eye. The other was squeezed shut, and with the cockeyed lashes, it looked like she had a squashed spider in her eye. "My mom had a dandelion seed fly in her eye as a kid and she said it almost blinded her. My fake lashes are much bigger than a tiny seed."

She could say that again. "But you can't go out there like one-eyed Willie."

"I can't go out there at all," she whined. "My makeup is a mess." She tore the sheet off her head and pulled Baby Jesus out from under her costume. "I didn't want to do this dumb play anyway. My mom was the one who forced me."

"Wait a minute," Savannah said. "You can't just run off. Who will be Mary?" But she was talking to herself because Mary was already gone. Savannah stood there in defeat until a shepherd spoke.

"Maybe we should just cancel."

Savannah turned on the startled kid like a rabid dog. "We are not canceling. Canceling is quitting. And Savannah Devlin Reynolds does not quit!"

"But who's going to be Mary? Who knows her lines?"

She snatched up the sheet and the baby doll. "I do." She yelled loud enough so every angel, wise man, and shepherd could hear. "The show must go on!"

There was a collective inhalation of shock when Savannah first stepped out on the stage. She didn't know if it was seeing a grown woman in a children's pageant that surprised them or her bright red dress, heels, and Cherry Tart lipstick. Dang, she should've used a baby wipe. But she ignored their shock and delivered her lines as if she were a contestant in the Miss Georgia contest. And she soon felt like the crowd got over her clothes and age and started to enjoy the beautiful story of the nativity.

She sighed with relief when the Angel of the Lord's finale was over and three wise men came walking down the center aisle—obviously, the third wise man had recovered. She remained in character and kept her awed gaze on the Baby Jesus with his slightly squashed head as the wise men delivered their gifts and their lines. She was so into character that she didn't look up until the third wise man spoke in a deep, familiar voice that made her heart bump hard against her ribs.

"I have some gifts too."

She lifted her head and stared at Raff, who was staring right back at her. He had on a western shirt, jeans, and cowboy boots. But instead of a cowboy hat, he wore the third wise man's purple turban with the ostrich feather. It looked good on him. Real good. He held a cardboard box with a lid that was jumping like her heart. Mumbling came from the audience. They seemed as confused as the kids on the stage. But Savannah wasn't confused.

Raff had come back.

He'd come back.

He set the box down in front of the manger and took off the lid. The cutest puppy Savannah had ever seen stuck his head out. Raff scooped the dog up and held the wiggling animal out to Luke. Around the puppy's neck was a strip of leather with an arrowhead dangling from it.

"I think every man should have a dog," Raff said.

Savannah's heart stopped jumping and melted into a puddle. Luke didn't react quite the same way.

"You don't have a dog," he said belligerently. But it was easy to see he was having a hard time not reaching for the puppy with the arrowhead collar that matched the one Raff had around his wrist.

"You're right," Raff said. "I thought I didn't want the responsibility. But the truth is I was scared. Scared that if I let my heart get too attached to something, it would get broken. It took a lot for me to finally figure out that some things are worth taking a chance on." He paused. "Will you give me another chance, Luke?"

Savannah held her breath until Luke nodded. He took the dog from Raff, and then laughed when it licked his face. Savannah figured that was as good a time as any to sing the final song and bring the program to a close. She and Raff needed to have a private conversation. She wanted to know why he left. She wanted an apology. And she wanted to find out if there was any chance that he could love her. But as it turned out, Raff didn't need privacy. Before she could start singing, he gave her everything she wanted. And more.

"I'm sorry, Savannah. I shouldn't have run off. Like I told Luke, I left because I was scared. I was scared of being hurt. But I didn't know what hurt was until I left you at Zane and Carly's. All my life, I've felt like I wasn't enough. Not enough for the townsfolk. Not enough for my parents. Not enough for myself. But you, Savannah, you make me feel like I'm enough. You make me feel worthy. You make me a better man." He got down on one knee and pulled a ring-sized box out of his shirt pocket. "And I want to spend the rest of my life being a better man for you." He opened up the box to display a simple engagement ring. "I love you, Savannah."

That was all it took for the waterworks to start. Tears spilled out of her eyes, and there was no way she could stop them. She had dreamed of wedding proposals all of her life, but they never came close to this one. "Oh, Raff," she breathed. "I love you too."

He lifted an eyebrow in question. A question she didn't hesitate to answer.

"Yes! I'll marry you." She waited for him to slip on the ring and stand before she dove into his arms.

The audience broke out in applause, and Raff kissed her. He kissed her until her knees grew weak and the angels started to giggle. He kissed her until Miss Pitty finally wiggled her way out of the donkey's arms to rub against Raff's legs. Seeing a furry friend, the puppy leaped from Luke's arms to give chase. The cat released a yowl and raced through the angels to climb the stable. Amid the children's shrieking, the puppy yipping, and the audience laughing, someone started singing "O Come All Ye Faithful." The rest of the congregation joined in. On the last verse, Raff and Savannah finally drew apart and smiled at each other before they joined the final chorus in their off-key voices.

The townsfolk of Bliss said it was the most memorable Christmas pageant ever.

"The first time, Melanie and Dax had been married in a large Atlanta church in June. The second time, they were married in a little white chapel on Christmas Eve."

CHAPTER TWENTY-FOUR

❦

AT ONE TIME, SAVANNAH HAD dreamed of being married in an expensive designer dress with plenty of hand-sewn sequins. She had dreamed of a huge cathedral that was filled with all the prestigious people in Atlanta. And she had dreamed of walking down a candlelit aisle to her groom—a perfect southern gentleman.

Her actual wedding didn't come close to her dreams.

It was much better.

Her gown didn't have one sequin. It was a simple, floor-length lace dress that Raff had found in his many travels. It seemed that Gus Arrington's mail-order bride had been a busty woman just like Savannah. The dress fit as if it had been made to order. Which was a good thing since there hadn't been enough time for alterations.

The church wasn't a huge cathedral or filled with prestigious people. It was a little white chapel decorated for Christmas with boughs of evergreen and a glittering Christmas tree. And it was filled to the rafters with the townsfolk of Bliss that she'd grown to love. Her dear friends sat in the first row with their husbands. Emery, Carly, Gracie, and even Becky, all looked back at her with tears in their eyes and smiles on their faces. She returned their smiles as she experienced the only part of her dream that mattered. She walked down a candlelit aisle to a handsome southern gentleman.

Although Raff wasn't dressed like a gentleman as much as a gunslinger. He wore solid black, from the toes of his polished boots to the tip of his felt cowboy hat. Next to him, Luke was dressed similarly—right down to the leather strip wrapped around his wrist with the polished arrowhead. He held Miss Pitty in one arm and the puppy in the other. The two animals still didn't like each other, but they seemed to have formed a truce for the ceremony. Dastardly Dax slept while Miss Pitty watched the puppy with wary eyes.

When Savannah reached the altar, she handed off her bouquet to Ms. Marble who looked stunning in a forest green dress and wide brimmed hat decorated with little red Christmas ornaments. She gave Savannah a tight hug as she whispered.

"Welcome to Bliss."

The words made Savannah's bubble of happiness swell to bursting. She hadn't just found a gentleman, she'd found a home. A home filled with loving, caring people. A home where she could make her own happy ending.

She hugged Ms. Marble back before she turned to Raff. The look of awe shining in his hazel eyes made her feel like the most beautiful woman in the world. Her happy bubble finally burst and spilled down her cheeks. Raff pulled a bandanna out of his back pocket and gently blotted the tears from her cheeks.

She sniffed. "I guess you should know that you're marrying the biggest crybaby on both sides of the Mississippi."

"You're not a crybaby." He put the kerchief away and took her hands, bringing them up to his lips for a kiss. "You're my baby."

The ceremony was short and sweet. As soon as the preacher pronounced them man and wife, Raff gave her a kiss that had his cousins whooping and Savannah blushing. Once the ceremony was over, they joined their friends and family in the pews to celebrate a more important event—Sweet Baby Jesus's birthday. The preacher gave a short sermon followed by the singing of Christmas hymns. They ended the night at Dirk and Gracie's new house where they ate Carly's braised beef and Ms. Marble's chocolate fudge wedding cake. It was almost midnight by the time they got back to the cabin. As soon as he helped her out of the truck, Raff swept Savannah up in his arms.

"You shouldn't pick me up, Raff" she protested as he carried her up the porch steps. "I've put on way too much holiday weight and you'll hurt your back."

"Hush up, woman. As your husband, I get to break my back any time I want to."

Her eyes widened. "Break? I did not say break. I am certainly not big enough to break your—" She cut off when he stepped in the door of the cabin. A fire was burning in the fireplace, the lights on the Christmas tree glistened like tiny stars, and candles flickered from every corner of the room. Lucy's childhood desk sat beneath one window, a bottle of champagne and glasses sitting on top.

"It's beautiful," she said in a hushed voice. "But when did you get time to do it?"

"I had Luke do it for me—with strict instructions not to open the champagne and help himself." He set her down and unbuttoned the sheepskin coat he'd buttoned her into before they left Dirk and Gracie's. He hung it and his hat on the hooks by the door before he took her hand and led her over to the couch. "Did you want some champagne?"

She hooked her arms around his neck. "I'd rather have some Raff." She kissed him, enjoying the heady flavors of her new husband. He pulled her close and deepened the kiss before drawing back.

"Before we get too into things, we need to get you out of that dress. If I get any more turned on, I won't have the patience to deal with all those buttons. I'm not even sure I have the patience now." He brushed his fingers along the high collar. "Maybe I should just rip it off."

She stepped back. "Over my dead body. I will not let you rip your great-great-great-grandmother's wedding's dress. This is an heirloom that needs to be cherished. I even hated to have it dry cleaned."

He shook his head, but a smile played on his lips. "Fine. Then turn around so I can tackle that row of buttons."

She turned and looked at the Christmas tree, finally noticing all the brightly-colored packages beneath. "You went Christmas shopping?"

His fingers brushed her spine with heat as he unbuttoned her dress. "I did a little shopping for you and Luke when I was getting your dress cleaned in Austin."

"But I didn't have time to get you and Luke anything."

He leaned in and placed a kiss on her neck. "You gave me the best gift I ever could've asked for when you married me. And I signed all the presents to Luke from both of us. We're a team now."

Her heart swelled with love, and she leaned her head back and kissed him. "I think I'm going to like being on your team as long as you let me be the quarterback occasionally."

"Just as soon as I get this dress off, you can be in charge all you want, sweetheart." He gave her another quick kiss before he went back to unbuttoning. She smiled as she looked at all the presents with Luke's name on them. She had married a good man. A good man who was a horrible wrapper. None of the packages had bows or tags. He had written Luke's and her names right on the wrapping paper with a magic marker. The only package that didn't have a name was the one wrapped in newspaper and propped against the wall. Even wrapped she knew by its shape what it was.

"Please tell me that you didn't get Luke a gun," she said.

"Of course not." He fumbled with a stubborn button. "Damn, how did men get to their women in the eighteen-hundreds?"

"Then what is in that package?"

He finished unbuttoning the dress before he glanced over her shoulder. "What pack—?" He cut off and walked over to the present. As soon as he picked it up, he laughed. "It looks like I wasn't the only one playing Santa today." He tore off the newspaper to reveal the Winchester rifle Savannah had pushed out of his truck.

She smiled. "I knew Luke would give it back to you eventually." She watched as Raff lovingly ran a hand over the circled A brand seared into the wooden stock. "So now that your parents don't want you to rebuild their house, what are you planning on doing with it?"

His eyes twinkled as he looked at her. "I'm going to sell it and build my bride a big, beautiful home to fill with antique furniture . . ." He paused. "And children."

She'd been worried Raff wouldn't want to have children after suffering through his mother's miscarriages. She was glad he'd released the past and was willing to move on. She was willing to do the same.

She walked over and took the gun from him, carefully placing it on Lucy's desk before she stepped into his arms. "I no longer want a big house. A little cabin will do me just fine. You can use the money to buy all those cows you've been drooling over . . . or you could just keep the gun and wait for your royalties from the final Tender Heart book to start your cattle ranch."

He pulled her closer. "I don't want to hang on to any more things from the past." He paused. "What would you think if I donated most of the things in the barn to a museum? I figure we can find some other antiques for your shop, but I think everything that has to do with Lucy or the mail-order brides should be enjoyed by everyone—especially Tender Heart nerds like you and your friends."

There were no words to describe how happy the

idea made her. She kissed him. "I love you."

"So I guess you like the idea."

She cradled his face in her hands. "About as much as I like the idea of spending the rest of my life with a junkman."

He smiled his lopsided smile that melted her heart. "Then let's get that life started." He slid Gus's bride's dress off her shoulders and let it slip to the floor.

☾

The Arrington Cemetery on Christmas morning was crisp and chilly. Ms. Marble shivered as she knelt and placed a bouquet of pink roses against the headstone. She ran a white-gloved hand over the inscription. *Lucy Arrington, a Tender Heart.* Usually, the words made her sad. But today, there was no sadness. Just a buoyant feeling of closure.

"We did it, Luce," she said. "We finally corrected our mistakes and brought a fitting ending to the story. All your nieces and nephews are happily married. We found Bonnie Blue, and she and your great-grandson Dirk and his three sisters have taken their place in the family. And the final book will soon be published and Tender Heart will get its happy ending. I must say that you did a good job of pulling all the loose ends together. Yes, I know. I promised I wouldn't read it until it was published, but I couldn't stop myself. When I see you again, I'm sure you'll give me a piece of your mind about that." She smiled at the thought of seeing her good friend again. "But for now, I need to get to the diner. Carly's cooking Christmas breakfast for the family and needs my help." She struggled to her feet, then patted the headstone. "Merry Christmas, my dear friend."

Lucy didn't answer, but as Ms. Marble left the cemetery the last words of the Tender Heart series drifted through her mind like the wind through the trees.

There were eleven brides that came to Tender Heart. Eleven strong women determined to find love and make Texas their home.

And they did.

ACKNOWLEDGMENTS

THERE ARE SO MANY PEOPLE I need to give a big hug and thanks to for making this series a success.

My wonderful readers who have never failed to show me their love and support. You are the best, and I love you right back!

My editor, Lindsey Faber, who jumped on mid-series and did an awesome job of keeping my story and characters on track.

My copyeditor, Rebecca Cremonese, who stuck with me through the entire series and is the most thorough, amazing copyeditor ever.

My beta readers, Margie Hager, Teresa Fordice, and Ada Hui, who took the time to check for all those little things that slip through the cracks.

My cover designer, Kim Killion, whose killer covers make me giddy with delight.

My formatter, Jennifer Jakes, who makes my words so pretty.

My Katie Krew who take the time to write reviews and spread release news.

My family and friends who shower me with the support and love I need to keep living my dream.

And last but not least, God who gave me this wonderful opportunity and walked with me every step of the way. I'm truly grateful.

If you haven't read the first novel in the
TENDER HEART TEXAS SERIES,
here's a sneak peek.

FALLING FOR TENDER HEART

❦

"EXCUSE ME, MA'AM."

Emery Wakefield looked up from the book she was reading—more like rereading for the hundredth time—and was disappointed that the man speaking wasn't a handsome cowboy with a sexy smile. He was just the businessman sitting next to her on the plane.

He was nice-looking, but not nearly as nice-looking as Rory Earhart. Although few men could compare to her favorite fictional hero—the key word being *fictional*.

Emery had a wee bit of a problem keeping fiction separate from reality. As an editor and avid reader, she loved to get lost in the fantasy worlds of her characters, which sometimes caused her to lose sight of her own life. Her two older brothers teased her about having her head in the clouds. And her close friends Carly and Savannah were always reminding her to live in the real world. In the real world, there were no perfect heroes. Just regular guys like this businessman who had ignored her the entire trip to play video games on his phone.

But if she ever wanted to be in a relationship again, she needed to lower her standards and make an effort.

She smiled. "Yes?"

He nodded at the aisle. "The plane's landed."

She finally noticed that people were out of their seats and collecting their luggage from the overhead compartments. "Oh! I didn't even realize." She pulled her laptop bag from beneath the seat in front of her and placed the tattered paperback in the side pocket.

"So you like those naughty romance novels?" When she glanced over, the businessman winked.

Emery felt her spine stiffen, but she quickly reminded herself that few men understood romance—books or otherwise. Romance to them was all about the sex. It wasn't about the first prolonged glance. The first heated touch. The first breathless kiss.

She blinked. *Reality, Emery, reality.*

"Yes," she said. "I like those 'naughty' romances. What genre do you read?"

"I don't do a lot of reading. I usually just wait for the movie."

Okay, she was willing to lower her standards, but not that much.

Since the conversation was pretty much dead, she busied herself by straightening the pages of the manuscript she'd been reading earlier. While most of the other editors at Randall Publishing did their reading and editing electronically, Emery preferred to have a hard copy. There was something about holding the pages in her hands that made the reading experience so much better. Although it hadn't made this particular manuscript any better.

After talking to the writer's agent and reading the first few chapters, she'd had high hopes for this book. The author had a fresh voice and a great ear for dialogue. Unfortunately, the entire plot had crumbled midway through, and there was little hope of salvaging it. Which meant that this wasn't the book that was going to give Emery job security and make her boss overlook the other books that had flopped. But hopefully, she had the key to the one novel that would. She looked at the zippered pocket where she'd carefully tucked the envelope she had received a month ago.

She was a firm believer in fate, and there was no other explanation for her having received the envelope. When she'd first opened it, she felt like Harry Potter getting his invitation to Hogwarts. And even if her boss was convinced it was a hoax, there was no way Emery could ignore it. That would be like ignoring destiny.

The Tender Heart novels were her favorite books of all time. The ten-book series about mail-order brides in the old West had gotten her through her horrific puberty years. The pimples and braces wouldn't have been so bad if she'd been a genius like her brothers and could've fit in with the geeks. But she wasn't a genius. She was horrible at math, couldn't have cared less about science, and hadn't gotten through one *Star Wars* movie without falling asleep. In school she'd been labeled the homely, weird girl who walked around with her nose in a book.

It was in those books that she'd found refuge from school bullies and the fact that she didn't fit in with the rest of her family of geniuses. And she was still struggling to fit in. She had yet to find her place in New York City and was only months away from losing her job.

Unless what was in the envelope turned out to be authentic.

"So what brings you to Austin?" The business-man pulled his briefcase out from under the seat.

She got to her feet. "I'm meeting my two best friends for spring break." It wasn't a lie. She had roped her two unsuspecting friends into joining her on this trip. They thought they were checking out the setting of their favorite series. They knew nothing about the letter Emery had received . . . or the chapter.

Something about her reply made the business-man's eyes light up. Probably the prospect of spring break with three naughty romance readers who were only interested in sex. "Really? I live here so I'd be happy to show you and your friends around if you'd like. Austin is an exciting town."

"I'm sure it is, but we're not staying in Austin. We're staying in Bliss."

He looked confused. "Bliss? Why would you want to go there? It's practically a ghost town."

She glanced at her laptop case, and a smile bloomed on her face. "In a way, that's exactly what I'm looking for. Ghosts." She didn't wait for him to ask any more questions before she moved into the aisle.

Since Carly and Savannah's flights didn't get in until much later, Emery planned to meet them in Bliss. Excited to get to the small town, she wasted no time picking up her luggage and renting a car. The entire drive from Austin, she couldn't help feeling like she was on the Hogwarts Express headed to a place that had only existed in her dreams.

Unfortunately, that excitement fizzled when she drove into Bliss and reality hit. She knew a modern town wasn't going to be like an old western town—especially a fictional western town—but she had expected to find something that reminded her of Tender Heart. A quaint knick-knack shop that sold souvenirs. A bookstore with the entire series displayed in the window. The 1950s diner where the author Lucy Arrington had plotted her famous stories. The pretty little chapel where all the mail-order brides had found their happily-ever-afters.

Instead, the two-lane highway Emery drove into town on was lined with vacant brick buildings that had fading signs and cracked windows. Rusty grain silos stood like aged sentinels, and weeds filled every empty lot.

The businessman had been right. It did look like a ghost town.

There were few cars on the road. So when a muddy pickup truck passed her going the opposite direction, Emery couldn't help but stare. The old guy behind the wheel stared back with a suspicious look. Or maybe it was her clean Hyundai that he found suspicious. The few vehicles parked along the street looked as dirty as his truck. It was hard not to feel disappointed. She had arrived at Cinderella's castle to find a hovel nothing like her fantasies.

She glanced at her laptop bag on the front seat next to her. The town might not look like what she expected, but there was still hope that her fantasies would be realized—if not in the town, then on paper.

Pushing her disappointment down, Emery searched for the Bliss Motor Lodge where she'd made reservations. It was the only place to stay in town, and she hoped she hadn't booked the Bates Motel. If she walked into the lobby and spotted a bunch of stuffed birds, she was out of there.

Since Main Street was only a couple of blocks long, she easily found the motor lodge. But before she pulled in, she couldn't help driving a little further to see if she could find a little white chapel with beautiful stained-glass windows. She didn't, but what she did find was a gas station that wasn't boarded up. In fact, two men sat at a table in front. And she couldn't help pulling in to see if she could get some information.

The old guy with the balding head looked at her just as suspiciously as the man who had driven past her on the street. She couldn't tell how the other man looked. He wore a brown felt cowboy hat that was tugged low on his forehead and shaded his face. But the hat turned in her direction when she got out.

Since she couldn't just start asking questions without adding to their suspicions, she decided to get gas. The pump didn't have a credit card slot, so she topped off her tank, then leaned into the car to get her purse from the front seat. That's when she heard one of the men speak.

"You gonna gawk? Or are you gonna play?"

She straightened and peeked around the pump in time to see the cowboy hat turn away. She had assumed he was the same age as the old guy. But on closer examination, she realized her mistake. The hard chest and broad shoulders that filled out the western shirt belonged to a much younger man. As did the dark hair curling on the back of his strong, corded neck.

She watched the muscles in that neck tighten as the old guy continued, "I thought you just got finished telling me that you didn't have time for women."

"Would you keep it down, Emmett?" the cowboy hissed as he picked up a domino. His hands were big, but agile enough to manipulate the small white tile into place on the table. Something about those long fingers made Emery's heart skip and her stomach feel all light and airy. The empty stomach she could blame on being hungry. She'd only had a bagel at the airport and a Cranapple and peanuts on the plane. The skipping heart was a little harder to explain.

"Now that was stupid." Emmett positioned a domino on the table, then picked up the pencil next to the notepad to put down his score. "Almost as stupid as wasting your time gawking at a woman who's just passing through. That's a rental car if ever I saw one, and no woman from around here wears heels that high unless it's Easter Sunday." He glanced over at Emery and noticed her watching. He smiled, revealing a chipped front tooth. "Howdy, ma'am."

Emery stepped around the gas pump, and both men stood up from their chairs. But it was the cowboy she couldn't look away from. If she'd thought his body was nice sitting down, it was nothing compared to how he looked fully stretched out. He had to be well over six feet tall with long, muscled legs that were emphasized by the fit of his well-worn blue jeans.

And his legs weren't the only things they emphasized.

Her gaze zeroed in on the bulge beneath the zipper. Not a small bulge, but a long, hard one. Before she could blink, his cowboy hat blocked her view. She lifted her gaze. Everything inside Emery went very still as reality collided with fantasy.

She had been searching for some sign of Tender Heart. Some small piece of the series she loved so dearly. And she'd finally found it. From the lock of raven black hair that curled over his forehead to the intense eyes as blue as a Texas sky at twilight, the man standing in front of her looked exactly like her favorite book boyfriend.

Her hero Rory Earhart had come to life.

If you enjoyed *Falling for a Christmas Cowboy*, be sure to check out the other books in Katie Lane's Tender Heart Texas Series!

Other series by Katie Lane

Deep in the Heart of Texas:

Overnight Billionaires:

Hunk for the Holidays:

Hunk for the Holidays
Ring in the Holidays
Unwrapped

Anthologies:

Small Town Christmas
(Jill Shalvis, Hope Ramsay, Katie Lane)

All I Want for Christmas is a Cowboy
(Jennifer Ryan, Emma Cane, Katie Lane)

ABOUT THE AUTHOR

❦

Katie Lane is a *USA Today* Bestselling author of the *Deep in the Heart of Texas*, *Hunk for the Holidays*, *Overnight Billionaires*, and *Tender Heart Texas* series. She lives in Albuquerque, New Mexico, with her cute cairn terrier Roo and her even cuter husband Jimmy.

For more info about her writing life or just to chat, check out Katie on:
Facebook: *www.facebook.com/katielaneauthor*
Twitter: *www.twitter.com/katielanebook*
Instagram: *www.instagram.com/katielanebooks*

And for upcoming releases and great giveaways, be sure to sign up for her mailing list at
www.katielanebooks.com

Made in the USA
San Bernardino, CA
24 November 2017